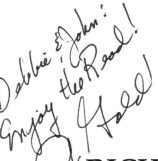

MW00936342

RICH GOLDHABER

VECTOR

A LAWSON SERIES NOVEL

This is a work of fiction by the author. All of the names, places, characters, and other elements of this written material are products of the author's imagination, are fictitious, and should not be considered as being real or true. Any similarity to actual events, locations, organizations, or persons, living or dead, is entirely coincidental.

All rights to this work are reserved. No part of this book may be used or reproduced in any manner whatsoever without the written permission of the author, except in the case of brief quotations as part of critical articles and reviews.

Copyright © 2012 Rich Goldhaber

ISBN – 13: 978-1467919616

ISBN – 10: 1467919616

ACKNOWLEDGEMENTS

The author would once again like to thank a wonderful group of family, friends and supporters, as well as the following individuals who deserve special recognition.

Lu and Kathlene Wolf have continued to help with editing and critical comments, and their efforts are greatly appreciated.

Bill Lamperes has provided many literary insights, and his inputs have greatly improved this literary effort.

ALSO BY RICH GOLDHABER

The 26th of June

Succession Plan

For: My wife Jeanne

PROLOGUE

Ali Santiani walked slowly along the street soaking up the warmth of the late afternoon summer sun. The fragrance from thousands of roses in full bloom along the parkway filled the air. The street echoed with children at play while young mothers pushed their Bugaboo strollers. The glorious day begged for enjoyment.

He had just finished his final exam in Statistical Thermodynamics, the last of his Senior year tests, and he knew with absolute certainty he had aced it. Good news, because an "A" in Thermo assured him of a full scholarship to Graduate School and a paid part-time position in Professor Wilson's laboratory.

He thought about his good fortune. Iran's decision to forgo its nuclear weapons program had been the key turning point in his life. The Student Exchange Program he participated in had been his ticket to success, and the University of Chicago ranked as one of the best schools in the world. It had been a sad day when he left his family in Tehran and boarded the flight to

Chicago, but his extended family had all agreed; he must take advantage of this opportunity.

The University had provided rent-free off-campus housing. His one-bedroom apartment, although past its prime, still had an understated charm about it. The old avocado appliances were far better than he could ever have hoped to afford in Tehran. The aging wooden floor had creaked with every step, but now an old Persian rug sent by his father covered the living room and completely deadened the sound. The electricity actually worked twenty-four hours a day, every day. Yes, he loved the good life in America, a testament to what a free democracy could create, even for a poor student. He used his key to enter the eight story building and walked up two flights of stairs to his apartment.

In the kitchen, he poured himself a glass of fresh squeezed orange juice to celebrate. He took a quick sip. The tartness of the fresh juice brought back wonderful memories of his hometown. His village, located near the southern coast, supplied the rest of the country with some of the best oranges in the world. He looked at his watch. He had a six o'clock date with his girlfriend Haleh, an exchange student from Yemen. Just enough time to check his e-mails.

One message from his mother caught his eye; strange, because she didn't know how to use a computer, let alone write an e-mail to her only son. Ali scanned the message written in Arabic and quickly realized it wasn't from his mother. He read it three times, more carefully each time. The taste of bile from his stomach reached his throat, his heart pounded, and he clutched his face with both hands and howled; not from sorrow but out of fear. He stood up, knocking his chair to the floor, as he backed away from the computer. He rushed to the bathroom just in time and threw up in the toilet. He lay on the bathroom floor embracing the old porcelain fixture contemplating his unfortunate fate. He hoped he would awake from this terrible nightmare and his wonderful life could resume; but Ali knew this was no dream, and definitely not a prank letter. No, this threat demanded total believability. He finally stood up and staggered back into his bedroom. A thousand thoughts raced through his mind as he sat back down at his desk and reread the message. The e-mail warned him not to speak to anyone, but he had to; he needed help, so he called his girlfriend.

"Haleh, I need to talk to you right now; it's an emergency; meet me at the Starbucks by your apartment; I'll be there in five minutes."

Ali printed a copy of the message and left his apartment. The full glass of orange juice still sat unfinished on his desk.

Haleh waited at the Starbucks, sitting at a dark empty corner table. An ashen-faced Ali quickly sat down next to her, and with tears in his eyes, handed her the copy of the e-mail.

As Haleh read the message, she placed both hands over her mouth and began to quietly sob. "What are you going to do?" she said. "Are you sure it's for real? This thing they're asking you to do, it must be terrible. How could they know these things?"

"All of the names and addresses of my relatives are correct. They even know where you live. The e-mail said if I don't follow their instructions exactly they're going to kill everyone, and I believe them. This must be from the Iranian Revolutionary Guards or the Quds. Who else would do such a thing? I have no doubt they'll do exactly as they say if I don't follow their instructions."

"Shouldn't we go to the police or the FBI?"

"No, the message says they're watching me to ensure I don't talk to anyone. Maybe these guys already know I'm talking to you. They could even be monitoring my phone. I can't talk to anyone or someone's going to be killed for sure. They'll do it, I know they will."

Haleh held his hands in hers. "So what are you going to do?"

Ali considered his options. "I don't know. The e-mail says more instructions will follow in the next few days. Let's wait to see what the next message says."

Outside Starbucks the two embraced. Haleh looked into Ali's eyes and saw no hint of the future. She began to cry and held him tightly, afraid to let go. Ali looked hopefully at her beautiful face and said, "Don't worry; somehow we'll get through this."

Ali left Haleh, their evening date cancelled, and walked back to his apartment. A light drizzle began to fall. He walked slowly, thinking about the family he loved so much. The unnoticed rain soaked his blue jeans and Polo shirt and dripped from his face. His earlier celebratory mood had now been replaced with a feeling of total despair. He had no idea what he would be asked to do, but one thing for sure, it would be something terrible and against the law.

¤   ¤   ¤

The second message finally arrived. Ali read the e-mail carefully.

Go to the Hertz car rental office at Midway Airport on July 3rd. A SUV has been reserved in your name. Use your credit card. Drive to the hardware store on the corner of Fifty-Fifth and State and buy a twenty-foot extension ladder. It will just fit in the back of the car.

On July 4th, at exactly 2:00 A.M., drive to the Denny's restaurant two blocks from your apartment. Behind the restaurant you will see a metal garbage can painted yellow. Inside the garbage can you will find a cardboard box. Place the box carefully in your car.

Next, drive to the alley behind 1267 Bridgemont Avenue. You will see a large yellow "X" painted in the road. Stop your car directly over the "X". Using the ladder, carefully place the box onto the roof of the garage next to the "X". Make sure the "this side up" arrow is properly positioned.

Drive through the alley two blocks west, and discard the ladder in the large refuse container at the construction site. Return the car to Hertz on July 5th.

If you value the lives of your family, girlfriend, and relatives, follow these instructions exactly.

God is great!

As with the first message, the e-mail written in Arabic lacked a signature. Ali thought, *why would anyone place a package in the middle of the night on the roof of a garage? It just made no sense. What would be the point of exploding a bomb on a roof, and if the box didn't contain a bomb, then what could it hold?*

Ali texted Haleh a coded message on her cellphone, made a copy of the second e-mail, and left the apartment by the back service entrance. He walked a half block and hid behind a large tree. He wanted to make sure nobody followed him.

Haleh sat waiting at the same table when he arrived. She read the message while he ordered a double espresso.

"It must be a bomb," she said.

"No, why explode a bomb on the roof of a garage?"

"Okay," she said, "let's say all we know is it's something bad, something really bad; otherwise, why would they go to all the trouble of getting you involved. Ali, I'm afraid you're going to be hurt. Who knows, there may be someone here watching us right now."

They both looked around the coffee shop, but the ragtag group of patrons looked just like normal people, mostly college kids enjoying an upscale coffee.

"Maybe I should call my father and let him know what's happening. He'll protect the family."

"Ali, do you really think the Iranian Revolutionary Guards or the Quds will not follow through on their threat? How's your father going to save them? "

They both sat silently, consumed by fear. There seemed to be no way out of the dilemma, but a plan did finally emerge. Ali would make copies of the e-mails and mail them to their friend Jamal. He would place the e-mails in a second envelope inside the first, with instructions to give the contents of the second envelope to the FBI if he was killed or went missing. Along with copies of the two e-mails, Ali would include a letter explaining the details of what had happened. His part of the bargain would have been completed, and his family would have been saved, but the

FBI would also know what had really happened and possibly be able to punish these people.

¤   ¤   ¤

Ali awoke suddenly the morning of July 3rd from a terrifying dream, his body drenched in sweat. He had just witnessed his entire family being lined up against a wall and executed, and he had been the person pulling the trigger. He showered, trying to cleanse himself of his upcoming sin. He walked out onto the sidewalk and hailed a passing cab. The trip to Midway Airport took twenty minutes, but seemed to last only a moment.

He anxiously approached the Hertz rental counter and waited in line. Finally, one of the representatives called out to him. No reservation would be his salvation, but unfortunately the woman behind the counter quickly found his name in the computer. He presented a credit card and driver's license, and after a few minutes sat behind the wheel of a large red Ford Expedition.

After leaving the hardware store, his thoughts turned once again to his family. He texted Haleh. *"I've got the car and ladder, and I'm going to park in front of my apartment. I love you."*

The day and evening passed slowly. Santiani's thoughts turning to his family and the sacrifice he would make to ensure they all lived. A somber Ali wrote a long letter to his father explaining everything, and he asked him to protect the family he loved so much. With mixed emotions the beaten down student dropped the letter in the apartment's mail drop just before getting into the SUV.

Ali drove to the nearby Denny's and quickly found the yellow colored garbage can partially hidden alongside several of the restaurant's waste containers. The young man slowly approached the garbage can and opened the lid. A cardboard box stared back at him from inside the otherwise empty trash can. Ali eyed the box with suspicion. What could it be? It looked innocent enough. He looked around the parking lot. The restaurant, open 24/7, still had a few patrons, but the parking lot appeared totally deserted. The exchange student cautiously lifted the box and placed it next to the ladder. It weighed about twenty pounds, a perfect cube, about a foot and a half on each side. The top of the cardboard box had been cut away, and lightweight brown Kraft paper had been used to reseal the top of the opening. Large black arrows on the sides and text on the Kraft paper clearly identified the up side.

The Bridgemont address, just northwest of Downtown, could best be described as transitional. Old brownstones were being torn down, and new single family two-story homes were the typical replacement. The working class neighborhood was trying to reinvent itself as a revitalized middle class community. Its location made it highly desirable, a mere ten minute bus ride to the Loop's mega-office buildings.

Ali easily found the address and circled the block once looking for possible witnesses. The entire neighborhood appeared asleep. The car stopped at the east entrance to the alley. His body shook with fear induced tremors and had been for the last hour.

A memory of his mother suddenly filled his mind, and for some reason he remembered his first day of school and his mother leading him by the hand into the classroom. She introduced a terrified Ali to his teacher and told him everything would be all right.

Ali pictured his father and two sisters sitting at the kitchen table having dinner and gained strength from the knowledge that by committing this act, their lives would be spared. A trembling hand turned off the car's headlights and the SUV entered the narrow alley. The car slowed to a crawl while Ali searched for the yellow "X", but it didn't really take a genius to find it. It glowed brightly, almost directly under a bright mercury vapor streetlight.

Santiani stopped the car directly over the "X" as instructed in the e-mail, turned off the motor, and looked around. The houses in the area were dark; everyone seemed asleep. His ears listened carefully for any hint of a human presence, but total silence prevailed. He had no idea what he would tell someone walking a dog. Fixing a satellite dish in the middle of the night wouldn't fly. Luckily, the entire alley seemed deserted.

Ali opened the back of the SUV and quietly removed the extension ladder. When extended it easily allowed access to the roof of the garage, and after a final search for unexpected visitors, he cautiously lifted the box out of the Ford Expedition. Clutching it in his left arm, he slowly climbed the ladder. He reached the top and placed the box on the garage's gravel-coated flat mansard roof. His heart beat loudly; his mouth was dry, and once again he felt like vomiting as he rushed down the ladder. He tripped on the last step, and the ladder made a loud clanking sound as it almost fell to the ground. A nearby dog barked in response to the sudden noise.

Ali, with new concerns about witnesses responding to the dog's alarm, quickly loaded the ladder back into the SUV. He started the car, and with the headlights still turned off, slowly headed west down the alley. As the e-mail had indicated, two blocks later a large refuse container sat next to a three story apartment building under construction. Ali removed the ladder from the car and quietly placed it inside the half-empty dumpster.

Driving back to his own apartment, Ali worried about whether he had been seen by anyone, especially after the dog had barked. He felt good about his chances of getting away without being caught. In hindsight he realized he should have covered up the license plate just prior to entering the alley. He concluded he wouldn't make a very good burglar. His heart raced; he breathed heavily, and he still couldn't imagine what evil sat inside the cardboard box. He hoped he could now return to just being a good student, but in the back of his mind, he sensed it would never happen. He had crossed a dangerous threshold, and his life would be changed forever.

He found a parking place a block away from his apartment, and walked slowly home. His entire body still shook as he entered his living room, and he didn't notice the shadow advance toward him. He never saw the person or heard the shot from the silenced pistol. The bullet struck him in the back of the head and splattered brain tissue on the floor as the front of his head split open from the large caliber bullet. He fell unceremoniously onto his beautiful Persian carpet, dead before his body reached the floor.

The sinister looking figure gazed dispassion- ately at his victim and removed the car keys from Ali's right front pocket. He then gloved up and proceeded to the computer on Ali's desk where he entered Ali's g-mail account and deleted the two incriminating e-mails. The man dressed in black then quietly ransacked the apartment throwing things haphazardly on the floor, apparently looking for valuables. He removed $256 from Ali's wallet and threw it down on the floor. It was all over in ten minutes. He left as quietly as he had entered using the front door, which he left unlocked. It took him only a few minutes to locate the Hertz red SUV and drive off in a northerly direction. He had one more job to complete before his work in Chicago came to an end.

The killer found a parking spot near Haleh's building and buzzed her apartment. Awakened from a restless sleep, Haleh asked, "Who is it?"

In an agitated voice the man answered, "It's Jeff Burns. I live on Ali's floor. He's been hurt and asked me to get you. It's terrible; please come quickly."

Without thinking, Haleh threw on some clothes and ran down the stairs leading to the front entrance. The stranger met her at the door and escorted her to his car.

"Is he Okay," she asked?

"I can't tell. It looks like he's been beat up and the apartment's a mess. I think someone tried to rob him. I wanted to call an ambulance and the police, but he told me to come get you."

Haleh remained silent, deep in thought, as they rode the six blocks back to Ali's apartment. Haleh used her key to enter the building, and they both ran up the stairs to the second floor. Haleh rushed ahead, opened the door to the apartment, and saw Ali lying on the living room carpet. Something was terribly wrong. Ali hadn't been beaten up. Blood covered the carpet. Too late, Haleh knew the truth. She turned back to face the killer who stood just inside the doorway, and even before she could react, the man shot her between the eyes. She collapsed, her body falling on top of her boyfriend.

The stranger then left the apartment and drove away in the Hertz rental car, his job completed and his $500,000 fee earned.

1

The Emergency Room at Northwestern Hospital was almost back to normal. The Fourth of July injuries, mostly from sparkler burns and misfired bottle rockets, had transitioned back to: automobile accidents, heart attacks, summer colds, and broken limbs.

Dr. Sally Lawson stood in the casting room setting a little boy's arm. He had fallen off his bicycle, and insisted he had been pushed to the ground by some mysterious invisible force.

Vicky stuck her head in the room. "Some medics just called. They're bringing in a man who looks really weird. They think you're going to want to see him immediately."

"Thanks Vicky. Can you ask Greg to finish up in here? I'm just waiting for the plaster to harden."

As Sally left the room she turned to the boy being comforted by his mother and said, "Billy, you be careful the mysterious force doesn't push you off your bike again."

The Medics rushed the gurney down the hallway with their patient, and Sally escorted them into the nearest vacant examination room. The middle-aged man moaned loudly, obviously in extreme pain. Barely conscious, he struggled with his words. Sally immediately noticed the red spots over the man's entire body, which she correctly identified as small hemorrhages under the skin. Her immediate subconscious reaction when she saw his red eyes was to pull her mask in place and glove up. Vicky, watching Sally, followed suit.

Sally turned to the Medics who she knew by name, "Joey, what's the story?"

"His wife said he's been sick for two days, and then today the red marks suddenly appeared. That's when she called us. His wife and their two kids should be here in a few minutes."

Sally, with a mixture of calmness and urgency said, "Vicky, when they arrive, please bring them back here. I'm moving him into the isolation area."

Vicky left to find the family while the medics helped Sally push the gurney into a walled room in the corner of the ER.

Joey asked, "What's with the red marks Doc?"

"I'm not sure yet, but I want you guys to wait around for a few minutes."

Sally now turned her attention back to the patient. "Mr. Morgan, I'm Dr. Lawson. What seems to be the problem?"

The man spoke with great difficulty. "I have a bad headache and a fever. Yesterday I could hardly move. All my muscles and joints hurt, and I have a sore throat."

The patient suddenly began vomiting. Sally passed him a small plastic basin to catch the fluid, and he filled it with a bloody liquid. Sally began cutting away the man's shirt. She figured he probably wouldn't want to wear it again anyway.

The red blotches covered his entire upper body. "Mr. Morgan, I'm going to remove the rest of your clothing so I can perform a thorough examination."

As Sally removed the man's shoes and pants, Vicky returned. "His wife and two kids are in the next suite. What have you got?"

"I need to check a few more things first."

Sally's skills at diagnosis were legendary within the hospital. Her photographic memory and ability to see patterns in what others perceived as random noise made her the envy of her colleagues. Now her brain compared her observations and the patient's comments to an array of possible explanations and the list kept getting shorter.

"Mr. Morgan, have you been having diarrhea, and has there been blood in your stool?"

"Yes doctor, the diarrhea began yesterday and it's bloody."

"Do you have stomach pain?"

"Yes."

Just then the patient coughed up some more blood. Sally, using a speculum, examined his mouth. His gums were oozing blood.

"Do you have blood in your urine?"

"Yes, for the last two days"

Sally noticed a cut on the man's left leg. A blister had formed with a black scab and the area was swollen. Sally remembered a picture she had seen of cutaneous anthrax, and this blister looked exactly like the picture. She could palpate swollen lymph nodes under his arms, throughout his lower abdomen, and his groin. Using her stethoscope, she detected fluid build-up in the patient's lungs. As she finished her examination the patient hiccupped. The hiccup was the clincher.

Sally's legs weakened as she struggled with what needed to be done next. She desperately wanted to deny the logic of her conclusion. She reviewed all of the man's symptoms again, and her mind raced toward the same almost impossible conclusion.

Sally walked to the next examination room and met Mrs. Morgan and the children. "Mrs. Morgan, I'm Dr. Lawson. Has your husband or anyone in the family been to a farm in the last few weeks or been in contact with any animals?"

Mrs. Morgan's replied with a quick no.

"Has Mr. Morgan or any of your friends been to Africa recently?

Again Mrs. Morgan's answered with a definite no.

Sally examined the Morgan family and observed many of the same symptoms on Mrs. Morgan.

Mrs. Morgan asked, "Doctor, What's the problem with my husband?"

Sally looked at the terrified woman and replied, "Mrs. Morgan, we'll have to do some additional tests to be sure, but it appears both you and Mr. Morgan have been exposed to a highly infectious disease. We're going to have to admit all of you and place you in isolation until we can determine exactly what you have."

Shock and desperation appeared on Mrs. Morgan's face. The children, who were too young to understand, sat quietly at a table with a coloring book provided by Vicky.

After explaining to Mrs. Morgan that she would be ordering more tests, Sally and Vicky left the examination room. Sally called her entire staff and the two medics together in the privacy of an unused examination area. "We have a major problem here. I believe the male patient has as a minimum cutaneous anthrax, but he also has all of the symptoms of inhalation anthrax and hemorrhagic fever. I think Mrs. Morgan is also expressing similar symptoms. I'm going to order some confirmatory tests, but as a precaution, I want to temporarily shut down the ER.

Joey, you and Peter have probably both been exposed and need to go into isolation. Vicky, you and I are also going to be quarantined. The rest of you guys, I want all of the patients presently being treated to be moved outside of the ER. Cathy, tell the receptionist we're closing down. She'll have to ask everyone to go to another facility."

Sally detected the smell of fear in the air, and it smelled like sweat, but slightly sweeter. She, suppressed her own fear and said, "Don't worry; we'll all be okay. We've all trained for this."

Deep down inside Sally knew the truth. These medical professionals had never trained for anything like this. If her diagnosis was correct, her team would be tested as never before.

The staff left to carry out Sally's orders. Sally then turned to Vicky. "Start all of the Morgans on Ciprofloxacin and intravenous Doxycycline. I want complete blood chemistries on everyone. I think the kids are symptom free, so separate them from Mrs. Morgan but keep them close enough so she can see them. Get urine and sputum cultures going. Set up spinal tap kits for Mr. and Mrs. Morgan, and ask George to collect the samples. Call Joe Klein in Hematology and Bruce Mathews in Pathology. Tell them what's going on down here. I don't want any panic, but they need to take personal charge of these samples to eliminate the contamination risk. Tell them both I'll call them within the hour, but right now I have to alert the boss."

Vicky had worked with Sally for over five years, but the head of the ER sensed uncertainty. "Vicky, what's the problem?"

"I'm scared shitless; I'm two months pregnant, and I'm afraid of getting infected."

"Vicky, listen carefully to what I'm telling you. Both anthrax and hemorrhagic fever are transmitted by direct contact with either blood or other bodily fluids. If we're wearing protective clothing and practice good infection control techniques, we'll all be okay."

A reassured, but cautious, Vicky left to carry out Sally's instructions. Sally sat down at her desk and tried to compose herself before she talked to Senior Management. She called the CEO's office and asked his Administrative Assistant to set up an urgent conference call between Harry Haskins, the Chief of Staff and Larry Becker, the CEO.

It took a few minutes before they were both on the line. Sally started out, "We have an urgent situation down here in the ER. We have two patients, a husband and wife, who have presented with what looks like highly contagious infections. They both appear to be infected with inhalation anthrax, but are also exhibiting the symptoms of hemorrhagic fever. The husband also has cutaneous anthrax, and he's in a highly advanced state. His prognosis is poor at best. His wife's condition has not progressed as rapidly. I've shut down the ER until we get test results to confirm the diagnosis."

Larry reacted as Sally expected. "What the hell do you mean, you shut down the ER? On whose authority?"

Sally, at five-foot four-inches, although petite, was certainly no pushover, and certainly not when her tiger instincts had been aroused. Her long dark-brown ponytail flipped up into the air as she jumped up off her chair and shouted into the phone, "On my authority Larry; I'm in charge of the ER, and it is my professional judgment we are in the beginning stages of a bioterrorism attack."

Dr. Haskins interrupted, "Sally relax; I'll support you on this, but why do you think this is a bioterrorism attack?"

"Harry, what's the probability of a person being subjected simultaneously to two lethal organisms, one of which is indigenous to Africa?

Larry jumped up from his chair and threw up his hands. "Are you guys both crazy? How can we just shut down the ER when we haven't confirmed the diagnosis yet?"

"Larry, Sally made the right call. Until we have contradictory information, we've got to assume the worst."

"Harry, this is going to be a financial disaster for the hospital."

Harry answered, "No it's not. Let's consider the possible outcomes.

"First possibility, Sally is right. Then we're perceived as having the best physicians and putting patient and worker safety concerns above financials. That makes for great PR, and I'm sure you'll figure out how best to spin the story.

"Second possibility, Sally is wrong. We still come across as a hospital putting the public interests above all else. Again we win. Either way we win. Think about it Larry."

Larry remained silent after his initial outburst, contemplating Harry's two possible alternatives. Meanwhile the Chief of Staff asked, "Sally, how can we give you the kind of support you're going to need?"

"Let me collect my thoughts and talk to Joe Klein and Bruce Mathews first. I'll call you when I'm done, but for starters you can alert security and have them prevent people from going into or out of the ER, and you can dig out our Bioterrorism Readiness Plan."

"Will do Sally. One more thing; I couldn't think of a better person to manage this problem. Just let me know what you need, and I'll make it happen."

"Thanks Harry, you're the best."

2

On a conference call with Joe and Bruce, Sally reviewed the facts, and stated her main concern about how long it would take to confirm her diagnosis. If she was wrong then she needed to know as soon as possible to explore other possibilities, and if right, then they needed to prepare for what Sally believed would become a major crisis for both the hospital and the city.

Bruce, who ran the clinical diagnostic lab, said, "Sally, Cook County Hospital is the designated repository for all of the rare diagnostic testing reagents. After Vicky briefed me, I called over there and they're sending the specialized reagents over by courier. I should have the results in about six hours."

Joe asked, "Sally, why are you so sure of the diagnosis?"

"Nate and I co-authored a paper two years ago for JAMA on the diagnosis of rare infectious diseases in the ER. I'm certain of the cutaneous anthrax; the lesion on the male patient's leg is characteristic and unmistakable. I'm a little less certain of the hemorrhagic fever. That's why I need the lab results to be sure. If it's both, this will be the first wave. We're going to see more patients here. We need to prepare for the worst."

After finishing the call, Sally left her office to find her Senior Resident, John Finley. The usually busy ER now looked strangely quiet, almost frightening in its emptiness. The usual noises: children crying, patients moaning, doctors and nurses shouting orders, lifesaving monitoring equipment screeching their warnings, had been replaced with an eerie foreboding silence. John, who sat with the Morgan children, met Sally near the central nursing station.

"John, I've talked to the bosses. They're setting up a security perimeter to ensure nobody enters or leaves the ER without authorization. I want you to organize a triage team just outside the perimeter. This may be an isolated event, but we need to plan for the worst-case scenario; this is probably just the beginning of a major epidemic. Review all of the symptoms of both anthrax and hemorrhagic fever with the staff. When the word gets out, and it will, there're going to be a lot of people who show up thinking they've been exposed."

"Should we plan on 24/7?"

"Yes, talk to Harry Haskins to get it staffed. Here's the key. We need to separate people into three groups. The people with advanced symptoms need to be immediately admitted and placed in isolation. The people with early symptoms need to also be admitted but separated from the advanced stage group. They're the ones we have the best chance of saving. For the people who do not have symptoms, we need to get their names, addresses, and telephone numbers, and ask them to come back again if they exhibit any symptoms."

John listened carefully.

"Work with the Infection Control group to print a list of symptoms for people to check for in both English and Spanish, and make sure anyone we do not hospitalize really understands how to check themselves. Everyone on the team needs to be in gloves, gowns, masks, and face shields; no exceptions."

"Sally, could this be anything else?"

"I'm sure of the cutaneous anthrax diagnosis, and I'm less positive about the hemorrhagic fever. The confirmatory lab work is underway and they say they'll have the results in six hours. I'll let you know as soon as we get confirmation. Also, when each person's shift is over, we need to sterilize their clothes and they have to take showers immediately. I know I'm being overly cautious, but we must assume the worst until we know exactly what we're dealing with."

As John left to set things up, Sally looked in on her four patients. The two children were still symptom free; Mrs. Morgan rested comfortably, still concerned about her husband and the children. Sally walked into Mr. Morgan's room. Vicky stood by his bed monitoring his condition closely, and he had rapidly deteriorated. In shock, his skin bubbled up in a sea of tiny white blisters. Lesions were now breaking out all over his body and hemorrhagic blood oozed from the rips in his skin. Sally knew death would occur within a few hours.

Sally returned to Mrs. Morgan's bed, sat down next to her, and held her hand. "Mrs. Morgan, your children are still okay and aren't exhibiting any signs of infection. I'm afraid your husband, however, is not doing well, and I must tell you his condition is rapidly deteriorating."

"Is he going to die Doctor Lawson?"

"I'm afraid you need to prepare yourself for that eventuality."

Mrs. Morgan began to weep, having already come to the same conclusion. She had been overhearing the conversations among the doctors and nurses and knew enough to understand her husband's pending fate, and Sally's pronounce-ment merely served to create closure. Her concern now focused on her two children. They looked so happy and unconcerned sitting across the room playing a board game with one of the nurses. What would happen to them if she died?

She regained her composure and asked, "Am I going to die?"

"Luckily, Mrs. Morgan, we began treating you at an earlier stage in the infection. The next twenty-four hours will be critical."

"Doctor, I gave the nurses the telephone number of my sister." Tears flowed down her face. "If I die, please have someone call Thelma and tell her I know she'll take care of the kids, and I love her very much."

"I'll do it Mrs. Morgan; you can count on it. Right now, however, I really need your help. We believe you and your husband were probably exposed to a bioterrorism weapon, and the exposure most probably occurred from inhaling the airborne particles. Do you have any idea where the exposure might have come from? It probably happened two to six days ago. "

Mrs. Morgan thought for a few moments and couldn't provide any insight regarding how she came into contact with the agent.

Sally left the woman's bed and returned to her desk. She needed to call Harry back and provide a list of areas where he could provide assistance. This was going to be unlike anything she had ever experienced. Excellence in medical staff skills would certainly be needed, but leadership would be the key to success. Dealing with the unexpected would now become commonplace, and she hoped everybody would be up to the challenge.

She tried to step back and see the big picture. Far from being an isolated incident, she knew this event foretold the beginning of a wave of new cases which would play havoc with the city's medical response capabilities. Her first conclusion was the most terrifying; all new cases identified should be brought to Northwestern Hospital until her facility couldn't handle the patient load. It made no sense to have all of the city's hospitals exposed unnecessarily to this unknown biological agent. Harry needed to interface with other hospitals and ambulance services to get the word out ASAP. Her hospital needed to become the primary treatment center for this crisis.

Sally worried about her staff's safety. There were certainly risks to the staff, but the use of Risk Category Four protective garments should go a long way toward easing anxieties regarding the risk of contagion, and Sally knew there were several dozen suits located somewhere in the hospital's off-site storage facility. Immunization against the anthrax would also be required.

They were going to need large quantities of drugs; antibiotics, antivirals, and the latest drugs the CDC recommended. Hemorrhagic fever, actually the more serious of the two infections, would require heroic efforts.

Vicky interrupted Sally's planning session. "We've got three more walk-ins. John indicated they're all exhibiting clear symptoms. I've placed them near Mr. Morgan who's fading fast. We've got him on a respirator now. Do you want me to initiate the same treatment régime for the new patients?"

"Yes, and I'm going to call Harry now. It looks like we're going to be facing the worst-case scenario."

Harry answered on the first ring. Sally started by thanking him for his support in the discussion with Larry Haskins. Harry replied, "So he's a dork; who cares; he does a good job on the administrative things, and once you get past his emotional reactions, he can be counted on to do the right thing."

"Well," Sally said, "we're going to test your hypothesis because we just had three more cases present with the same symptoms. Patient number one is going to die, and his wife may not make it, not if it really is hemorrhagic fever. Harry, I think you need to talk to the morgue about this. I think we're going to be taxing their logistical capabilities."

"I'll do it Sally. The security personnel should be in place already. What else do you have for me?"

She then explained the need for their hospital to become the primary treatment site. Harry thought for an agonizingly long few seconds.

"Wow," he said, "let me think for a minute. That decision has a number of major consequences."

Silence once again followed. Sally stared at the clock on her wall and counted off the seconds before Harry finally answered, "Yes, it's the optimum solution. Then all of the CDC and infection control resources can be focused in one facility. You're right, this is certainly going to test Larry's backbone, but let me handle Larry. If he doesn't agree then I'll go to the Board. When will you have the confirmatory lab results?"

Sally looked at her watch. "Should be another three hours."

"OK, what else do you need?"

Sally ran through the list, and Harry took notes as she rattled off item after item.

"As soon as you get lab confirmation, I'm going to activate the Bioterrorism Plan, and it's going to mean getting a lot of government agencies involved. I'll call a friend of mine at CDC and let him know what's going on here. You're going to be stage center on this, and I want you to extricate yourself from actual patient care as soon as the CDC says you're not contagious. I'm going to need you to interface with all the bureaucrats, the FBI, Homeland Security, the local police, and the Mayor's office."

"Why me Harry?"

"Because I trust your judgment. By the way, the anthrax vaccine is staged at Cook County Hospital, and one-thousand doses should be here in the hour."

"You're the best Harry. If you run for President, you've definitely got my vote."

"I'll remember your offer. I just may call in the chit someday."

They both laughed.

3

The results arrived shortly after three o'clock. Bad news, both the anthrax and hemorrhagic fever diagnoses were confirmed, but at least Sally now knew exactly what she was up against. Bruce Mathews also added a strange twist to the test results. The actual Ebola virus causing hemorrhagic fever couldn't be identified, but he did identify several of the protein markers associated with the disease. Sally immediately called Harry, and he activated the hospital's Bioterrorism Readiness Plan.

Harry first called City Hall. Luckily the plan included the Mayor's private telephone line. He answered on the third ring. "Mayor, this is Dr. Harry Haskins, I'm the Chief of Staff at Northwestern Hospital. We have just activated our Bioterrorism Readiness Plan. We have had an outbreak of anthrax and hemorrhagic fever at our Emergency Room."

Mayor Dobbins stunned by the news asked, "How many people are affected?"

"A total of five so far, but we expect the number to increase rapidly. We believe we're seeing the leading edge of the epidemic."

"Doctor, I'll have my Chief of Staff Sid Greenfield contact you shortly. He'll coordinate things from our end. In the meantime what can I do to help?"

"Thank you Mayor Dobbins. I suggest two things immediately. First, we believe calls need to be made to all medical facilities and ambulance services in the city. Until further notice, all patients should be brought to our hospital. We are in the process of transferring our patients to other facilities to allow us to accommodate up to several hundred patients. We believe it's best to minimize contagion by consolidating all patients into one facility."

"Doctor Haskins, I agree completely and appreciate your willingness to place your staff at risk. What else?"

"We believe it is critical to immediately inform the public about the problem and explain what they should do if they exhibit any symptoms."

"Well Doctor, I agree, but we need to make sure we don't cause widespread panic. Let's set up a conference call in one hour. I'll have my key personnel there so we can decide on the appropriate course of action."

"Mayor, I'm going to ask some of our people to attend the meeting as well. Shall we call your office?"

"Yes, Doctor Haskins, my Administrative Assistant will take your call and transfer it into my conference room."

"One final thing Mayor, I'm going to immediately notify the CDC, FBI, and Department of Homeland Security."

"Thank you Doctor; we'll talk again in one hour."

Following the call, Harry hustled down to the corner office to speak with Larry Becker. Harry expected a major fight over the decisions he and Sally had made. Uncharacteristically, Larry sat quietly behind his desk looking pale and staring blindly at the far wall of his office. Harry wondered whether his CEO would be up to the hard decisions ahead.

"Larry, it's as we suspected. The lab has confirmed it; it's anthrax and hemorrhagic fever. I just talked to the Mayor's Office and we've scheduled a conference call in one hour. I talked to Sally; we have three new patients. The first is about to die and his wife may be next. Here's what she and I have decided to do, and I don't want any arguments from you."

Larry suddenly turned his attention away from the wall and stared at his Chief of Staff.

"Northwestern is going to be the primary care facility for the city. All of our patients who can be moved will be transferred to other facilities. Our Bioterrorism Readiness Plan indicates the best way to expand our number of beds while providing good air handling isolation between these contaminated areas and the other facilities in the hospital.

Larry now looked fully alert.

"The entire South Wing will be sealed off and become the primary care area. If the patient load requires, we'll seal off the West Wing next and finally the North Wing. We'll save the East Wing for those patients we can't transfer to other hospitals."

Larry listened with glazed over eyes to the message Harry delivered. "Yes Harry, I agree; it's the right course of action. Now we have to be the good soldiers and do what's best for the city. I've been thinking about your earlier analysis. When this is all over, our hospital will be perceived as the premier facility in the nation."

Harry looked shocked at Larry's ready acceptance of the plan. He had indeed stepped up to the plate. "Thank you Larry. Now let's agree on who's going to be on the conference call. Sally should be our lead medical person. Sarah Feldman in Infection Control must also be involved."

Larry added, "Paula Flattery in Public Affairs should also be there, and we may need to add people to the team, but we can do it later."

"Sounds good. Why don't you set up the conference call, and contact Homeland Security and the FBI. Meanwhile, I'll inform CDC. They're going to want to send a team here ASAP. One more thing Larry; Sally is going to be our lead person on anything having to do with the care of these patients. She's the best and you know it. If anyone is going to talk to the outside world about what's happening here, it's going to be her; agreed?"

"Yes, you're right; we can count on her. She's the right choice."

Harry left the CEO's office with renewed respect for his colleague, and knew he'd be able to count on Larry to do the right things in this time of crisis. Back in his office, Harry called his good friend Al Shlepley at CDC. "Hey Shlep, it's Harry Haskins."

"I know; who else would call me Shlep?"

Harry filled in his old college buddy on the facts.

"Hemorrhagic fever and anthrax, how can that be?"

"I don't know, but I'm sure your people are going to help us find out."

"Okay Harry, I'll talk to the Director as soon as we're done talking, and we'll have a full investigative team in the air in the next few hours. I'll have them contact you when they arrive."

"Thanks Al, I think this is going to be a major epidemic."

Next Harry called Sally. He briefed her on his talks with the Mayor and Larry, and explained her role in the upcoming conference call. Sally informed him of the arrival of another four patients and stressed the urgency to expand the treatment area.

Sally asked for one additional favor. "Can you have a copy of the Bioterrorism Readiness Plan sent down to the ER. I want to review it prior to the conference call."

"Will do Sally, and I'll have my secretary patch you into the conference call. Hang in there; you're going a great job."

Sally thought, *great job my ass, my world is collapsing around me, and I just hope I'm up to the challenge.* She thought back to an expression she learned in Med School *"When you're up to your ass in alligators, it's hard to remember your job is to drain the swamp.* And this was one hell of a swamp needing to be drained.

4

The FBI Field Office in Chicago had been contacted by Northwestern Hospital, and Jimmy Davis, the head of the Chicago office, immediately contacted Director Jacobson in Washington to alert him to the problem. "Bruce, Hi, sorry to bother you, but we've got a problem here in Chicago."

"Well Jimmy, what a nice way to start the conversation. What have you got?"

"It looks like a bioterrorism attack. A couple of hours ago residents on the Near Northwest Side began walking into Northwestern Hospital's Emergency Room. Our friend Sally Lawson diagnosed anthrax and hemorrhagic fever as soon as the first patient arrived. CDC and everyone here are doing everything they can to deal with the problem, but right now I've got to put together a team to figure out whether it's really terrorism, and if so, who's to blame."

"Okay Jimmy, it looks like you've got things under control. Who do you want on the team?"

"Well, Alice Folkman as the Senior Agent, Benny Cannon in Tech-ops, and Glenda Beecher in the Forensic Lab. Then I want to ask Dan Lawson to be the liaison with the police, and Sally Lawson to be our medical expert."

"Sounds good Jimmy. Let me also recommend Brian Sawkowski, he's our lead agent in the Terrorism Section. He worked on the Florida anthrax case."

"A good choice Bruce. Have him pack his bag and get here as soon as he can."

"Will do, and Jimmy call me anytime if anything important comes up."

"I'll try to give you a call once a day to keep you current."

Jimmy called his senior staff together and gave them as much information as he knew, at this stage basically zilch. "Listen, I'm going over to Northwestern to see if I can get some more information. Alice, why don't you come with me?"

¤   ¤   ¤

Jimmy and Alice walked into a maelstrom of activity. Dozens of ambulances were lined up along Huron Street waiting to transfer patients to other hospitals, and the hospital's staff loaded patients as quickly and safely as possible. Police tried to maintain order amidst the chaos. Luckily, no TV crews had arrived on the scene, but Jimmy knew they would be there shortly. Engineering crews busily erected transparent sheet plastic walls to seal off the Emergency Room from the rest of the hospital.

Carefully avoiding dozens of gurneys filled with patients, they finally found the information desk in the main lobby and showed their FBI credentials. Jimmy said, "I'd like to speak with the person in charge of the hospital."

Both ladies looked like they were preparing to meet the grim reaper. Smeared mascara covered both of their faces. One of the women behind the counter answered, "That would be Larry Becker. Let me call him for you."

After a brief conversation, she escorted them both to Larry Becker's office. On his phone, he motioned them both to sit down. Larry was evidently talking to another hospital discussing the moving of patients. "Okay, so you can take another two-hundred patients, but no more. Great, they should be transferred over there within two hours. Thanks Jack, I owe you big-time for this."

After introductions, Jimmy said, "I'm sorry to have to bother you in the middle of a crisis, but you can understand why we're here, and why we need to start as quickly as possible figuring out what happened. What can you tell me?"

"Agent Davis, I'm sorry but we don't have a clue, except we now have eleven patients with anthrax and hemorrhagic fever who walked into the Emergency Room, and we're gearing up for what our medical people believe is going to be one hell of an epidemic."

"Is Doctor Lawson in the Emergency Room?"

"Yes, she's in charge. How do you know her?"

"We're good friends. I'll give her a call."

As soon as Jimmy and Alice moved into the hallway, Jimmy called Sally on her cellphone. "Sally, it's Jimmy; we found out about the bioterrorism attack an hour ago. What can you tell me?"

Sally proceeded to give Jimmy a quick summary. She concluded with, "Listen Jimmy, I know your first reaction will be to send people into the infected area, but don't unless everyone is fully protected. Talk to Glenda; she'll know what needs to be done."

"Will do Sally. By the way, I talked to Director Jacobson, and we both want you on the investigative team. He's going to talk to Larry Becker."

Sally responded as Jimmy expected. "Bullshit, I've got patients to take care of."

"I know, but we need you on the team. You can join us after things stabilize."

"Okay, but only after I'm done at the hospital."

"You've got it!"

5

Mayor Dobbins called the meeting to order at 5:15 P.M. The Mayor introduced: Sidney Greenfield, his Chief of Staff; Jack McWalden, his Chief of Police; Dorothy Reems, the Director of Public Affairs; and Rich Gantrey, the Director of Public Health and Safety. He also decided to record the meeting so minutes could be prepared without the usual human errors.

Harry Haskins then introduced the Northwestern team and the meeting began with Harry asking Sally to summarize the events for the entire group. As Sally began, she realized all of this had happened during the last seven hours. It took her almost twenty minutes to summarize the important points.

As Sally briefed the group, Larry thought about her being so insistent on the most conservative action plan. She had guessed right and his hospital now looked like the best in class.

After Sally finished her detailed summary, the Mayor's team took the lead on what specific actions should be taken, including how to communicate all of this to the general public. The Mayor wanted to know more about how the infection was transmitted between people.

After a long painful silence Sally decided to answer the question. "If this is a bioterrorism attack, then the agents were probably dispersed into the air. That would explain the inhalation anthrax. The cutaneous anthrax is probably nothing more than the same agent coming into contact with a cut on the first patient's exposed leg. The hemorrhagic fever had also probably been delivered through the air."

The Mayor and his team were hanging onto every word.

"We need to be concerned with two possible modes of infection. The first is from people breathing in any remaining agent from the primary dispersion, and the second is from cross-contamination between a contaminated patient and others. Luckily this second mode of transmission is unlikely as long as people do not come into direct contact with an infected patient's bodily fluids. Our medical personnel are using Standard Precautions to mitigate any possible retransmission of the infections."

"Doctor Lawson," the Mayor asked, "What's the risk of death from these agents?"

"Mayor, the prognosis is very poor indeed. Patients with inhalation anthrax, even with aggressive antibiotic therapy, are likely to experience a 60% to 90% probability of death, and the hemorrhagic fever, depending on the strain of Ebola virus, is likely to cause about a

90% probability of death. Put both agents together and I'm guessing at least 90% mortality.

If Sally had been able to see the faces of the people in the Mayor's conference room, she would have witnessed shock and disbelief, and then finally realization of the magnitude of the problem facing the city.

"My God," said the Mayor, "Where are we going to put all of the dead? Do we have any idea about the number of people who might be infected?"

Again Sally answered the question after realizing nobody else risked speaking. "It's too early to tell. All we know at this time is we're only seeing the beginning and the number of patients will grow exponentially."

The meeting then turned to specific actions to take. Everyone knew there needed to be a public announcement. Dorothy Reems had been getting calls from the local media all afternoon, and rumors spread rapidly. The Chief of Police wanted to avoid widespread panic. Everyone fleeing the city would create a major problem. Sally interjected, "People fleeing the city will only increase the risk of the infection spreading. From a public safety perspective, we need to quarantine people to ensure containment."

"What, lock people in their houses?" the Mayor's Chief of Staff said defiantly.

A loud heated discussion ensued between the Mayor's people. Sid Greenfield expressed concern about violating people's rights, and feared the panic created by any announcement. The Chief of Police felt widespread looting would certainly occur. Dorothy Reems argued for full disclosure and Rich Gantrey wanted to call up the National Guard and proclaim martial law.

Finally the Mayor said, "Quiet, enough already, the most important thing is what to do from a medical perspective. Then, we'll modify the plan as necessary to deal with the realities of an ignorant, terrified population. Doctor Lawson, you seem to be the person who knows the most about this from a medical perspective. If you were in my shoes, what would you recommend?"

Sally hadn't thought about this aspect of the problem before but knew intuitively what needed to be done. "Mayor, here's what I'd do. First I'd look at where all of these patients are living. Their locations in the city will probably tell us where the primary dispersal of the agent took place. The earliest patients are probably the ones closest to the point of dispersion. Then, I'd cordon off a half mile radius from where these patients live and have the police set up roadblocks to enforce a quarantine.

I'd have trained medical personnel check everyone within the perimeter to ascertain whether they're infected. If they are, then they go to the hospital. If they're not, they get anthrax vaccine and prophylactic antibiotics. I don't know if it's possible from a logistics standpoint, but it's what I'd do. We simply can't let this infection spread."

Mayor Dobbins listened carefully with both hands engulfing his chin. He turned to his Director of Public Health and Safety. "What do you think Rich?"

"Mayor, what Doctor Lawson is suggesting is the best course of action from a medical point of view. From a public safety point of view, containment is the key."

"Jack can the police enforce the quarantine?"

"Mayor, we're talking about literally thousands of officers needed to man a several mile long barricade. It's at least a four mile perimeter we'll have to manage twenty four hours a day. We can do it, but I can tell you opportunistic crime will go up throughout the rest of the city. Maybe the National Guard should be called up?"

"Jack, it'll take a couple of days to activate the Guard. We'll have to live with the increase in crime. We need to do the right thing, and do it now. We can consider the Guard if we can't manage the perimeter. Is anyone against Doctor Lawson's plan?"

The Mayor's question was met with silence. "Alright," he said, "I'll take your lack of response as we all vote in favor of the doctor's plan. Rich, I want you to work with Dr. Haskins to get the support of all of the hospitals in the area to supply medical staff to go from door to door to check out the people living inside the perimeter."

Dobbins said, "Jack, how long will it take you to cordon off the area?"

Jack McWalden thought for a few moments and answered, "About four hours. I'm also going to need Doctor Lawson to give us the addresses of where her patients are coming from so we can plan the quarantine area."

Sally said, "Give me your cellphone number, and I'll get back to you with the information as soon as we're done with this call."

Mayor Dobbins said, "I want everyone here to exchange cellphone numbers. Now let's turn our attention to the problem of communications. What do we tell people, who should tell them, and how do we tell them? Dorothy, what do you think?"

"I've been thinking about this since I first learned of the problem. We need to be honest, but without raising fears; we can't afford to have people panic. I think we should go on TV and radio; all the stations. The Mayor should start out and tell the people there has been a terrorist attack, but only a small area of the city is affected. Then someone from Northwestern Hospital should explain the medical issues, what the symptoms are, and where to go if you observe the symptoms. Then, Rich should discuss the public safety concerns, emphasizing medical teams will be visiting each house in the area to examine everyone, and ambulances will take them to the hospital if necessary. Jack should then identify the affected area he has cordoned off. The Mayor should finish up with a plea for people in the affected area to stay in their homes until they have been checked out by medical personnel. We should also set up a hot line, and be prepared to give press conferences at least once a day until the situation has stabilized."

Mayor Dobbins said, "I like it Dorothy except for the terrorism part. Until we know for sure, we should not use the word terrorism. Doctor Haskins, will Doctor Lawson provide the medical update?"

"Unfortunately she's in quarantine for a few days. I guess I'll present the medical perspective."

"Okay, we'll start the press conference at 9:45 P.M. A few more things; I want the police to cordon off the perimeter the same time we go on TV and radio. Doctor Haskins, please come up to my office one hour before we go live. I want a final review of everyone's speeches. We need to make sure we're not providing any contradictory information. Also let's send sound trucks through the area just prior to the TV presentation. We should alert everyone in both English and Spanish to turn on their TV for instructions. I'm going to call the Governor after our meeting to brief him on our plan, and indicate, depending upon how the population reacts, we may have to call up the National Guard."

After the conference call ended, Sally sat down at the nurse's station and listed all of the home addresses of the infected patients. She noted an additional six patients had been checked into the ER during the teleconference. Sally didn't recognize all of the streets, but many seemed to be clustered together, obviously good news.

She called the Chief of Police, and at his request, e-mailed the list to his assistant's computer. "Doctor Lawson," he asked, "would you happen to be related to Detective Dan Lawson?"

"Yes, he's my husband."

"Well, I've heard a lot about you, and the way you handled yourself in our meeting, I can see you've lived up to the advanced billing. It's going to be a pleasure to work with you. Please feel free to call me if the Department can be of any assistance."

"Thanks for the offer, and please call me Sally."

Now Sally needed to make one final call to her husband. Dan answered his cellphone. "Hi Honey, listen we've got a major crisis at the hospital. It looks like we've had a bioterrorist attack on the Near Northwest Side. It's anthrax and hemorrhagic fever."

"Oh shit! What else can you tell me?"

"I just had a meeting with the Mayor's Office, and we're going to cordon off the affected section of the city. All patients are going to be brought to our hospital. I'm going to be quarantined for the next few days, just to make sure I haven't been infected, but don't worry, I'm sure I'm okay. Before this is over, there're going to be hundreds if not thousands affected."

"I'll give our office a heads-up. I'm sure we'll be asked to help with enforcing the sealed-off area."

"The FBI has been notified, and Jimmy's involved. Oh, and one more thing, make sure anyone patrolling or entering the affected area is wearing gloves, masks and face shields. You can only get infected from breathing in the agent or if it comes into contact with a cut on your skin. Stay safe, I love you."

Dan sat at his desk after Sally's call. He bent a pencil in his hand until it broke. He knew his wife might be deliberately minimizing the risk to ease his concerns. Finally he turned his attention to the problem. This crisis would surely test the City's resolve, and he wondered whether widespread panic would break out as soon as the news of the attack hit the airways.

Involving the FBI was obviously necessary, and Dan knew the Chicago Field Office would be heavily involved meaning, Jimmy Davis would be busy for many weeks to come.

Jimmy Davis and Dan were best friends. They were roommates at college where both studied Criminology. Jimmy joined the FBI, and Dan decided to sign up with the Chicago Police Department and had recently been promoted to Detective. Both Dan and Sally had worked for the FBI in the past, and it looked like they would all be working together once again.

6

The police quickly analyzed Sally's patient data and set the perimeter: Ashland Avenue on the eastern edge, Western Avenue on the west, Grand Avenue on the south, and Division Street on the north. In total nearly two thousand officers were pulled from a multitude of other assignments.

At 9:30 P.M., the taskforce moved into position to cordon off the affected area. They quickly ran out of yellow crime scene tape, but used squad cars to block intersections and alleys. Simultaneously, sound trucks moved through the area announcing in both English and Spanish that the area had been quarantined, and everyone should listen to the TV or radio for a broadcast from the Mayor's office scheduled for 9:45 P.M.

Cars registered to residents living in the area were permitted to enter the zone. Cars passing through the area that had not stopped were allowed to leave, but all other cars and pedestrians were kept inside the perimeter. All requests for an explanation directed the person to listen to the TV or radio at 9:45 P.M.

Dorothy had done a great job of alerting the key media players, and there were hundreds of news people assembled for the press conference. Mayor Dobbins and the other speakers climbed onto the makeshift stage at exactly 9:45 P.M. The Mayor walked to the podium, and put on his reading glasses. It was the first time the public would see him wearing glasses. He knew his image as a young vibrant leader might be slightly tarnished; but he also knew he had to get the tone of this meeting right, and the glasses actually helped set the stage for a serious discussion.

"Citizens of Chicago, I am here tonight to brief you on a serious situation affecting the health and safety of the public. Several days ago an area of our city was exposed to two highly infectious agents, anthrax and Ebola. The cause of this contamination is not known at this time. Due to the severity of these agents I have ordered the following actions be taken.

"First, as I speak, the affected area has been cordoned off, and a quarantine is in effect. The area is bounded by Division Street, Grand Avenue, Ashland Avenue, and Western Avenue. No one will be allowed in or out of the area unless authorized. These boundaries have been chosen to ensure the epidemic is contained. We know everyone living in the area is not affected, but I want to ensure we contain this outbreak.

"Second, we are in the process of staging a large number of medical personnel within the cordoned off area. They will move from house to house to examine every person living inside the perimeter. Those who have been infected will be transported to Northwestern Hospital, which has been designated as the primary treatment center. For those not infected, prophylactic treatment will be initiated. This will include antibiotic drugs and vaccinations as appropriate.

"Finally, it is absolutely necessary for everyone in the quarantined area to follow instructions from police and medical personnel on the scene. If necessary the National Guard will be called up to maintain law and order, but I am certain this will not be necessary. I know the people of this great city will act in a responsible manner. I have been assured by my medical advisors, if everyone follows the instructions we will be issuing in a few minutes, then this emergency should be over in a few days."

As he spoke, a person standing next to him translated his comments into sign language, and simultaneous Spanish translations appeared at the bottom of the TV screen.

"I would now like to introduce Doctor Harry Haskins, the Chief of Staff at Northwestern Hospital, who will discuss the outbreak."

"Thank you Mayor Dobbins. Earlier today, infected patients began arriving at the Northwestern Hospital Emergency Room. Fortunately, our medical personnel were able to quickly diagnose anthrax and hemorrhagic fever. Later diagnostic tests confirmed these preliminary diagnoses. We immediately shut down the Emergency Room to everyone except infected patients and have been transferring our non-infected patients to other medical facilities. We are converting our hospital into the primary point of treatment for all infected patients. A triage center has been set up just outside of the Emergency Room entrance on Erie Street. Anyone outside of the cordoned off area who believe they have been infected should come to the triage center for examination. The following symptoms are indicative of the infection, but must be seen collectively, not individually: blood in the urine, stool, and saliva; headache; red spots on the skin; flu-like symptoms; and muscle and joint pain. Now I'd like to introduce Rich Gantrey who will discuss some public safety issues."

"Thank you Doctor Haskins. I want to discuss the safety precautions the public should take to avoid secondary infections. These diseases can only be retransmitted by contact with infected fluid from sick patients or by inhaling the agent from particles dispersed from a sick person's cough or sneeze. Therefore, the best precaution is to avoid contact with sick patients and if contact is necessary, then protective precautions such as gloves and facemasks must be used.

"For those within the cordoned off area, you will notice all medical personnel are fully protected with gloves, gowns, masks and face shields. This is for their protection, and to ensure we successfully contain the epidemic. Please do not interfere with police officers or medical personnel. They are trying to do the best they can with limited resources. Chief of Police Jack McWalden will now discuss some security measures."

"Thank you Mr. Gantry. The police will maintain law and order within the affected area, and we will take all necessary steps to ensure people do not enter or leave the area without the approval of the Mayor's Office."

Mayor Dobbins once again stepped up to the microphone. "We will be holding news conferences daily. We have set up a twenty four hour telephone hot line to answer any questions. The number is 1/800/555-5555. As you can appreciate, we are trying to respond to a very fluid situation, so please try to listen to these news conferences for the latest information. Finally, we have prepared fact sheets for those in attendance today, and we will be taking questions from the press at the next news conference which I am scheduling for ten o'clock tomorrow morning. I thank you for your attention, and my prayers go out to the families of those infected."

Amidst a chorus of yells and screams from the press, the Mayor's team left the podium and the auditorium.

¤   ¤   ¤

Sally didn't have the opportunity to see the news conference. Instead, she supervised the completion of the South Wing's conversion to an expanded Emergency Room facility. The quick actions of the hospital's dedicated staff amazed Sally as she watched the expanded emergency room take shape. Everyone knew the urgency of the situation. Patients were moved; rooms were modified to accommodate multiple beds; plastic sheet barriers were erected to isolate the South Wing of each floor from their central lobbies.

The engineers built a special isolated corridor in the basement to allow for the dead to be brought to the morgue. Also, sterile pass-throughs were created on each floor to allow for food, medicine, and equipment to be transferred into the quarantine areas, and contaminated refuse to be moved safely out.

The anthrax vaccine had arrived, and many patients and all of the staff had been inoculated. A large supply of scarce antibiotics and antivirals were being sent from other hospitals along with a large number of respirators to manage the worst patients. The death toll had now reached six, and surprisingly Mrs. Morgan somehow still hung on tenaciously to life. The will to live and to take care of her children trumped the known pathology of these diseases, and most unexpectedly, the Morgan children were still asymptomatic. A total of 128 patients had now been admitted to the hospital, and the trend rose along an exponential curve.

Sally looked around the ER with growing apprehension. *My God, how did I ever get into this business?*

Sally thought back to the quintessential moment many years ago. She had helped some strangers who had been involved in a head-on car crash with a truck. It had been the transformational moment when she decided to become a doctor and specialize in emergency medicine. After completing her B.S. degree in Nuclear Engineering, she had been accepted at Northwestern Medical School, and the rest was history.

She had been through many crises in her life; the early deaths of both parents in an accident, and being drafted by the FBI to help solve a bizarre terrorism case. In fact, it's how she met Dan. She had fallen in love with him from the first moment they met, and every day they spent together reaffirmed their decision to get married. She had thought career was everything until she met Dan, and now both saving patients and loving her husband consumed her days.

This crisis, however, would test her in a way that defied prediction. She could easily imagine the horror of the next few days. Hundreds if not thousands would die. Parents were going to be without children, children without parents, families thrown into chaos, and friends never to be seen again; all because of some asshole terrorists who were after something they thought couldn't be accomplished in any other way. Indeed, some shitty people inhabited the planet.

She put on gloves over a disposable full body protective jumpsuit, donned a facemask and placed a face shield over her head. She first checked with the triage team on Erie Street. Hundreds of people were lined up waiting to be examined. Sally knew most were not infected, just the usual reaction from the general public who had seen the news conference. Nurses had handed out masks to all the people waiting in line just in case any were actually contagious. Doctor Goodwin headed the triage station. "Hey Doris, how's it going?"

Doctor Doris Goodwin, the head of Pediatrics, looked up to see who had called her name, a look of extreme fatigue stared back at Sally through two face shields. "Sally, it's getting worse; the line keeps getting longer and longer; we're running out of facemasks; I've ordered more, but if they don't get here in ten minutes, we'll run out."

"I'll check on the masks as soon as I get back inside. How are we doing on the vaccine; do you have enough?"

"We're okay. I'm only vaccinating people who are either from the affected area or have been there in the last week."

Sally said, "The line is only going to get longer. We'll need to staff a second triage center on the other side of the driveway. I'll ask Harry to get us the extra staff. How long have you been here?"

"Doris looked at her watch; about four hours."

"Okay, we're going to go to six hours on, six hours off shifts. I have medical staff rest areas set up on the sixth floor. They should be ready in another hour. When this crew goes on break have everyone shower with the bactericidal soap, and make sure you have all of the disposable gowns double bagged and placed in the refuse area near the sixth floor lobby."

Sally walked over to some cops standing near the line maintaining order. She motioned for them to come over. "Thanks for your help guys, but if you're anywhere near these people I want you fully protected just like the medical staff. Talk to Doctor Goodwin over at the triage center. She'll get you some protective clothes."

Sally then walked back to her desk and contacted Larry Becker. "Larry, I need your help. We've ordered more facemasks, but they haven't arrived at the triage center. We're going to run out in ten minutes."

"I sent over the head of Purchasing to the local distributor to pick up ten thousand. He just called to tell me he's on his way back, but he's stuck in traffic. A lot of people are fleeing the city. From now on, I'm going to have the police act as couriers. How's it going down there?"

"We've admitted 128 patients, and we have over one-hundred people waiting in line at the triage center. The South Wing should be ready in another hour, and that's good because we're out of room in the ER. The staff is holding up pretty well, but we're going to need more people manning the triage area. I'm going to talk to Harry as soon as he gets back from the Mayor's office."

"He got back five minutes ago. He's in his office. Hold on and I'll ask him to come over."

Sally waited until Harry got on the speakerphone. "Sally, how's it going?

"Good, but the lines outside are getting longer and we're going to have to set up a second triage station."

"I'll get it staffed in the next hour. Over ninety percent of our people agreed to work extended hours. I never would have expected such commitment."

"Harry, we have a great group of professionals, even down to the janitors. They all recognize the need and will respond accordingly. How did the news conference go?"

"Great Sally. The Mayor set exactly the right tone. Now we'll have to see whether the public panics. I'm betting they won't, but we'll know for sure in the next couple of hours."

Vicky interrupted, "The South Wing is officially opened."

"Harry, we're good to go on the expanded area; I've got to go."

7

Dan manned the perimeter along with what seemed like half of the police force. Suddenly, a dark-blue Toyota Corolla raced toward a narrow gap in the barricade. The car couldn't possibly fit through the narrow opening, but the car's driver thought he'd give it a try. As the police ran for cover, the Toyota collided with a police car and wooden barricade and stopped. The police surrounded the car with pistols drawn and ordered the terrified man out of his car. His body, covered with red marks, staggered from the car. He collapsed to the ground, begging to be taken to the hospital.

Dan ordered a nearby ambulance to bring the man to Northwestern Hospital. The driver and his partner, dressed in protective suits, placed the man on a gurney, rushed him into the back of the ambulance, and accelerated down the street with sirens blaring.

Prior to this incident, the epidemic had not been up close and personal, but the presence of the infected man covered in a bright red rash brought the officers manning the barricades face to face with the realities of a life threatening biological terrorist attack. Those officers not wearing gloves and facemasks began a frantic search for protection. Dan wondered how many other citizens were going to panic and try to break through the quarantine.

A caravan of emergency medical vehicles pulled up to the blockade at the corner of Augusta Boulevard and Ashland Avenue. A man dressed in a full protective jumpsuit walked over to the barricade and asked for the person in charge. Dan as the senior Detective at the station figured out he was the one. Dan introduced himself to the man who looked like he could be ready for a walk in outer space. The body behind the plastic helmet turned out to be Doctor Eli Fineman.

"Detective Lawson, we're the medical team from Cook County Hospital. We're probably the first to arrive. My team is going to go to what we believe is ground-zero and begin examining residents. I want one of your sound trucks to alert the residents. Each family should assemble by their front door, but remain inside their homes or apartments. Can four police officers accompany us in case we run into any problems? Whoever goes into this area needs to be fully protected in the same type of Hazmet suit I'm wearing."

After calling for the sound truck, Dan called out the names of three other officers from his precinct and explained the situation. The four were handed protective suits and instructed in how to wear the gear. The fully protected officers split up and Dan entered the lead doctor's ambulance. They talked as the emergency vehicle caravan slowly proceeded west on Augusta. "Dan, we have no idea of what to expect, but we know it's going to be pretty bad. If nobody answers their doors, we're going to need to break in. Some people may be too sick to come to the door or may already be dead."

"What are you going to do?"

"We're going to examine each person and ask them some questions. If they show signs of the infection, then we're going to load them, and the rest of their families into the ambulances, and bring them over to Northwestern Hospital."

"What if they're asymptomatic?"

"Then I've got a card to fill out for each patient. They'll be given anthrax vaccine, antibiotics, antiviral drugs, facemasks and gloves to wear. They'll keep a copy of the card to bring to the hospital if they get sick, and we'll keep another copy to know what they've been given just in case they lose their card."

Dan, listening to the doctor, decided to move his holster and gun to the outside of his protective suit. He called his three buddies in the other ambulances and asked them to do the same.

The caravan, led by the sound truck, stopped just west of Damen Avenue. With the loud speakers blaring the message in English first and then Spanish, residents were asked to assemble their families inside their front doors and wait for the medical team to arrive. The sound truck then explained what the doctors planned to do and what would happen if the medical team determined they were infected.

The four medical teams, each accompanied by a police officer, split up and began systematically checking each building on the street. Dan followed Doctor Fineman's team. The doctor rang the doorbell on a corner single family home, and a terrified family appeared at the door. The mother carried a small toddler and the father held tightly onto a young girl about five years old. The doctor asked if they spoke English, and the man answered yes. Fineman then confirmed the people had watched the news conference. The doctor then requested permission to enter their home and received a quick yes.

"Good, I'm going to examine each of you." He looked into the living room and asked them to please sit on the couch. "Have any of the family experienced any of the symptoms discussed at the news conference?"

The woman answered no, and he then wanted the parents to strip the children down to their underwear. He carefully checked them out, paying particular attention to the presence of any rashes and blood in their mouths.

He then moved to the two parents. The woman appeared nervous at having to undress in front of strangers, but she was more concerned about what the doctor would find. The examination of the family took less than five minutes and they all seemed symptom free.

The family smiled when Fineman told them they appeared to be in good health. He told them to call a number on the card if any of the listed symptoms were observed.

The doctor then explained the pathology of anthrax and hemorrhagic fever, and easily convinced the parents to agree to take the anthrax vaccine, antibiotics and antiviral drugs.

One of the other medics in the team inoculated each family member while Doctor Fineman filled out eight cards. He filled in their names, the address, the results of his examination, and noted the medications each had received. One of the medics handed out facemasks and gloves and stressed the importance of the masks being worn by each family member at all times for the next few days.

The man asked, "When will the quarantine be lifted?"

Fineman replied, "I don't know, but it will probably last at least another week."

The father looked distraught, "We're going to need to get food for the children in the next few days."

Fineman looked startled. "We haven't thought of that."

He took out a cellphone from his pocket and dialed a number. "Dave, it's Eli. I'm at the first home; the family checks out okay, but the father wanted to know how he would get food for his children if there's a quarantine in effect. You need to pass this message up to the Mayor's office. We're going to have to get food and all kinds of other things to these people if the quarantine is going to last more than a few days."

Fineman then spoke to the family. "The request for food and other things will get to the mayor's office. I don't know how they'll work out the logistics, but I guarantee you'll get what you need."

The family thanked Fineman and escorted the team to the front door. Fineman looked at his watch. "Ten minutes for an easy one. Get ready for a long night."

As they left the first house, a medic attached a large sign to the front door informing others this family had been examined.

At the next house, loud knocks on the front door and repeated ringing of the doorbell went unanswered. Fineman said, "Dan, it's your show now."

Dan looked at the front entranceway. The door had sidelights. Dan used the butt end of his pistol to break one of the glass panes. He carefully reached inside, released the deadbolt lock, and opened the door.

Fineman said, "Well done Detective," as he entered the home. He shouted, "Is anybody here?"

No answer, so the team began searching the house. On the second floor Dan found an elderly couple lying in their bed. Doctor Fineman quickly confirmed they were both dead. He left two of the medics to fill out the paperwork and transfer the bodies into one of the ambulances.

Meanwhile, they proceeded to the next home, actually a two-flat apartment building. They started on the second floor unit and were greeted by a middle-aged woman with two children. "My husband is in the bedroom, and I think he has the infection."

Dan looked at her and suspected she also was infected, but perhaps at an earlier stage. Her eldest child, a boy about nine years old, also had a rash on his face. Proceeding to the bedroom, Doctor Fineman confirmed the woman's suspicions. A quick examination of the others also confirmed all but their two-year old were infected.

Fineman explained they would all have to be taken to the hospital for treatment. The woman expressed concern about the children, but

Fineman explained even their youngest son would need to be quarantined within the hospital. The woman started to pack some things, but Fineman explained they would need to leave now. One of the medics escorted the family down to an ambulance and then returned with a stretcher to help move the husband. Dan assisted while Fineman proceeded down to the apartment on the first floor.

By the time Dan and the medic returned, Fineman had already confirmed the middle-aged couple living in the first floor apartment were also infected, and they both were escorted to the same ambulance. The emergency vehicle wasn't really set up to handle six patients, but crowded or not, the driver turned on his siren and headed off toward Northwestern Hospital.

Fineman spoke to Dan, "I'm surprised we haven't found people who refuse to come. I guess they're all really scared. The Mayor's news conference must have been pretty effective at explaining the severity of the situation. It just goes to show you, you're always better off leveling with people."

Dan asked, "How long do you think it's going to take to examine everyone inside the perimeter?"

"Well, I heard there'll be a total of thirty-two medical teams helping out. We're estimating there are about 100 residents on each block, and we have about one hundred blocks to cover. That gives us about ten-thousand people to check. If there are a total of four doctors on each team, then we've got about 128 doctors. So far we've spent about thirty minutes to look at twelve people."

Fineman did some quick calculations in his head and concluded, "I'm guessing we'll need about four to six hours in total."

Dan felt encouraged, "That's a lot less than I thought. Of the twelve people we've examined, you've sent half to the hospital. If that's typical, then about five-thousand patients will need to be taken to Northwestern Hospital. My wife's a doctor there; I know they can't handle that many patients."

"Remember Dan, we're probably at the central point in the contaminated area. As we move further out toward the perimeter, I'm hoping we'll be sending fewer people to the hospital. What's your wife's name?"

"Sally Lawson."

"I know Sally. I saw her give a paper last year at the AMA conference in Chicago."

8

Sally tried her best to manage a logistical nightmare. A little over four-hundred patients had checked into the hospital. Three triage stations had been activated, and thankfully very few people were being admitted from them, just the usual group of terrified citizens fearing they had been infected, and needing nothing more than reassurance from the medical staff. Sally guessed the South Wing would be filled to capacity in about two hours, but Larry had assured her the next wing would be ready within the hour.

She made her rounds, starting with the most severe patients, all in serious condition, and about half on respirators, a sure sign they were probably terminal. Mrs. Morgan miraculously seemed to be getting better. Sally sat down by her bed. "Mrs. Morgan, it looks like your condition has stabilized. I think you're going to make it. You'll be one of the lucky ones."

The woman started to cry. "My Jacob didn't make it. The nurses told me."

"That's right, but your children seem to be free of infection, and that's good."

Mrs. Morgan brushed away her tears and with a weakened voice said, "You're right, I have to focus on taking care of my children."

Sally patted her on her hand and said, "I'll visit your children in a few minutes. Is there anything you want me to tell them?"

"Yes, tell them I love them very much. Don't tell them about their father; I want to do that. One more thing doctor, the nurses told me if it hadn't been for your immediate diagnosis I probably would have died. I don't know what to say except thank you."

"Thank you Mrs. Morgan, those words mean a lot to me."

Tears wet Sally's cheeks as she left to check on other patients, but her face shield prevented her from drying her eyes. She knew Mrs. Morgan was right, if the correct diagnosis had been missed, many more people would be dead, and she took great comfort in this fact.

As she moved to higher floors, the patients' condition improved. The people without symptoms had been placed on the highest floor, and Sally questioned the large number of very young children. *Why were there so many uninfected young children? Yes, there were indeed infected children on the lower floors, but not many.* She didn't have an answer to the question of why, but somehow she intuitively felt being able to understand why would help explain something about how this infection began. Right now, however, Sally needed rest, feeling too tired to think about the why. She headed for the area the doctors had set aside for their brief breaks and stripped completely, discarding her contaminated clothes in a container filled with bleach. She took a shower with bactericidal soap, dressed in some clean scrubs, grabbed some food at a makeshift kitchen, and sat down at a table with six of her colleagues.

"Fred Collins, a middle-aged surgeon, spoke first. "This reminds me of my days as a Resident, not really knowing what the hell I was doing, too proud to ask for help, and overstressed from not enough sleep."

The group of doctors and nurses laughed together, both in complete understanding and total agreement. George, one of the Med-Techs in the ER asked, "Sally, how bad is this going to get?"

"George, I'm not really sure. The problem's still growing exponentially, but I'm guessing it could last as long as a week before things level out. For sure we're going to be in this mode for at least another two weeks. When the CDC gets here, they'll be able to make some predictions. Their epidemiologists are really great."

Fred always the comic said, "The least they could have done is supply us with clean underwear. Now I have to go commando."

Vicky took a look under the table and said, "It's alright Doctor Collins; it's no big deal."

It took over two minutes for the group to stop laughing, and everyone except Fred high-fived Vicky.

Sally said, "You know guys, in all seriousness, I've never been prouder of our people. I'm not aware of a single person in the hospital who refused to help out in any way they could. I hear the other hospitals had to turn away staff who wanted to help examine patients inside the affected area, and I still don't know how Engineering totally reorganized the South Wing in only a few hours. I think we're going to look back at this in a few weeks and feel an immense sense of pride."

Fred replied, "You're right Sally, but we've also got to find out who did this. I'm thinking Al Qaeda. How about you?"

"You know Fred; I really haven't had time to consider that question. I'm going to leave it to the FBI.

After relaxing for a few more minutes, Sally found an empty bed in one of the ex-patient rooms and immediately fell asleep.

9

The call from Cook County Hospital to Sid Greenfield had alerted the Mayor's Office to the first problem they had not anticipated. How were they going to get food and other supplies into the quarantined area? Mayor Dobbins convened a staff meeting and posed the problem. Sid said, "The city's in a real budget crunch Mayor. We can't just give it away."

"You're right Sid, but we'll have to if there's no other way. Why don't we call Homeland Security and see what they can do. In the meantime, what else can we do?"

Dorothy Reems said, "Mayor, why don't we ask people to donate food and other supplies. There's no doubt in my mind, people will do whatever they can to help out."

Rich Gantrey added, "We could publicize a list of supplies we need and ask volunteers to bring everything to Soldier Field. The Salvation Army and Red Cross could organize the logistics and the TV networks can publicize the effort. Dorothy's right, we don't need Homeland Security for this. We can do it ourselves. Let Homeland Security focus on the things we can't do."

Mayor Dobbins smiled, "Just like how the city pulled together after the Chicago Fire, we'll do it again. Make it happen!"

¤   ¤   ¤

The local TV stations were up to the task. They quickly alerted the public to what types of food and supplies were needed. Within hours, donations came in from the large food chains and thousands of people. Cars and trucks began lining up in the Soldier Field parking lots where donations were consolidated and then placed onto delivery trucks and brought to distribution points inside the affected area.

¤   ¤   ¤

Sally awoke to the sun shining through the hospital room's window. She grabbed some coffee and a blueberry muffin and sat down at an empty table. Her cellphone rang. It was Harry. "Sally, the CDC team just arrived. I want to schedule a meeting with them in forty-five minutes. Engineering loaded Skype software on the computer in the doctor's break area. Can you be at the meeting?"

"Sure Harry. I just got up, so let me check on what's going on at the triage stations and with the patients. Call me when you're ready."

Sally hurriedly dressed in clean protective gear and headed out onto the street. The lines had dramatically shortened compared to last night, and only two new patients had been admitted from the triage stations. Sally found Vicky inside the ER at the nurse's station. Sally received updates from Vicky, and several doctors added their own take on things. About five-hundred patients had now been admitted, sixty-seven had died, and an additional three-hundred were failing rapidly, and would probably expire in the next few hours. The CDC had contacted the staff during the night and made some recommendations on new drugs to try and changes in the doses. The North Wing had been opened, and if things continued at the present rate of increase, the hospital would be at full capacity sometime tomorrow. The good news, as if there might be any, was the rate of new admissions had stopped growing exponentially.

Sally returned to the doctor's break area, showered and sat at the computer terminal making notes waiting for Harry's call. Sally looked at the picture of the hospital's largest conference room on her computer screen. Bodies filled the room to capacity. Every Department head seemed present along with five people who Sally didn't recognize. In the back corner of the room stood two familiar faces, Jimmy Davis and Alice Folkman, both looking concerned and ready to start their investigation.

Harry introduced Sally and then asked Doctor Greg Raster to do the same for his team. Greg stood up and said, "Thanks Harry, I've brought some very experienced people from our Atlanta office. Mary Higgens is an epidemiologist who worked in Uganda during the last outbreak of hemorrhagic fever. Jeff Sarma is a pathologist in our Special Pathogen Section, specializing in bioterrorism agents, and Silvia Flowers is an

Investigative Scientist specializing in infectious diseases. I've been involved on several teams investigating Ebola induced hemorrhagic fever outbreaks as well as the anthrax outbreak in Florida in 2001."

Harry then introduced Sam Watts from Homeland Security. He had been assigned to act as liaison between Northwestern Hospital and the Federal Government. Finally, he introduced Jimmy and Alice.

Harry then asked Sally to summarize the events of the last twenty-four hours. Sally gave a concise detailed review and concluded with a dire warning. "If the rate of increase in the number of new admissions doesn't begin to decrease, then we'll run out of bed space by tomorrow morning."

Harry replied, "Sally, I've been in contact with Cook County Hospital, and they're preparing to take additional patients. The medical teams inside the affected area now estimate a total of about 2000 patients will be hospitalized before this is all over."

Doctor Raster added, "Our limited experience with hemorrhagic fever is that the maximum rate of infection should occur at about five days from the initial infection, however that's with naturally occurring outbreaks, not a bioterrorism introduced agent."

Harry asked, "Doctor Raster, how can we assist your team?"

"Well Doctor Haskins, we're going to want to begin to talk to patients and send blood samples back to the Atlanta office for analysis as soon as possible. We'll also help Doctor Lawson acquire the best drugs possible for treating the infected patients. We'll try not to interfere with the actual treatment of the patients. In all honesty, we wouldn't do things any differently than what you are doing right now. You should all be commended on a job well done."

The meeting broke up and the CDC team prepared to enter the isolated area with some of their specialized equipment. Sally met them on the sixth floor where they decided to have lunch and more discussions before touring the emergency response areas.

Doctor Raster started, "Doctor Lawson, I want you to know your early diagnosis of the infection has undoubtedly saved hundreds of lives and most importantly probably prevented a pandemic. How did you get the diagnosis right? I can tell you most medical personnel would have assumed these were just flu-like symptoms."

"First Greg, let me tell you everyone in this hospital is on a first name basis, regardless of rank, so please call me Sally; and as for getting the diagnosis right, I coauthored a JAMA paper two years ago on the diagnosis of rare infectious diseases in the ER. The lesions and the rash were consistent with pictures I had remembered seeing, and the hiccups clinched it."

The epidemiologist then asked, "Have you noticed any unusual patterns in the patient population?"

"Strange you should ask that question Mary. Whenever a person is admitted with symptoms, we also admit the rest of the family, assuming there is a high probability of their also being infected, but just at the earlier stages of the disease. With only a few exceptions, children under the age of five have continued to be asymptomatic."

Mary thought for a moment and answered, "I've never seen this type of response before in young children; in fact it's usually the kids who are the most vulnerable. I'll follow up on your observation; I think it could help us understand what's happened here."

Sally then began what turned out to be a two hour tour of the emergency treatment center and introduced the CDC people to her senior staff.

◘   ◘   ◘

After the tour, Doctor Mary Higgens sat down at the nurse's station on the first floor. She began a laborious process of entering all of the patient data for anyone who had been admitted to the hospital, their present medical status, and the severity of their condition at the time of admission. The special software program she used had been custom designed to look for patterns in the data.

At a high priority, she wanted to determine the point of origin of the outbreak. Under normal circumstances this would mean trying to identify the primary source of the infection. This situation, however, was a bit different. They were dealing with a terrorist attack most assuredly, meaning they were looking for the point of origin of the attack, the actual location in the city where the aerosol dispersion of the infectious agent took place. She knew the FBI would need this information.

After entering the data, she would begin the process of interviewing patients, at least the ones capable of speaking. Her skills as an investigator would be tested during these interviews. The patients almost always held the key to understanding how the disease spread. As in trying to solve any complex problem, finding the correct answer always boiled down to asking the right questions, identifying distinctions between those who were sick and those who were not. As important as why some patients became sick, was why others didn't, and Sally's observation concerning the children could be very important.

Mary found it useful to focus on a few important areas. First, where were people located who became sick, and where were people located who did not become infected? Second, when did the initial dispersion of the agent take place?

If the problem being studied concerned an outbreak of salmonella, then identifying the source of the problem almost always came down to finding out what foods people were eating in the past few days and then tracing the source of the suspected food. This problem, however, didn't fit the pattern.

Mary solicited help from one of the nurse's aides. She taught her how to enter the data, and after Mary confirmed the aide knew what needed to be done, she left to interview patients.

Meanwhile, the rest of the CDC team collected blood samples from all of the patients admitted to the hospital. Sally told Greg Raster, "We need to prepare a Chain of Custody document."

Doctor Raster answered, "I'm going to do it as soon as we've collected all of the samples."

"Greg, I'm friends with Jimmy Davis. You met him at the meeting. He's the head of the FBI's Chicago Field Office. Do you want me to call him to arrange transport of the samples?"

"Good idea Sally. Otherwise one of our team will need to accompany the samples."

Sally then called Jimmy and arranged for an FBI agent to hand-carry the samples to the CDC's

Atlanta diagnostics laboratory on a Government jet.

Sally asked Greg, "What are you going to test the samples for?"

"A couple of things. First, we need to confirm the presence of the anthrax and Ebola virus. We've either got a bioterrorist weapon with both organisms or a genetically engineered agent. I hope it's the former because at least the anthrax vaccine we've got will be efficacious, but I'm thinking we're going to find it's genetically engineered, because your people were unable to visually identify the Ebola virus, which means we'll be dealing with something we've never seen before.

"Secondly, we're going to have to begin culturing the organism, the necessary first step in preparing a vaccine against the agent. That, of course won't help the people who have already contracted the infection, but if this has happened once, it could happen again, and eventually we'll need a vaccine to defend ourselves."

"Greg, I get the impression you think we could be in really deep shit."

"Best to plan for the worst and hope for the best."

10

Jimmy called Dan. "Hey, where are you?"

"I'm manning the barricades at Ashland and Ohio Street. I feel like one of the freedom fighters in *Les Miserables*."

"Well, I've got news for you. Director Jacobson has contacted your boss's boss's boss, and you're one fortunate dude, because effective immediately, you're going to be the liaison between the FBI and the Chicago Police Department. As of this minute, you're on my team."

"Well Jimmy, anything is better than waiting here for the unexpected blockade runner. What are you thinking?"

"Benny, Alice, Glenda, and a few of the techno-geeks are going to enter the restricted area. We've got some instruments to help sniff out anthrax. I want to nail down as quickly as possible the exact location where the agent was dispersed."

"Have them meet me here. I walked pretty close to ground zero last night. I'll be their tour guide."

"Great, they'll be there in an hour. Hey keep in touch. Sally's going to join the team as soon as she gets done saving patients."

¤   ¤   ¤

Dan suited up in his protective gear just as the FBI group pulled up to the barricade in three emergency vehicles. Benny Canon, the first out of the lead truck, walked up to Dan. "Didn't you get the memo; we're wearing blue protective suits today."

"Benny, they give out the red protective suits to the team leaders."

"Bullshit, Glenda's the team leader. I know because she's already told me three times."

Dan put his arm around the smartest techno-geek in the FBI, a bit difficult given their full battledress. "It's good to see you again. How've you been?"

"Pretty good, until this mess."

Glenda, who emerged from the lead truck said, "Okay guys, enough of the love fest. Let's get to work. Dan, Jimmy told me you're going to lead us to ground zero."

"Well, I know the area where we found the most infected people. I guess for now we can assume it's the place."

Dan entered the lead truck with Glenda and the caravan passed through the blockade. Dan led them to what he felt might be near the point of origin. Glenda explained they were going to take samples of the environment for analysis of anthrax back in the FBI lab. She wanted to develop a precise map of anthrax spore concentration throughout the area. Glenda assembled her crew on the deserted street and reviewed the plan. The group then dispersed to begin the process of sample collection. Each of the technicians held a small vacuum cleaner device that sucked air samples into glass test tubes.

The team took samples every one-hundred feet, holding their vacuum cleaners close to the ground; the assumption being the biological agent had fallen to the ground, and had become embedded in the grass and dirt.

Dan did some quick calculations in his head. The affected area covered about one square mile, meaning about 2500 samples. "Glenda, are you really going to collect 2500 samples?"

"No, as soon as we move outside this high infection area, we'll change to every one-thousand feet. We should be done here in a couple of hours."

Dan told Glenda he wanted to walk around the area to look for evidence, although he really had no idea what to look for. Finally, Dan had the chance to switch from manning the barricades to investigative mode. He slowly looked around the deserted street trying to decide how to start. The technical people believed the biological agent must have been somehow dispersed into the air.

Dan remembered the movie *Goldfinger* where an airplane sprayed nerve gas into the air. He considered the possibility. During a low level attack, people would have heard the plane, and an attack from higher altitude would have affected a larger area of the city. He could talk to residents to find out if anyone remembered a plane flying overhead.

Doctor Fineman had mentioned the initial infection probably took place between the second and sixth of July. Just like a technical person. Why not just say on the Fourth of July. They always wanted some weasel room. Of course, the one thing about the Fourth of July, nobody would pay particular attention to an explosion in the air.

The more Dan thought about it, the idea of an airburst from something like a skyrocket made sense. He'd need to talk to some experts on how this type of agent might be dispersed.

Dan had helped provide security once for a barge loaded with fireworks for the City's annual Fourth of July celebration a few years back. He remembered the launching systems as nothing more than vertically mounted tubes directing the explosive projectile up into the sky. A timed fuse then ignited the fireworks at the appropriate height.

Well, if the terrorist launched something on the Fourth of July, he'd certainly want to do it at night and not in plain sight of anyone. Therefore, the terrorist would probably launch it from an alley or other out of the way place. Dan entered an alley and began moving east toward Ashland Avenue. After walking a few blocks he moved over one alley to the north and headed back toward Western Avenue. Chicago Avenue, a fairly busy commercial street located one block further north, appeared empty. The whole place looked like one of those science fiction movies after a plague had killed off civilization, and in fact, this seemed pretty close to reality.

Nothing appeared out of place as Dan covered block after block. Finally he came to a bright glow-yellow "X" painted in a concrete alleyway. From his early school years, he remembered using chalk to make hopscotch designs in the alley behind his house, but kids probably had nothing to do with this, more likely something a surveyor would do, except much bigger.

A few blocks further west he came to a dumpster on a new construction site. He looked inside and noticed a brand new ladder in the half-full waste container. Why throw away a perfectly good ladder? The five story apartment building under construction had been recently topped out.

Confined inside his protective suit, he struggled up the concrete stairs to the roof of the building and looked around. This would have been a good place to launch the dispersion, but nothing seemed out of the ordinary, except for a large amount of construction materials. He systematically examined the roof looking for evidence of the launching of fireworks, but the most exciting things he found were a Nestles Crunch Bar wrapper, and a container of half-finished McDonald's Super-Sized fries, now being consumed by an army of ants.

Dan approached the edge of the roof and surveyed the streets below. Except for a few of Glenda's lab techs taking samples and some ambulances transporting patients, everything appeared totally deserted. Dan moved along the perimeter of the roof, and everywhere he looked the streets appeared empty.

Dan took the stairs back to ground level and tried to find Glenda. He had been searching the area for almost two hours and didn't see any need to stay with the forensic team. He really needed to talk to an expert on biological weapons and find out how these agents would be dispersed.

He found Glenda taking samples in a nearby front yard. A small child looked at her through the window with her mother standing behind her. Dan waved to the little girl and she waved back. The child's mother beckoned for him to come to the front door. He climbed up the stairs in his protective suit as she opened the door. "What are you doing," she asked?

"We're taking samples to analyze back in the lab. Please stay inside your house."

The woman nodded and closed the door. Dan wondered how he would react to being quarantined. Not knowing what people were doing would drive him crazy, and the fear of the City Government lying to prevent widespread panic would always be there.

Dan said, "I'm going back to the office. When do think you'll have results on the samples?"

"About seven hours. I'll see you back at the office."

It took Dan about twenty minutes to return to the perimeter and have the outside of his protective clothing sprayed down with bleach at a hastily organized decontamination center.

After returning to the barricade, he called Chief of Police Jack McWarden. "Detective Lawson, I was just about to call you; what can I do for you?"

"Chief, I was just inside the infected zone with the FBI. They're analyzing for residual anthrax. One of the residents asked me what we were doing, and I told her. I think we need to send the sound trucks through every couple of hours to tell people what's going on inside the perimeter. I think it will go a long way toward relieving their anxieties."

"A great idea Dan, I'll give the order immediately. By the way, I met your wife Sally at a meeting with the Mayor. She's one hell of a lady."

"That's why I married her Chief."

"Listen, I got a call from Director Jacobson at the FBI, and he insisted we appoint you the liaison between the FBI and the Police Department. I talked to Joey, and we both agree. So effective immediately, you'll be working on the FBI investigative team. Please call me if I can be of any help."

"I sure will Chief. I'll head over to the FBI office as soon as we're done talking."

11

Dan interrupted a discussion between Sally and Jimmy. "Listen, Dan just got here. Let's start the meeting in ten minutes. We'll call you."

Jimmy hugged his best friend. A hug from Jimmy always represented a challenge. At a biscuit shy of three-hundred pounds, when he hugged someone it became a full engulfing embrace. "Sally and I have organized a task force. We're going to have the first meeting in ten minutes."

Jimmy then asked his secretary to have Brian Sawkowski and Alice Folkman come to his office.

When he returned, Dan said, "I left Glenda and Benny inside the infected zone. They're still collecting samples."

"Yep, I talked to Glenda thirty minutes ago. She says they'll be done in two hours. We need those sample results for two reasons. First, we need to get a more precise location of ground zero, and second, Homeland Security needs to find out which areas within the zone need to be decontaminated."

Alice entered Jimmy's office with a person Dan didn't know. Jimmy made the introduction. "Dan this is Brian Sawkowski. He's the FBI expert on bioterrorism and was involved on the anthrax case in Florida."

Dan shook his hand, "Good to meet you Brian, and I've got plenty of questions for you."

Jimmy's secretary interrupted, "I've got Sally and the CDC people on the line. Do you want to take the call in your office?"

"Yes Marge, thanks."

They gathered around Jimmy's desk, and Jimmy transferred the call to his high tech conference call system.

Sally introduced the CDC group and Jimmy introduced the people sitting around his desk.

Jimmy started, "Our team is going to focus on figuring out who's responsible for all of this, and we're going to need to work closely with you and the people at the CDC. I think a daily meeting where we can exchange information may help your team as well."

Greg Raster added, "We also think the meeting is a good idea. Let me tell you what we've been up to so far. Mary Higgens is working the epidemiology part of the equation. The information we get will help us treat the patients who have been infected more effectively, and if we're lucky, we'll also be able to tell you where the initial dispersion took place."

Jimmy said, "We're looking at trying to identify ground zero as well. I've got a number of our people in the area now measuring anthrax levels within the perimeter. We should have results by the end of the day."

Dan asked, "Mary, when you talk to patients, will you try to have two questions answered. First, did any of them hear or see any low flying planes on the night the agent was dispersed; and second, on the Fourth of July, did any of them see or hear a fireworks explosion near where they live."

"Dan, I'm interviewing patients now, and I'll definitely ask both questions. I should have information for tomorrow's meeting."

Greg Raster spoke, "We've sent several hundred samples to the Atlanta laboratory. Hopefully they'll be able to identify the strains of anthrax and Ebola we're dealing with. They're also going to begin growing whatever they find so we can start vaccine development."

Brian asked, "Greg, when do you think you'll have the results on the identification back?"

"I'm hoping some time tomorrow. I'll call you as soon as we get an answer."

Sally then reviewed the clinical situation. "There are now 896 patients admitted to Northwestern, and an additional 345 patients at Cook County Hospital. Of these 1241 patients, 412 have died, and an additional 356 are in critical condition and not expected to survive. The other patients are in earlier stages of the infection or remain uninfected. Also a large number of young children, for reasons still not understood, are not infected."

Greg added, "We've been tracking the admission rate, and believe new admissions will peak tomorrow. Then we'll see decreasing numbers of new patients for the next several weeks. Jimmy, I want to see your anthrax location mapping. We can make some recommendations on how to decontaminate the infected areas after we see the data."

"As soon as Glenda Beecher has the data, she'll send it to you. Does anybody have anything else for today's meeting?"

Interpreting the silence as a no, the meeting ended with the next meeting scheduled for the same time the next day.

With the meeting over, Dan asked Brian, "Explain what a terrorist would have to do in order to create an aerial dispersion of this agent."

"Well Dan, for the anthrax it's pretty straightforward. It's the biological warfare weapon of choice. It's stable when it's in the form of a spore. When it's inhaled by a human, it becomes activated. To disperse the agent, you could spray it into the air, or place it in an artillery shell designed to explode overhead."

"What about placing it inside fireworks, and shooting it off like a mortar?"

"Absolutely, you just need to make sure the anthrax doesn't get burned up from the heat of the blast, but there're lots of ways to protect the agent."

"How would you disperse the Ebola virus?"

"That's a little more difficult to understand. It could be dispersed as an aerosol, but not much is known about Ebola as a biological agent. Let's wait until we get feedback from the CDC."

Dan said, "Here's what I'm thinking. The doctors are guessing the dispersion of the agent took place around the Fourth of July. I don't think people would have paid much attention to somebody shooting off some fireworks from their neighborhood on the Fourth of July. Hopefully Mary's interviewing of the patients may tell us something, and we can also interview people inside the infected zone tomorrow. Glenda should have the results back by then."

12

Doctor Clifford Bales took possession of the Chicago blood samples and moved them into a Class IV containment laboratory. While he dressed in his protective clothing, several scientists began unpacking the blood samples and entering patient identifications into the computer.

The first blood sample had been prepared for viewing on the custom designed scanning electron microscope just as Cliff entered the fully isolated laboratory. He sat down at the computer terminal controlling the costly instrument, punched in a moderate magnification, and began looking at the prepared sample. He perused the image. He wasn't looking for any of the normal blood constituents, but rather something special, known in the scientific community as *Bacillus anthracis*, and to the rest of the population as anthrax. Eventually he saw something and zoomed in on the area. And there it sat right before his eyes staring back at him. "There you are you little bugger. Hey guys, we've definitely got anthrax. Come take a look."

A group of seven scientists gathered around the electron microscope and stared at the computer screen. Bales said, "Maggie, I want you to do the detailed workup required to identify the strain of anthrax we're dealing with, but right now let's see if we can find our other little virus friend."

Bales turned up the magnification and began scanning the sample for the proverbial needle in the haystack. The Ebola virus had a characteristic shape, almost like a Sheppard's staff but with a loop at one end. Bales moved the controls in order to view different parts of the sample, and also adjusted the focus and magnification to be able to see deeper into the material. He stopped, unable to believe what he saw on the computer screen. It wasn't the Ebola virus, but something much more menacing, a plasmid.

As Bales adjusted the focus and enlarged the image, the group moved closer to the computer screen to get a better look. With one exception they all looked intrigued by what they were seeing. The lone outlier, Brad Woolford, looked absolutely terrified.

"So," said Bales, "It looks like we're not dealing with a naturally occurring Ebola virus, but a genetically engineered biological agent. It's a vector, not the native virus, meaning someone attached Ebola proteins to this plasmid and probably inserted it into the anthrax.

"Bobby, I want you to start a workup on the plasmid. We need to identify which one it is, and then run the genetic sequence on the part of the

Ebola virus that's been inserted. I want the rest of you to focus on how we can create a vaccine against this vector."

Bales left the laboratory and sat down at his desk. He looked at his watch, too late to call Greg Raster, but he did send an e-mail with the essential facts and scheduled a conference call for early the next morning.

¤   ¤   ¤

Dan called Sally on her cellphone. "How's it going Hon?"

"It could be a lot worse. It's almost becoming routine. We're up to full capacity now. We're down to only one triage station. I guess people are mostly over their fear about having been infected."

"Hey, I heard Jacobson pulled both of us out of our regular daytime jobs. I guess we can't escape the long reach of the FBI."

"I told Jimmy I'm not leaving the hospital until we're past the crisis."

"How many more days do you have to spend in quarantine?

"Tomorrow, as long as my blood test comes back negative, I'll be a free woman."

"That's great news. I'm going home now. I want to get an early start looking at Glenda's mapping of the infected area. Can I get you anything?"

"Clean underwear would be good. Bring it up to the sixth floor, and give the bag to one of the staff. They'll make sure I get it"

"Will do; love you Honey."

13

Glenda had worked late into the night completing the anthrax level mapping in the infected area. Linda Higgens had forwarded her the data on hospitalized patient locations, and the patient data had been superimposed onto the anthrax level map.

Dan, Jimmy, Brian, Alice and Benny now gathered around the conference table looking at copies of the map with Glenda describing the data collection process and providing her interpretation of the information. Luckily, the anthrax spores seemed to be concentrated within a six by eight block area, and not surprisingly all but one of the hospitalized patients whose blood tests confirmed the infection, lived or worked within the contaminated area, and this unlucky person had been delivering a pizza order late on the Fourth of July, probably just after the air-burst.

Benny said, "So, do we think ground zero must be in the center of the contaminated area?"

Dan said, "I don't think so. The highest concentration of anthrax comes from the eastern edge of the contaminated area, and the pattern's not a perfect circle. We need to check with the weather bureau to see the wind direction on the Fourth of July, but I'm guessing the wind blew from the east. I put ground zero right around the corner of Superior and Damen."

The others agreed with Dan's analysis. Alice asked, "So what do we do now?"

Jimmy replied, "We suit up in our protective armor, get our asses over to Superior and Damen, and canvas the area for clues."

¤   ¤   ¤

Dan volunteered to search the area where he had been looking for clues the day before. For some reason the large glow-yellow "X" painted in the alley seemed out of place, and he had been thinking about it since yesterday afternoon. He still favored the exploding fireworks theory as the method the terrorists used to disperse the biological agent, so he focused on looking for remnants of the explosive device.

Standing in front of the glow-yellow "X", he carefully began searching for clues. He knelt down on his hands and knees, rather difficult considering his confining protective suit. He crawled closer to the garage next to the yellow mark, being extra careful not to puncture his protective garment and noticed some small shards of broken glass reflected in the bright sunlight. The small pieces looked similar to what you'd get if you broke a light bulb on a street, except there wasn't any light bulb base. He turned on his open-mic radio, "Brian, this is Dan. Could the biological agent be enclosed in glass?"

"Dan, glass would be the best way of containing the agent until it's dispersed."

"I might have something here, but I'll let you know after I've done a little more searching."

Dan thought about how the terrorists would have launched the weapon. They launched it most certainly at night. Also, some type of timing device must be involved, so they could get away before it exploded. No point in committing suicide.

Of course some fanatical terrorists might be willing to martyr themselves, but why waste a perfectly good suicide bomber unless absolutely necessary.

They wouldn't come back later to pick up the device; why get exposed to the biological agent. So where was the launching device? Dan opened a gate and walked around the garage; Nada! Some idea began forming in the deep recesses of his brain, but it swirled around unable to reach his conscious mind.

Suddenly, he remembered the new ladder he had seen in the dumpster two blocks west of where he stood. He looked upward focusing on the roof of the garage. It had a mansard roof, perfectly flat, a good place to launch an explosive projectile and not likely to be seen by any passers-bye before it launched.

Dan walked to the dumpster as rapidly as his bulky suit permitted and looked inside. The ladder rested against the side of the large container just within reach. Leaning over the edge of the dumpster, he lifted the aluminum ladder and placed it on the ground. Although the ladder seemed rather light, it was still an awkward load when carried two blocks to the glow yellow "X".

Sweat dripped down Dan's face as he arrived at the garage. He paused to catch his breath after slamming the ladder against the edge of the roof. He rested a full two minutes; he was definitely getting out of shape. He figured it must be all the cheeseburgers and fries he consumed each week. Finally, he slowly climbed the ladder, being very careful not to slip on the metal treads. As he reached the top, he looked out at the gravel coated roof.

There, only a foot from his protective suit, sat the charred remnants of a cardboard box and a still intact fireworks mortar launching system complete with battery and timer attached to the base of the mortar. It looked similar to what Dan remembered seeing when he guarded the fireworks barge years ago.

Dan turned on his microphone and said, "I think I've got it guys, I think I've got it!"

Within twenty minutes each of the other agents had climbed the ladder and agreed with Dan's assessment. Glenda called in a special team of her forensic people to take charge of the evidence and bring it back to the FBI lab for analysis. The team now focused on the area downwind from the mortar and eventually found additional glass fragments as well as the remains of the explosive charge used to launch the weapon. The lab techs carefully transferred everything into evidence bags.

Jimmy asked, "What do you guys make of the glow-yellow "X"?"

Brian answered, "I think we're dealing with a group, not a lone terrorist. One person decided where to plant the mortar, and marked the spot with something easily recognizable for a second person to locate, and I'm guessing the two people never even knew each other."

Dan thought Brian had a good point and added, "We need to check the ladder for prints. I'm guessing the guy who placed the weapon also used this ladder."

Dan had a list of priorities engrained in his brain. They were developed over the years and had led to critical evidence on other cases. Since the launching point of the weapon had now been identified, he began searching for any surveillance cameras in the area. In the last decade, companies and individuals had been adding these devices for obvious reasons. Dan knew there were even people who would place fake cameras in places where a burglar would see them in order to convince the would-be felon to seek easier marks.

He carefully scanned the area for cameras, and his instincts were soon rewarded. A four story office building almost directly in line with the alley had a camera on the roof pointed almost exactly in the direction of the glow-yellow "X". As Dan liked to say at times such as these, *once in a great while the blind pig does indeed find the acorn.* He pointed out the location of the camera to the others and began his one block walk to investigate.

The building inside of the infected area looked deserted. A small sign on the front door indicated the Rochelle Management Company managed the facility. Dan called Jimmy. "Jimmy, we need to get inside. Can you have one of your people get someone to come down here to open up the place? Tell them we need to look at their security cameras."

"Will do Dan."

Jimmy called his office on a private line and gave them the telephone number of the management company. Ten minutes later Jimmy called Dan to let him know a Mr. Jerry Adams, the office manager, would be brought over by an agent as soon as possible.

¤   ¤   ¤

Within the hour, Mr. Jerry Adams, dressed in protective garb and looking absolutely terrified, was escorted to the front of the office building by one of Jimmy's agents.

Dan approached Adams who had been given a communications headset and said, "Thanks for agreeing to come into the infected area."

"Well agent Lawson, I can tell you I'm scared to death. I know I'm probably going to get infected."

"Don't worry Mr. Adams; the medical people tell us this protective gear and the right precautions will keep us safe. We're all just being extra cautious. The reason I've asked you here is we think we've found the location where the terrorists launched their weapon, and it appears to be exactly in line with the camera on your building's roof, the one pointed directly west. We need to look at your surveillance video to see if we can identify the people who were responsible."

As Adams unlocked the front door of the building, he said, "All of the surveillance equipment is located on the fourth floor in our management office. The system is designed to take a picture every ten seconds, and the pictures are stored on the computer's hard drive. We installed the equipment a few months ago. We're doing the test marketing of the system for the manufacturer. It's really great, and we got it for free just by participating in the marketing trial."

Adams unlocked the security room and switched the computer monitor to show camera eleven. Dan looked at the picture through his protective gear. The resolution and clarity brought everything into sharp focus. He could clearly make out the FBI team still located at ground zero. "Mr. Adams, we're going to need to take your hard drive as evidence."

"No problem Agent Lawson. The system uses an external hard drive, but I would like the original or a replacement returned as soon as possible."

"Our lab people will get what they need in a few hours. I'll get you a replacement by tomorrow. If you leave the building unlocked, our people will re-attach the hard drive to the computer system."

Adams handed Lawson the key to the building and asked him to return it to the management office after the Mayor lifted the quarantine.

After Adams left with the agent as an escort, Dan called Jimmy. "Jimmy, I've got the pictures, and I think we lucked out. I'm going to bring the hard drive back to Benny and have him look for the terrorists."

"Okay, we'll be done here in another hour, and I'll see you at the office."

At the outer perimeter, one of the forensic people carefully decontaminated the hard drive and double bagged it for safe transfer to the FBI lab while Dan once again felt the concentrated bleach spray hit his protective suit.

14

Dan had three more hours until the daily meeting with the Northwestern people. Benny sat at his desk working with the security camera hard drive data, trying to get it into a format allowing the pictures to become visible on his high resolution video equipment. Finally a picture appeared on Benny's oversized computer monitor.

The camera was centered on the glow-yellow "X", and Jimmy and the other members of the team were clearly visible gathering evidence around the garage. Benny located the earliest pictures and set them up on the screen. The date in the lower left corner of the picture, May, 17th, was probably close to the original start-up date for the system. The glow-yellow "X" remained clearly visible, and as Benny moved forward picture by picture, the story unfolding was one of a typical city scene with people walking down the streets, kids playing in their backyards, and cars and garbage trucks moving along the alley.

Benny, can you advance the date to the third of July?"

Benny played with his computer and finally a picture appeared on the screen for July 3rd, 9:00 A.M. He began advancing the pictures, frame by frame, stopping whenever a car or person appeared in the alley. July 3rd transitioned into July 4th. Dan and Benny carefully reviewed the pictures. At 2:46 A.M. a red SUV without lights entered the alley from the east and stopped exactly over the glow-yellow "X", perfectly illuminated by the mercury vapor streetlight.

A man removed a ladder from the back of the car and positioned it against the garage. He then lifted a cardboard box from the rear of the car, carried it up the ladder, and placed the package carefully on the roof. He climbed down, pushed the ladder back inside the car, and proceeded down the alley toward the west. The car stopped by the construction dumpster and the man discarded the ladder in the waste container. The SUV finally moved out of the camera's field of view.

"Wow," said Benny, "I can't believe what we just saw!"

"Benny, can you zoom in on the car when it's under the light to see if we can get a license plate number."

"Sure, no problem."

Benny worked with his mouse to zoom in on the car while it remained parked by the garage. An enlarged license plate filled the screen. Benny then played with some computer commands to refine the picture and improve the sharpness. When he finished, they had a clear view of an Illinois license plate with the number 366 2601.

Benny said, "Now let me try to get a picture of the man in the car."

After playing with the computer for a few minutes, he was able to find a good frontal image and printed a blowup of his face.

Benny continued advancing the picture. At 9:45 P.M. the camera captured a bright flash of light coming from the top of the garage. The actual airburst must have occurred between pictures, but the evidence seemed perfectly clear. They had found their terrorist.

"Well done Benny. We've got to get to the daily meeting now, but can you have one of your people run a trace on the car. Have them bring the car's registration up to the meeting as soon as they have something."

Benny yelled across the room, "Hey Sarah, can you log in the picture on my monitor and the external hard drive into the evidence room and put a trace on the license plate? Bring it up to Jimmy's office as soon as you get the information."

Sarah began searching for the registration on the plates as Dan, holding the picture of the terrorist, and Benny left for Jimmy's office and their scheduled meeting.

¤   ¤   ¤

Jimmy, Alice, Brian and Glenda had already arrived in Jimmy's office. Dan tossed the picture onto Jimmy's desk and explained what Benny and he had just found on the security camera's hard drive, and the happy group of agents, recognizing the importance of the new lead, gathered around the desk and stared at the picture.

As previously agreed, Sally's team, along with the CDC people, called into Jimmy's office. Sally started with an update on the clinical situation at both Northwestern and Cook County. The new admissions during the last twenty-four hours had decreased from the previous day, certainly good news. The epidemic had evidently peaked. The death rate on infected patients now exceeded seventy percent, and the CDC estimated the final death rate would reach over eighty percent.

Homeland Security, without any public announcements, had brought in dozens of refrigerated trucks to store the dead prior to their release for burial. A newspaper reporter had somehow learned about the effort, but had been convinced, in exchange for an exclusive interview with the Mayor, not to publish the information until after the quarantine had been lifted.

Greg Raster presented the preliminary results on the blood samples sent to the Atlanta lab. "Well, we have something none of us have ever seen before. Our lab confirmed the presence of anthrax in all of the infected patients. The Ebola virus, however, is a different matter. We haven't found the virus yet, but what we have discovered is a plasmid. It's evidently being used as a vector, and our guess is the vector contains Ebola virus DNA, and proteins made from the DNA are infecting the patients."

Jimmy said, "Wait a minute Greg; I don't have any idea what you're talking about. You've got to explain it in plain English."

Greg replied, "I'll give it a try. In genetic engineering when you want to manufacture a human protein, you first isolate the human DNA sequence coding for the protein. Then you take a plasmid, which is a type of bacterial DNA in the shape of a circle, and you break the circle. Using some genetic engineering tricks, you attach the protein DNA into the plasmid DNA chain and reestablish the circular structure."

Jimmy interrupted, "This all sounds like witchcraft. Is there any oil of dog or eye of newt involved?"

After everyone laughed, Greg continued, "Well Jimmy, there is a bit of magic involved, but let me assure you, this is all first year biology stuff in college these days. Okay, so this new genetically modified plasmid is called a vector because it's inserted into a host cell, in our case the anthrax, but for most proteins it might be e-coli.

The plasmids are taken up by the host, and the plasmids use their host to replicate and produce the protein of interest from the inserted DNA. So in our example by growing the e-coli in mass culture, you can produce your protein of choice and then go through some additional steps to separate the protein from the e-coli and purify it."

"You mean you can make any protein you want," Jimmy asked?

"That's right Jimmy. In our case somebody probably identified the Ebola proteins creating the clinical symptoms we're seeing and created the plasmid as a vector, using the anthrax as the host to produce the protein. When people inhaled the biological agent, the anthrax began to reproduce, but also the Ebola virus proteins causing hemorrhagic fever also replicated."

Glenda, who understood Greg's analysis, said, "What an elegant and terrifying way to create a biological weapon. You make this sound very simple, but aren't there only a few groups in the world who would be able to pull this off?"

Greg answered, "Glenda is absolutely correct. The real trick is being able to do the testing to confirm the DNA extracted from the Ebola virus actually produces the proteins causing the hemorrhagic fever clinical symptoms. For Ebola a large colony of primates would be required to validate the process."

Sally offered another interpretation, "Maybe we're witnessing the definitive final test. The terrorists used humans as the species to confirm their evil concoction produced the desired results. This may be the final experiment."

The ensuing silence reinforced Sally's point.

Jimmy said, "Sally I think you're right."

Glenda asked, "Did you guys get the map I sent of the anthrax concentration inside the infected area?"

Sam Watts, from Homeland Security answered, "We did. I took the liberty of contacting a special decontamination unit in the Department of Defense. I sent them a copy of the map, and they propose decontaminating the entire area with a combination of chemicals; a special fog based on peracetic acid and hydrogen peroxide for the insides of the buildings, and a variety of germicidal foams for the outside. They should be starting the cleanup tomorrow. The Mayor's office is going to be reviewing the operation at today's news conference, and we're preparing a full written explanation for each of the residents within the infected area."

Jimmy said, "The timing is good. We were inside the infected area today and located what we believe is the launch system for the weapon. It appears to be based on a simple fireworks design. Dan, why don't you review what else we found."

"We located a security camera system appearing to have pictures of the launch site. We've identified a car in the area around 2:45 A.M. on the Fourth of July. An unidentified man placed the launch device on the roof of a garage. We're tracing the license plate number now, and hopefully it will be a significant lead. We'll know more by tomorrow's meeting."

Just as Dan finished, Sarah brought in a note for Benny. "Here it is." he said. "The car is registered to Hertz."

Dan said, "We'll call Hertz right after the meeting."

Mary, the epidemiologist, said, "That's consistent with what some of the patients are saying. They recall hearing a loud explosion about ten o'clock. They all assumed somebody was shooting off a skyrocket."

Jimmy scheduled another meeting for the next day, and everyone left feeling upbeat for the first time in several days. The epidemic might be peaking, and there were significant leads.

15

It took Dan and Alice thirty minutes to determine Hertz rented the car to Ali Santiani, and an hour later a group of ten agents surrounded Ali's apartment building and stood quietly in the hallway outside his unit. Benny inserted a small endoscopic like instrument under the front door and saw the two bodies lying on the living room floor. He whispered, "Two bodies down with nothing else visible."

Jimmy directed two agents with a battering ram to open the door, but Dan turned the door knob first and found it unlocked. Jimmy said, "But the battering ram's more fun."

The group smiled as Dan and the others quietly entered the apartment with guns drawn. The stench from the two decomposing bodies overpowered their senses. The apartment had clearly been ransacked. It gave the appearance of an armed robbery, but they all knew better. These murders were clearly the work of a terrorist group eliminating two people involved in the plot who would no longer be able to provide any further explanation of their crime.

Dan alerted the local police and explained the FBI would take charge of the crime scene. The group of agents fanned out inside the apartment building, interviewing everyone to determine whether they knew anything. Benny began working on Ali's computer to pull any useful information. Wearing gloves, he placed the entire computer in an evidence bag for analysis back in the lab.

Dan, Alice, Brian and Jimmy stayed with the bodies. Jimmy asked, "What do you think Detective Dan?"

"A couple of things: First, the killer is a professional. Both shots were perfect shots to the head. Second, he shot the man first, and he fell to the floor. Third, the killer wanted the police to think this was a burglary gone awry, so he ransacked the apartment and threw things on the floor. It looks like the ransacking took place afterwards because nothing's under the man's body. Fourth, the girl somehow comes upon the scene of the murder and she's shot. You can see some of the things thrown around are under her body. After he shot her, she fell down on top of those things."

Alice gloved up and looked inside the girl's purse. "They're not married; neither is wearing rings; given their age, she's probably a girlfriend. Her name's Haleh Aboud, and she's also a student."

Alice then turned her attention to Ali's wallet and found his student ID. The picture looked the same as the picture Benny had taken from the security camera.

Jimmy called in the forensic people, and left to go back to the office. Dan on the other hand headed over to the University of Chicago Administrative building to check out Santiani and his girlfriend.

¤   ¤   ¤

The school administrator expressed shock to learn two of her students might be involved in terrorist activities. She pulled out both of their records. "Ali is a student on the exchange program with Iran. He's been a straight "A" student majoring in Chemical Engineering. He's been accepted to our graduate school program and Professor Wilson is going to offer him a part-time job in his lab."

Dan found it interesting the woman referred to victims in the present tense. Some people couldn't accept death. "Had he been involved with the campus police, or is there anything negative in his record?"

"No, nothing; he's been a perfect student."

"What about the girl?"

"Haleh Aboud, she's an exchange student from Yemen. She's a Junior majoring in Education. She's also a good student and has nothing negative in her records."

"Who might be the best person to talk with about Ali?"

"You might try Professor Wilson. Here's his cellphone number."

"Thanks for your help. I'll try him."

Dan left the Administration Building and dialed the number. "Professor, this is Detective Dan Lawson with the Chicago Police Department.

I would like to talk to you about one of your students, Ali Santiani."

"What's this in regard to Detective Lawson?"

It appears he may have been involved in the recent terrorist attack in the city."

"I find it very hard to believe Detective Lawson, but I'll be happy to talk to you. I'm in my office now in the Chemical Engineering Building."

Professor Wilson provided Dan the directions to his office and soon they were meeting face to face. "What can you tell me about Ali?"

"Well, he's a remarkable student. He came to the University as part of a special exchange program with Iran. My wife and I have sort of taken him under our wings. He's very bright and a wonderful person to be with. I can't believe he's involved in some terrorist plot. He doesn't seem like a political person at all."

"Doctor, Ali and another woman were killed in his apartment probably on the Fourth of July under very strange circumstances."

Professor Wilson became visibly upset with the news. He began to cry and reached for a box of Kleenex on his desk. "Terrible, terrible, I can't believe it. Was the other woman Haleh Aboud?"

"Yes, what do you know about her?"

"Haleh and Ali were very close friends. No Sir, I'm sorry, I just can't believe Ali and Haleh would have anything to do with terrorism."

"Professor, did Ali have other friends?"

"I really don't know, but I know Ali and Haleh were members of the Muslim Fellowship Club. You can try them."

Wilson looked up the telephone number of the club in the school directory, and Dan thanked him for his help.

After leaving the Chemical Engineering Building, Dan called the Muslim Fellowship Club, but nobody answered. Dan decided to try later and headed back to FBI Headquarters.

16

Deep into the analysis of Ali's hard drive, Benny Cannon rubbed his temples. Given the circumstances, he gravitated toward Ali's e-mail account. A missing password; not a problem; Benny had some special software to bypass the password protection feature. After all, nobody could outwit the BennyMeister. Unfortunately, the e-mail account held nothing more than a variety of messages to family and friends. Benny had enlisted the help of one of the agents fluent in Arabic, who translated the e-mails as Benny pulled them up onto his screen. Of course the e-mails could have been written in a type of code, but code breaking was something for the cryptography experts to figure out.

Benny then ran a special software program collecting a history of all e-mails deleted forever. Forever, for techno-geeks was a relative term, and although the user might think the message had been permanently deleted, never to be retrieved, in actual fact, messages could be resurrected for many months after they were deleted from the person's personal account.

A few minutes later, Benny and the other agent reviewed a number of deleted messages. The two critical e-mails were easily located. As Benny listened to the agent translate the messages, he knew he had found some important evidence. He called Jimmy, and in short order the full team sat together reviewing copies of the translated e-mails.

Benny said, "I think this URL address is used by the Quds and the Iranian Revolutionary Guards. I'll check with a friend of mine over at the CIA to be sure."

Jimmy said, "So, the world has changed, and now it appears Ali may have been forced to plant the weapon."

Jimmy's cellphone rang. He took the call and after hanging up said, "Somebody by the name of Jamal Mamoude just showed up. He says Ali Santiani gave him a letter to give to the FBI if he was killed or disappeared. He's in the interrogation area now. Benny, why don't you follow up on the URL address while the rest of us talk to Mr. Mamoude."

¤   ¤   ¤

Jamal sat in a conference room free of one-way mirrors, but nonetheless wired for sound and video. When a person comes forward with important information, the critical thing is to put them at ease and make them believe you are on their side. The tricks are many, but Jimmy preferred the sharing of food. A psychiatrist once told him the mere act of sharing is an important first step in building trust.

Jamal initially refused the coffee, but as the others poured themselves a cup, he changed his mind, and soon the tension of the meeting had been broken, and Jamal felt more at ease.

"Yesterday, I received this letter from my friend Ali. I opened it and saw this other envelope and a message from Ali. I tried calling him, but he didn't answer, so I went over to his apartment, and I saw all the police. Then I came here."

He handed the message and envelope to Jimmy who opened the envelope. As he finished reading each page he passed it onto the others and finally asked Jamal to translate the two e-mails written in Arabic.

After Jamal translated the messages, he asked, "What's this all about?"

Jimmy answered, "Well I can't tell you everything right now, but clearly people forced Ali into doing something he knew wasn't right, and he wanted to make sure we got the information so we could find the people who killed him."

Jamal, under the weight of several hours of stress and sorrow, knew he had done the right thing, and it appeared to be enough to lift a heavy burden from his shoulders.

Dan asked, "Jamal, what can you tell us about Ali or Haleh?"

"Ali wanted to be a great chemical engineer and go back to Iran and help build the country's infrastructure. He loved being here in a country so inclusive, and wished Iran could be as well."

Jimmy asked, "Was Ali political?"

"I don't think so. We both belonged to the Muslim Fellowship Club, but it's just a group of Muslim students here at school. We meet once a week and do social things together. I wouldn't call it very political. I know he hated the ruling party in Iran. Any student, who comes from those repressive régimes, hates their government, especially after experiencing what a truly free democracy is really like."

Alice asked, "What about his girlfriend Haleh?"

"I didn't know her very well. We went on a few double dates together. I know she's from Yemen and majoring in Education, but not much more. She and Ali seemed to be in love."

After thanking him for coming forward, Jimmy gave Jamal his business card and asked him to keep in touch in case the FBI needed to talk to him again. Jamal wrote down his address and telephone number and Alice escorted him to the front entrance.

The team then met in Jimmy's office to review the data collected to date. Benny had confirmed the URL address on the e-mails, and it did come from an Iranian server used by the Quds to communicate to their operatives.

Jimmy summarized. "Okay, here's what we've got. An Iranian terrorist organization forces an innocent student to plant a weapon and then kills two people to prevent anyone from talking. We don't know why they exploded the weapon, but we think it might be a small scale test prior to the big event. We still don't know who actually decided on the launch site because the terrorists painted the glow-yellow "X" before the security camera became operational. We also know they used a sophisticated biological weapon, and only a handful of countries would have the technical knowledge to develop the device. I'm thinking we need to focus on the Iranian connection, and if it can be proved they're responsible for this, it's clearly an act of war. What do you guys think?"

Alice and Benny bought into Jimmy's argument, but Dan remained strangely silent. Jimmy, sensed Dan's uncertainty and asked, "What do you think Dan?"

Dan sat quietly for a moment, not sure of where his thought process would take him, and then it clicked. "I think there's another possibility. I'll start with a very basic premise; whoever did this knew what they were doing. They're sophisticated in both their technical ability and operational skills. I agree using Ali was a set-up, but there're some strange thoughts spinning around my brain; some of these things seem inconsistent with professionals."

"Like what," Jimmy asked?

"Why did the primary terrorist paint the glow-yellow "X" on the alley months before the launch date, and before the security camera became operational? Maybe the City or a resident of the area would have seen the mark and had it removed. Why did the security camera happen to be perfectly lined up with the "X". Why place the "X" directly under a bright streetlight, the worst possible place to put it unless you wanted to make sure the security camera would be able to read the license plate in the middle of the night?"

Jimmy said, "Keep going Danny boy, you're on a roll."

Dan smiled. "Then, the e-mail specifically tells Ali to use his credit card at the Hertz counter. Why would anyone in their right mind use their own credit card, unless they wanted Ali to get caught? The real primary terrorist must have known any reasonable FBI agent would look for security cameras once ground zero had been located, and technically, they must have known we would have been able to identify the general area of the launch. So therefore, it is intuitively obvious to the most casual observer, the real terrorists knew we would find Ali, and, in fact, wanted us to find him, and of course the cops would investigate a double murder, so they knew we would look at his computer. I know Benny is a super geek, but they must have known he would have been able to dig up the deleted e-mails."

Benny asked, "So where does that take you?"

"It takes me to a simple conclusion. Whoever did this wants us to believe the e-mails came from an Iranian terrorist group's web site. Of course my logic all falls apart unless Benny can explain how a person skilled in the art of computer hacking can have an e-mail sent from a remote e-mail account without the owner of the account knowing it."

Dan pointed at Benny, "So my super-geek, can it be done?"

Benny laughed and said, "Are you kidding me; a piece of cake. Any hacker worth his salt could have a virus inserted in the e-mail account and the virus would send the memo, and the owner of the account would never know it."

Dan asked, "I'm assuming the CIA would be monitoring this site. So the real question is, will whoever did this be able to hide it from the CIA as well as the Iranians?"

Benny thought for a second. "Sure, no problem."

Dan smiled, "I rest my case."

Jimmy asked, "What do we do to prove your theory?"

Dan thought for a moment and said, "Why would a security company do a marketing evaluation in an unimportant office building? I think we need to talk to the building manager again and find out more about how he came to get a free expensive security system. I think the bad guys wanted the camera in the exact location it was located, and maybe we can lift some fingerprints or other evidence from the video system."

Jimmy smiled at his good friend. "That's why I wanted you on the team Dan; you think outside the box. I like your theory better than mine. But if it isn't the Iranians, then who did it and why?"

The four contemplated the question but no answer emerged.

17

Ralph Crawford listened to the news from Chicago with growing interest and concern. When the news services expanded on the breaking story, it became clear he had every reason to be worried. As the death toll mounted, he thought about what he had done. The opportunity had been presented as one of corporate espionage, one company trying to steal a biological agent from another. He knew it happened all the time.

At least he had used this rationale when first approached by the sinister looking man with the piercing dark-black eyes. One million dollars to remove one vial of biological material, one million dollars for ten minutes of an illegal act. But this was very different; the material used in research and development was okay, but as a terrorist weapon, absolutely not.

He couldn't tell the FBI, because he'd surely go to jail. After rationalizing the need for silence, he worried how he might be caught, and how to cover a trail he knew would inevitably lead to him.

Ralph could have purchased a large home with his newly acquired fortune, but he knew the purchase would have raised many questions among his colleagues. Instead, he decided to keep his small condominium just outside the city. As he pulled into his one car garage, he felt both remorse and guilt, but knew he couldn't do anything about it. There seemed to be no way out of the dilemma.

He threw his briefcase onto the living room couch, grabbed a beer from the fridge, turned on the TV, and looked at the mail. He never saw the shadow move slowly across the room, never heard the silenced shot, and never realized the problem of what to do had been solved for him, and without his having a say in the matter.

The killer with the penetrating eyes systematically ransacked the condo, and placed small things of value in a plastic garbage bag. He found a stack of one-hundred dollar bills under the mattress in the bedroom. How original he laughed. Most of the one million dollar bribe probably sat untouched in some bank. No matter, it certainly wasn't his problem; he'd only been hired to terminate this link in the evidence chain.

He'd used a small crowbar-like device to jimmy the backdoor's lock. He knew the police would incorrectly assume a burglary in progress had been interrupted by the owner returning at an inopportune time.

After leaving the scene of the crime, the stranger carefully avoided the security cameras placed throughout the condominium complex. Whoever had been contracted to place the cameras had placed them in such obvious places as to be totally ineffective. Only the most stupid criminal would be caught in the act by these cameras, but then again, the stranger knew there were some pretty stupid criminals.

◘   ◘   ◘

The killer's next contracted assignment was not as simple to execute as this one and had required some careful planning. His employer had sent him a key to the small laboratory located in a high-tech industrial park along with the code for the building's security system. He entered the laboratory and began preparing the scene.

The lab served as the manufacturing site for the genetically engineered biological material. After a long search, his employer had been able to find two young Muslim scientists with strong ties to a radical masque in Dearborn Michigan. They had agreed to produce the material, believing its ultimate destination was an Israeli settlement in the West Bank, and a salary of ten-thousand dollars a month would help support their families for many years to come.

The biochemical factory made use of a number of volatile chemicals, including ether, as part of the purification process. The stranger examined a diagram of the lab supplies and glassware used for the synthesis, and located the necessary equipment. Setting the stage reminded him of his high school chemistry class, which he had enjoyed immensely. He took pride in being able to complete the fairly sophisticated setup.

By 1:00 A.M., he looked at his work with satisfaction and waited for the senior scientist to arrive. The Muslim man had been told to meet a person at the lab alone at 2:00 A.M., and transfer the biological agents for shipment to the Middle East.

At two o'clock the scientist arrived and looked suspiciously at the stranger. The dark-eyed man was clearly not Muslim, and the stranger, who sensed the scientist's concern, said, "Do you think our group would be foolish enough to have a Muslim smuggle this material. I do things like this for money; I'm not political."

The unknown person's admission seemed to ease the scientist's concern. He dressed in a protective suit, walked to the lab's freezer, removed sixteen sphere shaped glass storage containers, and placed them carefully inside two custom designed Styrofoam shippers. The scientist never noticed the arrangement of glassware on one of the many lab benches. He totally focused on the safe packaging of the device and didn't see the man pull out his nine-millimeter Glock. The scientist turned around after completing his task and came face to face with the front end of a pistol pointed at his head.

The stranger ordered him to back away from the package and turn around. As the scientist faced the far wall, the unknown man removed a wad of gauze from his pocket, poured a liberal dose of ether onto the gauze pad, placed his gun quietly on the bench, and forced the gauze over the scientists face. After a short-lived struggle, the man collapsed onto the floor.

The man with the dark eyes then dragged the unconscious scientist to the bench in front of the setup, and out of sight of the front door. He then put the ether impregnated gauze pad in a glass beaker, covered it with a petri-dish, and placed the covered container on a desk.

At 2:30 A.M. the second scientist arrived in the lab. He had been told not to talk to the first scientist and to arrive at exactly the appointed time. The message asked him to prepare the biological weapons for transport. Needless to say, he didn't expect to see the unknown person sitting in a chair with a gun pointed directly at his head.

The man told him to walk over to a bench near the desk, face the bench, and then the stranger used the ether once again to render the second scientist unconscious. He moved the man's body close to his partner. As instructed by his employer, the unknown person then lit a Bunsen burner under a glass flask containing ether, placed the open bottle of ether near the setup, picked up the two packages containing the biological agent, and left the building.

The evil looking man drove to a nearby parking lot with an acceptable view of the laboratory, turned off the car's motor and waited. Inside the lab the Bunsen burner began heating the ether inside the glass flask. The temperature rose until the flash point was reached.

The ensuing explosion scattered the hot solution and glass shards across the lab and in the process ignited a second open bottle of ether. A second explosion erupted and fire spread rapidly throughout the lab, igniting additional chemicals in a nearby open storage area. The fire spread throughout the building, and as flames became visible, the stranger smiled, started the car, and slowly drove off down the deserted street and away from the scene of the crime.

Thirty minutes passed before the first fire truck arrived. By then, the building was too far gone for the firemen to do anything other than prevent its spread to other buildings in the industrial park.

In the stranger's mind, another perfect double murder had been committed, and any crime scene investigator or coroner would confirm the two scientists were killed in a terrible industrial accident. The police investigation, if conducted in a professional manner, would identify the two scientists as radical Islamists who had prepared the biological agent used in Chicago.

18

Dan found the name and telephone number of the security camera company on the external hard drive. He called the company's help line, identified himself as an FBI agent, and asked to speak to the CEO. Dan had the luxury of being able to identify himself as either a Chicago Police detective or an FBI agent dependent upon the circumstances.

It took only a few minutes for the head of the company to confirm they did not have any marketing trials going on, and even if they did, they wouldn't have been for free. Dan asked, "If we get you the unit's serial number can you tell me who bought it?"

"Sure, but we sell through distributers, so you probably won't be able to trace it to the final customer, unless they registered for our warranty program."

Dan thanked the CEO for his help.

Dan then called Jerry Adams, the building's manager. "Jerry, we need your help again. We have reason to believe the free marketing trial for your security system is a sham, and the person who talked to you is involved in the recent terrorist attack. Tell me about what happened."

"Well, like I told you last time, this man, I forget his name, but I have his business card in my office. Anyway, he calls me and explains the company wants to test market a new security system; and he says all we need to do to get the system for free is agree to complete a survey and appear in a TV ad if asked. After I agreed, he said an installation specialist would show up the next day to set up the system."

"And did they install it the next day?"

"Yes, their technician showed up the next day with a simple contract. It seemed very straightforward, and we could tell them to remove the equipment any time we wanted. We agreed on a location for the computer system, and I had their technician work with our maintenance engineer."

"Can we get a copy of the agreement?"

"Sure it's in my desk. Anyway, it took them almost a week to complete the installation. My engineer said their technician bordered on incompetent. The system is really great. I would be more than willing to appear on a TV ad to recommend their system."

"Jerry, I want our forensic people to lift as many fingerprints from the cameras as we can. If we get lucky, we may be able to find out who their technician really is. Do I have your permission to go up on the roof?"

"Sure, and if you want I'll get dressed up in the protective suit again and get you the guy's business card and the contract we signed."

"Thanks Jerry, how about if I have someone pick you up at your home, say in about twenty minutes?"

"Sure, I'll be ready."

¤   ¤   ¤

As Dan had suspected, a call to the surveillance camera company confirmed the man's business card and contract were a fake. Meanwhile, the forensic people lifted fingerprints from the vast number of cameras throughout the building and on the roof.

Dan joined the team on the roof and scanned the area. On the edge of the quarantined zone, military trucks began their attempt to decontaminate the area. Volunteers delivered food and other supplies to the quarantined residents. Now only a few ambulances moved in and out of the area. It seemed the City had weathered the storm, and he guessed the medical people would confirm this fact at their next meeting.

Dan thought about Sally, a strong and determined person; in fact, it's one of the reasons he loved her so much. He knew, however, this crisis had seriously tested her resolve. It had seemed like an eternity since he had last seen her, and even though only a few days had passed, he couldn't wait to hold her in his arms once again.

Dan reflected on this act of terror. In many cases of terrorism the *why* could easily be understood, even though the act itself was horrific. For this act, however, the *why* eluded him. What did the people responsible for this terrible act hope to accomplish? It remained the key question, and being able to answer it would undoubtedly help find, and ultimately punish, those responsible.

¤   ¤   ¤

Brad Woolford, the CDC scientist, had been struggling with the decision of what to do since he first saw the electron micrograph of the plasmid. Several years ago he had seen similar pictures while working for the Government as a genetic engineer. He had signed an agreement to never disclose anything ever seen or worked on in Building 257 on Plum Island, but never in a million years did he ever think the pledge would come into conflict with disclosing what he knew about a terrorist attack on his country.

The decision to break his agreement came as the death toll mounted in Chicago. He walked into his boss's office with determination. His legs were shaking and his dry mouth made speaking difficult, but he began the incredible story.

"Cliff, what I'm about to tell you is something I've pledged never to divulge, but I feel the circumstances justify my decision to break my promise. Before coming to CDC, I worked for the Department of Agriculture on Plum Island. Our group worked on trying to predict what types of biological weapons the country might be confronted with and how to defend against them; top secret research kind of stuff. We were heavy into creating genetically engineered agents, and then trying to figure out how to defend against them."

Cliff Bales looked at his colleague in utter disbelief. The more Brad told him, the more it sounded like a development program for biological weapons.

Brad continued, "One of the scientists isolated a DNA sequence from Ebola virus and attached it to a plasmid, the exact type of plasmid I saw yesterday. The animal testing carried out seemed to indicate the Ebola proteins induced all of the symptoms associated with hemorrhagic fever. He told me the research wasn't for weapons, just to understand what could be done. Within a month of establishing the symptoms in primates, the project closed down, and they reassigned the lead scientist to another facility."

"Brad, are you telling me the U.S. Government made this genetically engineered agent?"

"Yes, Cliff, that's exactly what I'm telling you. I believe the scientist continued to work on the project in some secret facility and figured out how to use it as a vector in anthrax. It's not some foreign terrorist's biological agent, it's ours."

Cliff thought for a few moments. "We've got to push this information up the organization. I'm going to talk to the head of CDC. I'll try to keep your name out of it. One more thing Brad, thank you for bringing this to my attention. It took a lot of courage. You made the right decision."

¤   ¤   ¤

Benny had entered the prints lifted from the security system into the FBI and Interpol data bases. Some would obviously be from the building's maintenance engineer, but others, and there were definitely two different sets of prints, would hopefully be from the primary terrorist.

The analysis took several hours to complete, but the results were better than Benny expected.

One set of prints belonged to a person by the name of Darrin Blake. His name appeared in the search because of the time he spent in the U.S. Army. Benny looked up his file in the military database, and the file was sparse to say the least. After entering the Army, Blake had specialized in Military Intelligence, and then, after two years, entered the Rangers. From then on, nothing existed inside the file except a notation that Darrin Blake had been honorably discharged sixteen years ago.

After seeing the information from Benny, Jimmy immediately contacted Bruce Jacobson on his direct line. "Bruce, hi, we've had a possible breakthrough in the case. It looks like the primary terrorist is named Darrin Blake. We lifted his prints off the security system. We believe he specifically located it there to lead us to the person who actually placed the weapon on the roof. Blake served in the Army, and became a Ranger, but from then on the file is strangely missing several years of information. The file looks like it's been redacted. We need to find out what he really did in the military. It looks very suspicious."

"I'm on it Jimmy. I'll get back to you as soon as I've got some information. I'll have to go up to the top on this one, but given the circumstances, I'm sure we'll get the support we need."

19

The taskforce meeting began with a higher than normal sense of expectation. Sally provided a clinical update. New admissions had decreased dramatically over the past twenty-four hours. The death rate for infected patients had reached eighty-six percent.

The army said the decontamination of the infected zone would be completed in a week. Ongoing testing of non-infected residents within the infected zone, had established a very low probability of new patients emerging from within the area. Everyone agreed the quarantine could be lifted after decontamination of the area had been completed.

No longer could this be portrayed as anything other than an act of terrorism, and Jimmy felt the pressure to hold a news conference, which he had scheduled immediately after the meeting of the taskforce.

Greg then reviewed the latest information from Cliff Bales. "I spoke with Cliff earlier today. He's the lead scientist at the Atlanta Lab. One of his scientists working at the lab identified the plasmid containing the Ebola virus proteins. It apparently comes from a U.S. Government facility."

"What," echoed everyone in the room?

Jimmy asked, "Let me make sure I understand. You're telling us the U.S. Government initiated this attack?"

"No, all I'm saying is whoever developed this weapon got the vector with the Ebola virus protein from a U.S. Government facility. Maybe it was stolen. I really don't know. All I know is our lab has identified the source of the vector, and I can tell you the person who identified it is a respected scientist who is scared to death right now because he feels he violated a secrecy oath he signed when he worked at Plum Island."

Dan asked, "Greg, what's Plum Island?"

"Dan, Plum Island is located near Long Island in New York. The Government conducts research there on diseases affecting animals, but obviously, the development of this type of vector has nothing to do with safeguarding our livestock population."

Jimmy added, "Well, you've certainly added a new dimension to this problem. We'll follow up. I'll check with Director Jacobson on this, but I'm sure we're going to want to talk to your scientist who identified the vector."

"Jimmy, he really wants his name kept out of all this; he's afraid of what will happen to him."

"We're still going to need to talk to him. I'll see what we can do to ease his concerns.

Changing the subject, we've got some good leads on the primary terrorist who painted the glow-yellow "X". This information is confidential for obvious reasons, and as the case progresses, we'll pass the information along on a need to know basis. I'm sure you can all understand the reasons for the secrecy."

As the meeting broke up Sally said, "Dan, I'm out of here effective right now. I'll see you tonight. It's going to be a restaurant night. I've been barely surviving on sandwiches and coffee."

Jimmy overhearing Sally said, "You may think you're going home, but I need you here. You're full time on my team as of right now."

Sally replied, "I'll come over, but not until I've had a chance to shower and change my clothes."

Jimmy laughed, "Well I guess we don't want you smelling up the place."

Sally said, "It's not the smell Jimmy, I don't think you want your agents walking around in surgical scrubs."

"I don't know; it would be a step up from Benny's dress code."

Benny looked at Jimmy and expressed mock shock and disbelief as he pointing to his bright orange sweatshirt, madras pants and polka dot Van gym shoes.

¤   ¤   ¤

When Sally arrived at the FBI Field Office, she found Dan standing in the back of the press briefing room. She snuck up behind him, and squeezed his ass. Dan said, "Oh Betty, not in front of everyone." Dan turned around, knowing full well the identity of the intruder, and held Sally tightly in his arms. He placed his hands on the back of her head and brought her lips to his. He kissed her gently and smelled the exotic perfume he knew so well. "I missed you Honey. You must have been going through hell."

"You have no idea. It felt like a war zone, only worse, but we all did our job, and I know we saved hundreds of people who otherwise would have died. We'll talk more tonight."

Jimmy stepped up to the podium and read a short prepared speech. It basically said nothing more than the FBI was in the early stages of investigating what appeared to be a terrorist attack using a biological weapon. Of course the speech took almost five minutes to deliver, but divulged very little.

Jimmy then opened the meeting to questions and the shouting began. The Mayor's office, because of the early decision to share as much information with the public as possible, had been feeding the media enough information to keep their papers filled with interesting special interest columns. The heroic efforts of the Northwestern Hospital staff created heart wrenching stories of personal and family tragedies. But now, because the epidemic appeared to be under control, the media turned its attention to the terrorist attack. Jimmy answered most questions with the same *no comment* response.

After the meeting the full FBI team met in Jimmy's office. "Okay, we've made a great deal of progress on this case. First, we now know Darrin Blake is probably the primary terrorist. Director Jacobson is trying to dig out more information on Blake.

"Additionally, it seems the vector, this plasmid as the medical people call it, originated within our own Government. It seems hard to believe some of our own people did this. Maybe the material was stolen from the Government, and then an outside terrorist group set off the weapon."

Sally said, "Jimmy, there's a long way to go from having this vector to creating a functional biological weapon.

"Okay Sally, I agree, but either way our own Government or an outside terrorist group is involved."

Sally asked, "What's the motive here. If it's a terrorist group, then why aren't they bragging?"

Dan answered, "Sally, you said so yourself. This may have been the final test before the big attack. Maybe the terrorists want to stay quiet on this until the big weapon goes off."

Alice said, "Let's not forget the Iranian terrorist e-mail site used for the messages to Ali. I agree with Dan, it was probably a set-up to convince us the Iranian Government is involved, but maybe they really did do this. It makes a lot of sense."

Jimmy's secretary interrupted the meeting with a call from Director Jacobson. "Have you got something for us?"

"I do Jimmy. Here's what I found out. Darrin Blake became involved in a covert Ranger group specializing in black operations. The military asked him to retire from the group after he needlessly killed civilians in a number of missions. Unfortunately, because of his proficiency at killing, he's been on retainer with the CIA, and used from time to time on special foreign assignments. I talked to his handler at the CIA who confirms Blake has the profile of a person who could easily do this type of thing. He has a reputation as a ruthless killer for hire, and is known to have been involved with foreign governments on special assassination missions."

Jimmy said, "Sure sounds like he's our man. Do they have any idea where he can be found?"

"No, they only communicate with him by e-mail, and they believe he has no permanent address, but just moves from assignment to assignment."

Jimmy thought for a moment and said, "We've been discussing the case. Everybody's in my office now, and here's what I think we should do.

Sally's our medical expert; she and Dan should follow up on trying to work on the origin of this vector. They need to see if they can figure out who's responsible for building the weapon. Meanwhile, Alice and Brian can work on locating Darrin Blake. He may lead us back to the mastermind of this operation and help prevent a second bigger attack."

Jacobson replied, "I like the idea Jimmy, and we can respond with more resources as needed. You need to be letting me know the status of things every day. The President is now asking for daily briefings on this, and I want to make sure I can fill him in with the most current information."

After the discussion with Jacobson, Jimmy asked Dan and Sally what they were going to do.

Dan said, "We need to get to Plum Island and see what we can find out there."

Sally said, "First, I want to talk to the CDC scientist in Atlanta to find out more about what actually happened at Plum Island. I'm betting he has a lot of useful information."

Jimmy agreed with Sally and then asked Alice and Brian about their next steps. Brian said, "We need to talk to Blake's handler at the CIA. We need to find out as much about him as we can."

Jimmy concluded the meeting. "I want Benny and Glenda to stay here. You guys can use them as your internal resources. If we have to, we'll add them and others to your teams."

After making airplane reservations to Atlanta for the early morning flight, Dan and Sally left for home and what they knew would be the last good night's sleep they would have for the next few days.

After dinner at their favorite neighborhood restaurant, they hit the sack. Proving the old adage, *absence makes the heart grow stronger*, they wrestled under the bed's duvet. With Sally straddling his waist, she dangled her breasts just above his face; something she knew drove him crazy. His pavlovian response, a tongue driven down her throat, led to a torrid lovemaking session.

Totally spent, they lay quietly entwined. Sally said, "I've never been so terrified in my life as when I saw the first patient. I finally narrowed the possible causes down to only one, but the full impact didn't register at first. When the third patient arrived, I knew we were in deep shit. I kept thinking the number of infected people could reach tens of thousands, and I knew if the number got that high, we could never respond."

"Honey, you guys are heroes. I've been reading the papers each day, and what you all accomplished was an absolute miracle."

"Don't believe everything you read. It became a public relations bonanza for Larry Becker. Harry called it alright; Northwestern Hospital is now the premiere hospital in the country. But I'll tell you this; the real heroes are the engineering staff. They completely rearranged the hospital in two days. It's amazing what you can get done with plastic sheeting and duct tape"

They both laughed, and then quickly fell asleep, getting some much needed rest before what they both knew would become an all-consuming race to avert a second and perhaps more deadly biological attack.

20

Sally and Dan arrived at the Atlanta airport shortly after ten o'clock, and drove to the CDC campus located in a northeast suburb of Atlanta. A security guard escorted their rented car to a relatively new building housing Clifford Bales' office and lab.

The security guard at the lobby's front desk asked them to remove their pistols. Sally handed hers in without objection. She hated the constant pressure of the gun and holster on the side of her body.

Cliff Bales met them in the lobby and led them to his fourth floor office. Cliff definitely had a professorial look about him, and his reading glasses hanging from an ugly yellow-braided lanyard added to the effect. He noticed Sally staring at the yellow yarn and said, "A gift from my daughter. She's an Indian Princess. I've got to wear it or I'm toast."

They all laughed as Cliff directed them to a sitting area in the corner of his office. Dan said, "Thanks for agreeing to meet with us on such short notice. I understand you canceled a trip to be here."

Cliff responded, "It became the perfect excuse to miss an outside meeting I never wanted to attend anyway, and besides, I wanted to meet the doctor who made the diagnosis. You know most doctors would have confused the symptoms with the flu. You saved a lot of lives doctor."

"Thanks Cliff, but I was lucky.

"So, in addition to your being a great doctor, you're an FBI Agent, and married to an FBI Agent. I'll bet there's an interesting story there."

Dan laughed, "It's an interesting story, but we can't tell you about it except to say we met on a case, and I couldn't resist her charms."

Sally just smiled in agreement.

Dan continued, "So as you know, we're following up on the vector one of your people identified. We're going to try to find out how terrorists got hold of it."

Cliff asked, "So you don't think our Government is somehow involved?"

Dan answered, "That's a possibility, but there're other more likely explanations."

"Such as?"

"Such as, we're not at liberty to discuss those other possibilities."

"Well, let me tell you about Brad Woolford. He identified the plasmid. He's one of the hardest workers in the group. He's a detail oriented scientist, and when he comes to a conclusion, we accept it as fact because he never jumps the gun until he's absolutely positive. I can tell you, if he's sure he's seen the plasmid before, then it's the same plasmid."

Sally asked, "Is there anything else we need to know about Brad?"

"Yes, he's scared. He signed this secrecy agreement when he worked at the Plum Island facility and promised never to divulge what he had seen there. Now he sees this plasmid and he's torn between keeping his promise and doing what he knows is the right thing."

Sally said, "Yes, I can see the dilemma. We'll be sensitive when we talk to him."

Cliff led them down to the second floor. The labs containing a large number of Class III cabinets were located in the center of the floor and separated from the perimeter offices by multiple containment walls. Isolation and containment of the various nasty infectious agents within the small laboratories was absolutely essential.

Cliff knocked on Woolford's office door, and a voice answered. Cliff led Sally and Dan into the small office and introduced them to Dr. Brad Woolford, whose hands felt damp and cold. Cliff then left the office and asked Brad to bring Dan and Sally to his office after they finished talking.

The three stared at each other not really knowing how to begin. It didn't take a psychiatrist to see Brad clearly feared the pending conversation. Sally and Dan had already agreed; Sally would take the lead, and she wanted to put him at ease. "Thank you for agreeing to meet with us Brad. As one of the treating physicians at Northwestern Hospital, I can tell you your willingness to come forward with the information on the vector helped us save many lives."

"Well Doctor Lawson, I saw it initially as a genetically modified plasmid. It didn't become a vector until someone decided to introduce it into the *Bacillus anthracis*."

"Please call me Sally, and of course you're correct. We're trying to trace who introduced the plasmid into the anthrax. We know you had nothing to do with it, but we're here because we want you to tell us as much as you can remember about what happened at Plum Island, and maybe you can start by giving us some history of the Plum Island facility."

Brad began to relax as he explained the history of Plum Island. "You see, the island is located near Long Island and early on the military recognized it as a strategic location for protecting the New York harbor. The government bought the island and built Fort Terry during the Spanish American War. Then, in 1952 the Army Chemical Corps took over the facility and began research and development on chemical agents. In 1954 the Department of Agriculture began running the place, and biological weapons research moved to Building 257. Work on the weapons continued until President Nixon ended all biological weapons research in 1969. Now, the island is run by Homeland Security and the research focuses on formulating countermeasures against foreign animal diseases."

Sally asked, "So you were working on those types of projects when you were there?"

"Yes, I specialized in foot and mouth disease. I helped develop new vaccines to fight the disease."

Sally asked, "I thought we eradicated the disease a long time ago?"

"We did, but it's still pervasive in other countries, and we wanted to eradicate the disease worldwide."

Dan asked, "So how did you happen to stumble on this plasmid?"

"One day I was working in the Electron Microscope Lab. All of the research teams shared this facility. I happened to see a picture on the computer monitor of this plasmid, but it wasn't just a plasmid like many of the research teams had used before; it looked really strange. I hardly knew the scientist at the computer, but I asked him about his project.

He said his team worked on Ebola virus and they discovered the group of proteins responsible for hemorrhagic fever. I thought wow, really neat, and asked him why their team had inserted the DNA code into the plasmid. He said the group thought it would be easier to create a vaccine from the modified plasmid instead of the inactivated Ebola virus.

I didn't think using a plasmid would work, and we talked for a while, but I remembered the unusual shape of the DNA structure of those Ebola proteins. The structure of the plasmid in the region of the inserted Ebola DNA was unlike anything I had ever seen. It made a lasting impression."

Sally asked, "So what happened then?"

"A couple of months later, I saw him on the ferry, and he said management had cancelled the project, and transferred him to another project. So there's the full story."

Dan asked, "What's the man's name?"

"His name is Waterford, Doctor Paul Waterford."

Sally asked, "Did he leave Plum Island?"

"Not as far as I know. He just moved to another facility on the island. Most of us who worked there lived on Long Island, and we sometimes took the same Government ferry home at night. I still saw him from time to time."

Dan asked, "Could there have been biological weapons work going on at the facility?"

"Biological weapons are illegal. There's a treaty against developing biological weapons."

Sally asked, "Were there military people at the facility?"

"Sure, the military had some active projects.

As Sally and Woolford then discussed technical facts beyond Dan's ability to understand or care about, he inspected Brad Woolford's office. Pictures of his wife and children cluttered the credenza behind his desk. Other pictures worthy of hanging in many modern art museums, and obvious gifts from his children, filled the empty spaces on his wall.

Two framed diplomas on the wall behind his desk testified to his exceptional credentials; an undergraduate degree in Biology from Caltech and a PhD from MIT in Genetic Engineering.

In spite of his super background, he seemed like an average person, except he looked scared to death because of what he had witnessed.

Sally and Dan spent the next hour talking to Brad, but they weren't able to extract any additional useful recollections from his memory. After their meeting, Brad walked them back to Cliff Bales' office, and after saying goodbye, they left the CDC campus.

They stopped for lunch at a restaurant at Hartsfield-Jackson International Airport. After ordering lunch, Dan called Director Jacobson on his private line. "I'm sorry to bother you; this is

Dan Lawson. We're in Atlanta, and just spoke with the scientist who identified the vector. Now we're going to visit Plum Island and need your assistance. We believe there's some highly classified work going on there and we're going to need your help in getting people to talk to us. Can you make a few calls?"

"Sure, I'll lean on some people. Give me a call when you get to New York and I'll have the name of a contact."

After talking to Jacobson, Dan turned to Sally, who stared intently at her i-pad. "What are you doing?"

"I've looked up the Biological Weapons Convention Treaty, and listen to what it says. *The treaty bans the development, stockpiling, acquisition, retention, and production of biological agents and toxins of types and in quantities that have no justification for prophylactic, protective or other peaceful purposes.*

"I'm no legal expert, but I recognize all types of weasel words, and, I'd say the treaty doesn't ban research, because research isn't really development, and under the guise of research, I'll bet the Government could justify the development of the biological weapon we're looking for."

"What are you saying?"

"I'm saying after Paul Waterford discovers this vector, the military moved him into another facility where they work on this kind of stuff. They figured out how to transfer the vector into anthrax."

"You're saying the U.S. Government did this?"

"No, I'm just saying maybe the Government developed it."

The first call for their flight to New York interrupted their discussion.

21

Alice and Brian flew to Washington to meet Darrin Blake's CIA handler at Langley. Dennis Jones met them in the lobby and led them into the bowels of the building to his private office. "So you think Darrin did this?"

Alice answered, "It sure looks like he did. We found his fingerprints on a security camera perfectly placed to get a picture of the person who actually placed the weapon. They wanted us to ID the person who planted the weapon, but we have other evidence showing the person was blackmailed into doing this and then killed, probably by Blake."

"Well like I told Director Jacobson, Darrin is clearly capable of doing this. All it would take is the right price. For him, it's all about the money."

Brian asked, "So how do we find him? Do you know where he lives?"

"He lives out of his suitcase, and moves from mission to mission. When we want to use him, we communicate using an e-mail account."

Alice said, "We want to find him and get information off his computer and cellphone without his knowing it. Any suggestions?"

Dennis Jones thought for a few minutes, finally smiled and said, "I know this is a bit complicated, but it's the kind of covert operation I enjoy planning. Let's say I contact him with a job offer. I'll tell him we're willing to pay big money if he'll break into somebody's house and exchange a fake document for a real one. It's something right up his alley. I'll ask him where he wants us to send the fake document, and when he picks it up, you can find out where he's staying. Then, when he breaks into the place, you guys can get the information while he's busy."

Alice asked, "But he may keep the computer with him."

"No problem," Dennis said, "we'll tell him the home has very sophisticated security and can pick up any electronic presence, and he can't enter the building with anything electronic."

Brian said, "For this to work, we'll need to convince him the person who has the real document is a big-time player."

"No problem, we'll use Director Jacobson as the target. Blake will easily believe there's a turf-war going on between the FBI and the CIA, and he knows we wouldn't want to use one of our own agents to pull this off. If you get Jacobson to go along with the ruse, then I'll make it happen."

Alice called Jacobson and briefed him on their plan for locating Blake. Bruce said, "Now Alice, I don't want you spending too much time with this CIA fellow. He's teaching you some bad things.

But I do like the plan. On the night of the robbery, I'll make sure my wife and I are out of town. Brief me on the plan when it's finalized, and make sure the guy doesn't break any windows."

Alice smiled at Dennis, "It's a go, but Jacobson said you're teaching me bad things."

They all laughed and got down to work planning the mission. By late in the afternoon everything had been worked out and an e-mail had been sent to Blake's anonymous e-mail account asking if he would be interested in the job for $50,000.

An hour later a response came back, "Yes, but for $75,000, and what are the details?"

Dennis then sent back the following e-mail. *A Top Secret document will be brought to Director Jacobson's house by courier tomorrow afternoon. The Director is leaving town for a speaking engagement with his wife the same afternoon and will not return until the next day. Protocol requires he store the document in the wall safe located behind the picture in the laundry room. We need you to remove the document from his safe, and replace it with a fake document we will supply. The security code for the alarm system is 55587943, and it is located inside the front hallway closet.*

In addition to the normal security system, a prototype state of the art system is designed to detect the movement of any battery powered electronic device. Therefore, entrance to the house must not be made with any cellphone, PCD, or even a battery powered watch. The combination to the safe is 33-45-16-77-89. After exchanging the real document with the fake one, the original document should be returned to us at a dead drop site specified by you. The exchange must take place tomorrow night. How should we get you the fake document?

The response came back an hour later. *FBI Director's house as the target requires a new price of $100,000. The dead drop site for the fake document will be supplied to you tomorrow morning. A different dead drop site for the real document will be sent to you the next morning at nine o'clock. Wire funds, half now, half after completion of mission to my usual offshore account.*

Dennis sent a message back confirming the new price, and then said, "We've got him. I'll have our best covert surveillance people follow him after we drop off the fake document. You can follow behind as long as you don't interfere."

Alice asked, "What's wrong, you don't think we're good enough to conduct covert surveillance?"

"You may be good, but not as good as the people I'm going to use."

"You're forgetting one thing Dennis; you're out of your jurisdiction inside the U.S. We'll take care of the surveillance."

"Okay, what if we provide backup support with one of our silent surveillance drones? We can operate it out of Andrews Air Force Base."

Brian replied, "We'll take you up on the offer."

After leaving Langley, Alice contacted Jimmy and briefed him on the plan. Alice asked for Benny's help in getting the data off Blake's electronic devices, and Jimmy agreed to send the BennyMeister to Washington as soon as possible.

22

Dan and Sally arrived at LaGuardia late in the afternoon. An FBI helicopter waited for them at the civil aviation terminal and flew them over to Long Island MacArthur Airport. They rented a SUV and drove east toward their final destination, the Orient Heights Inn, a small Bed and Breakfast located near the eastern end of Long Island.

After checking in and unpacking, they both wanted a nice dinner, only their second together since the terrorist attack began. The receptionist recommended a small restaurant across the street from the Orient Harbor Yacht Club. It was the only restaurant within a half-hour's drive, so they decided to try the ocean-side recommendation.

They arrived at the restaurant a little before sunset, and, as they stepped from the car, Dan deeply inhaled the salt air breeze. Saltwater air had the ability to rejuvenate the body. The

Sailfish looked more like a small café than a full-fledged restaurant, and a chalkboard by the front door described the daily specials. The menu emphasized seafood, understandable given the name and location. A dozen tables filled the small dining area. The owner, multitasking as host, sous chef, and server, sat them by a large bay window overlooking the yacht club.

Over a bottle of the house Chardonnay, they sipped away the last few days of stress. They both ordered the Swordfish, which their server assured them was both fresh and delicious, and then, while waiting for their salads, reflected on the past few days.

Sally looked beautiful in her jeans and a loose-fitting white cotton sweater. Her long dark-brown hair, held in a ponytail by a simple yellow ribbon, fell down to her shoulders. Dan reached out across the table and looked her in the eyes. "What was it really like Honey?"

Sally reflected for a moment, smiled and said, "It had to be the most terrifying and rewarding experience of my life. The magnitude of the epidemic exceeded anything I had ever trained for. The entire staff just ran on instincts, nothing more. When the first patient arrived in the ER and I examined him, I couldn't believe it. It just hit me; he has all the symptoms of inhalation anthrax and hemorrhagic fever. I thought this can't be a naturally occurring disease; it has to be an act of terrorism. I felt scared to death, but knew I couldn't show it; the others in the ER counted on me to lead, not to panic."

"But you saved a lot of people."

"We saved more people than we should have. With an outbreak of both hemorrhagic fever and Anthrax, the death rate should have been almost one-hundred percent. The entire hospital staff rose to the occasion. I still don't know how the facility engineers transformed the entire hospital in less than two days."

Sally sat silently for a few moments; tears began falling from her eyes. Dan held onto her hand, and gently kissed it. Sally then recovered and said, "The first patient's wife. Now there's a real hero. She should have died, but I honestly believe she willed herself to live. That's what surprised me; seeing those people hanging on tenaciously to life. We didn't save them; we just helped them. They saved themselves."

Dan then shared some of his thoughts, "When I first heard about what happened, I thought you would be infected. Then, when this doctor Eli Fineman shows up in a spacesuit, I really became terrified. You know it's what you can't see that's the most terrifying. You can see a tornado or hurricane coming, and when it's over, it's really over. But this thing; I stood outside the perimeter, breathing in the air, not knowing if it was infected. We were all scared, but nobody would admit it. We all did what we had to do."

Sally said, "We've got to find out who did this. We can't stop until we find them."

"Honey, we will find them! I'm just hoping it wasn't the Iranian Government, because if we can prove it, then it's definitely an act of war. I'm hoping it's a group of people who want us to believe the Iranian Revolutionary Guard or the Quds did it. If we catch this guy Blake, he may have more information. It's interesting that Blake isn't a Muslim, and if the Iranians did this, I can't believe they would use a non-Muslim to execute the plan. I'm betting on a U.S. sponsored terrorist group, but we need more information to be sure."

A young family arrived at the restaurant. Obvious regulars, the hostess greeted them all with hugs and kisses. The youngest child, strapped in an infant seat, responded to the lady's facial gymnastics with a gleeful yell. The mother, enjoying the spectacle said, "She should be asleep by now. It's way past her bedtime."

Sally, watching the exchange with a certain amount of envy, suddenly understood the answer to a mystery. "That's it," she said!

Dan replied, "What Honey?"

"At the hospital, very few of the young children became infected. None of us could figure out why, but it's so clear now. They were all asleep in their beds. Only the older children were allowed to stay up late and watch the fireworks show. They were all outside and exposed to the anthrax spores, but the little kids were inside, asleep and protected from the spores. The answer stared us in the face all the time."

The salads arrived and they began decompressing as they ate. By the time they finished their dinner, both felt rejuvenated, anticipating the next day's investigation on Plum Island.

23

Director Jacobson had instructed them to meet their helicopter ride to Plum Island at the Orient Point Ferry terminal. When they arrived, the chopper waited in a grassy field alongside a parking lot. As they approached the helicopter, the door opened and Director Jacobson stepped out to meet them. He hugged Sally and shook hands with Dan. The last time Dan and Sally talked to Bruce Jacobson had been in his office after having stopped a group of terrorists from exploding a nuclear device in the nation's Capital.

Of course Bruce had also attended their wedding ceremony, but they never had a chance to talk to him because he had to leave the celebration early after receiving an emergency call from the President.

Sally said, "Bruce, it's nice to see you again, but what are you doing here?"

"Well, there're a couple of reasons. Solving this case is the most important thing on my docket; and we're about to enter a facility with a lot of secrets, and believe me when I tell you, a lot of bureaucrats want to keep the FBI out of this probe. So, I'm here to clear away the bullshit and make sure the truth sees the light of day."

Dan asked, "Why the secrets?"

"It turns out we've been following the letter of the law as related to the Biological Weapons Treaty, but we haven't been very good at following its spirit. For a number of years we've been conducting research on biological weapons on the island. Of course it was all done with the intention of developing defenses in case foreign countries chose to use those same weapons, but nonetheless, we now have a considerable number of biological agents stored there."

Sally said, "We thought as much after talking to Brad Woolford."

"I'm going to stay here for the day to make sure everything's disclosed, and then I'll leave the actual investigation to both of you."

The ride to Plum Island took less than ten minutes, and their chopper landed at a heliport located alongside the Plum Island Animal Disease Center. With advance notice of their arrival, a small entourage stood at the heliport waiting to meet them. After introductions, the Director of the facility, Doctor Robert Grimes, led them inside the main building. Director Jacobson walked next to Grimes and informed him they needed to talk to him without his staff.

Jacobson asked Dan and Sally to join him in Grimes' office. Bruce Jacobson began, "Doctor Grimes, I'm here today because I've been stonewalled and bullshitted for the last two days. The President finally had to step in and tell the Secretary of Defense and the other cabinet members in no uncertain terms that he expected them to have their departments cooperate fully with our investigation. I am told you have already been ordered to disclose everything, and I do mean everything."

Grimes interrupted, "Director, I can assure you my team has nothing to hide."

"Doctor Grimes, I expect more than complete disclosure. I demand full assistance from your people. Working together, we need to figure out what really happened here. I'll leave this afternoon if I feel my two agents receive the help they're going to need. Dan, Sally, where do we start?"

Dan began, "We want to talk to Paul Waterford, the scientist who we know worked on the plasmid used as the vector, and then we'll want to trace the development program from beginning to end. Somehow your people lost control of this biological agent, and we need to understand how it happened."

Grimes made a telephone call, and five minutes later Doctor Paul Waterford entered the office. Grimes made the introductions and informed Waterford the participants were cleared to receive the most classified information. Waterford looked visibly distressed. At this point, he had no idea why the Director of the FBI came to Plum Island and wanted to talk to him. But being a smart person, he intuitively knew he was in deep shit. The middle-aged scientist appeared rather short and looked anorexic. He couldn't have weighed more than one-hundred-twenty pounds

Sally and Dan had discussed how to proceed with the interrogation of Waterford. Due to the technical nature of the subject matter, Sally took the lead. "Doctor Waterford, I'm sure you've been following the recent events in Chicago, but what you probably don't know is the biological agent used in the attack used a vector containing a plasmid, probably developed in this facility.

Paul Waterford's face turned ashen. He now understood the significance of Sally's comment and thought, *it's my plasmid, and they think I'm involved.*

Sally continued, "We talked to Brad Woolford yesterday. He told us the plasmid came from this facility. He saw a picture of it one day in the electron microscope room and talked to you about it."

Sally handed Waterford a picture of the plasmid given to them by Cliff Bales. Paul Waterford looked at the picture, fell back in his chair, and exhaled deeply. His face turned red and tears came to his eyes. "Is this the agent used in Chicago?"

"Yes Doctor Waterford. Could you please give us the history of the project you're working on, and its present status?"

Waterford struggled with where to begin. "Well Agent Lawson or should I call you Doctor?"

Sally interrupted, "Call me Sally."

Sally had a way of getting people to relax, and with the tension lifted, Paul Waterford began the story. "I've worked with Ebola virus for the last ten years. We were concerned it might be brought into this country by accident or by terrorists, and we wanted to understand how to prevent a pandemic. After a number of years I isolated the DNA code for the proteins involved in producing the hemorrhagic fever symptoms. We had this DNA sequence coding for the proteins and I thought it might be easier to create a vaccine if we incorporated the DNA into a plasmid. It wasn't any big challenge since I had the DNA sequence already isolated."

Sally asked, "Is that when you talked to Brad Woolford?"

"Yes, we talked for about half an hour. He's really smart. He didn't think it would work, and he had some good ideas of alternate approaches. Anyway, it's the only time we talked about the plasmid."

Dan asked, "What happened next?"

"About a week after I talked to Brad, Colonel Clarke came to see me. He's in charge of the Offensive Agents Group. He wanted me to transfer to his group and work exclusively on developing defensive strategies against the vector. It was exactly what I wanted to work on anyway, so it seemed like a perfect opportunity, and I received a promotion."

Jacobson asked, "Does this Offensive Agents Group report to you Doctor Grimes?"

"It's a dotted line reporting point. He also reports directly into the Head of the Joint Chiefs."

Bruce Jacobson didn't like dotted line reporting relationships. They were a source of confusion, and often as not, led to employees keeping neither boss in the loop on key decisions.

Paul Waterford continued, "Colonel Clarke asked me what a terrorist would do if they wanted to take advantage of this plasmid. I told him a vector needed to be incorporated into another organism to act as the delivery system, and I thought e-coli and anthrax offered two good choices. The e-coli could be added to a city's water supply and the anthrax could be delivered as an aerosol. Clarke asked me to develop both

delivery   systems   and   then   develop
countermeasures for each."

Sally asked, "Didn't it seem like you would be
violating the Biological Weapons Treaty?"

"No, not at all. It seemed a reasonable
approach to me. You've got to know what the
terrorists are doing before you can develop the
countermeasure."

Waterford's answer struck Sally as logical, but
fraught with potential risks, such as the one they
were now facing with terrorists managing to steal
the biological agents.

Waterford continued, "I've been working on
the project for the last few years. I successfully
incorporated the vector into both anthrax and e-
coli, and my group has been trying to develop
vaccines against both agents."

Jacobson said, "Thanks for your help Doctor
Waterford. Doctor Grimes, could you ask Colonel
Clarke to join us? We need to talk to him about
this program."

Grimes called Colonel Clarke and asked him
to come over immediately. While waiting for his
arrival, Grimes had coffee served.

Bruce Jacobson asked, "Tell us about the
Montauk Monster."

Grimes lifted his head and laughed. "Back in
2008, a dead animal washed up on shore near
Montauk, New York. The creature, at least what
was left of it, was a quadruped, and the experts
said it looked like a raccoon, but others thought it
couldn't be a raccoon because it looked like it had
a beak, and of course the conspiracy theory
people said it came from Plum Island because of
the water currents. I saw a picture of the animal,
and it didn't look like any raccoon I've ever seen."

Sally added, "And because of the work with biological agents here on the island, local residents assumed your people had something to do with it."

"You've got it. A good conspiracy is always more exciting than the truth."

¤   ¤   ¤

Colonel Jack Clarke entered the office with a noticeable limp. Sally could see the unmistakable signs of two artificial legs. He slowly scanned the room, and with a great deal of suspicion, he introduced himself, and then moved his chair to sit next to Grimes. The movement of the chair clearly attempted to create an us versus them environment.

Jacobson took the lead. "Colonel Clarke, we're here to investigate the apparent use by terrorists of a biological weapon developed in your lab, and we'd like your assistance in trying to figure out what happened."

Colonel Clarke, with fire in his eyes, looked directly at Jacobson and said, "Director, I report directly to the Head of the Joint Chiefs, and he has not given me permission to release any information on our projects to the FBI or any other organization, regardless of your clearance level."

Here was the big power play. Sally wondered how Jacobson would respond to this insult. Bruce Jacobson pulled out his cellphone and dialed a number. "Andy, it's Bruce. I have an emergency situation with regard to the recent terrorist attack. The head of the team working on the plasmid, a Colonel Jack Clarke, says he won't work with us unless directed to do so by General

Burke. I really don't have the time to put up with all this crap. I want you to ask the President and the Head of the Joint Chiefs to call me back right now. I need a direct order from the President before he'll cooperate. Call back on Doctor Grime's phone."

Grimes gave Bruce the telephone number, and after hanging up the phone, Jacobson stared at Clarke. It was a stare down contest of epic proportions, and how quickly the President responded to Bruce's request would dictate the winner. The silence became a painful exercise, as everyone just sat there waiting. After fewer minutes than Sally thought possible, Grimes' phone rang. An operator began trying to connect everyone into the conference call. Clarke fidgeted in his chair, and his face flushed.

The teleconference began, "Bruce, this is James. How can I help you today?"

"Mr. President, thank you for talking with me on such short notice. Let me introduce the people in our meeting. Director Grimes is in charge of the Plum Island facility, Colonel Clarke is in charge of the team of scientists working on the plasmid project, Doctor Waterford is the lead scientist on the project, and I think you might remember Doctor Sally Lawson and Dan Lawson, the two FBI agents working on the case."

Dan and Sally, yes of course I remember both of you, except when we last talked I believe Doctor Lawson was Doctor Graff. Sounds like the two of you got hitched."

Sally smiled and said, "Yes Mr. President, Dan made me an offer I couldn't refuse."

"Well good for him. Let me thank you both again for your heroic efforts on that other case.

The country will always owe both of you a great deal for your efforts.

I also have General Burke on the line, and I understand we need to clarify some levels of authority. Let me get right down to the nitty-gritty, because I have a meeting with the British Prime Minister in five minutes. Colonel Clarke, as the Commander and Chief, I am ordering you to provide all of the help and assistance to the FBI and others as they may deem necessary. Do you understand?"

A meek Colonel Clarke answered, "Yes Mr. President, I will obey your order."

The President then continued, "General Burke, do you agree with my order?"

General Burke responded, "Yes, Mr. President, we must do everything in our power to find the terrorists who committed this horrific act. Colonel Clarke, I also order you to provide all of the assistance to the FBI as they require."

It was the most impressive example of power politics Sally had ever witnessed. Clarke fumed in his chair, being rebuked by not only his boss, but also the President of the United States. The conference call ended in less than two minutes.

Director Jacobson began, "Colonel Clarke, how do you think this agent fell into the hands of terrorists?"

Clarke answered, "I honestly don't know Sir."

"Well then, I guess Sally and Dan will have to figure it out. Since we now have your full cooperation, I'm sure they'll be able to get to the bottom of this. Meanwhile, I have to get back to Washington for an important meeting. Dan and Sally are in charge of this investigation and have my total support. Any request from them should be viewed as a request from me."

Bruce Jacobson stood up, shook hands with everyone, asked Dan to call him later from their hotel for an update, and then left the office.

Dan, recognizing Colonel Clarke was still too pissed to be of any real help said, "Paul, Why don't we go back to your office and get started, and later today we'll check in with Colonel Clarke. Robert, we're going to need a way to get back to the Ferry Terminal at Orient Point."

"No problem Dan. There's a ferry leaving for the terminal every hour. Paul can show you how to catch it."

The meeting broke up, and Paul Waterford brought them to the facility's cafeteria for lunch. They sat in a corner of the lunchroom and talked casually about the meeting. Paul said, "I can't believe I actually attended a meeting with the President of the United States. My wife won't believe it."

Sally said, "I've never seen a person get dressed down before like Clarke, but he deserved it. He didn't know who he was up against."

Paul defended his boss. "He's really a good person. He served in Desert Storm. He's a double amputee. He's just absolutely focused on defending his country, and I think he didn't like someone intruding on his turf."

Dan interrupted, "Yea, well he picked the wrong person to stick it to."

Sally brought the group back on topic. "So how do you control the biological agents? You must have some pretty tight security measures, right?"

"We have security up the kazoo, too much security. We keep track of every agent we remove from storage. If it's not returned to the freezer, then we burn the biological, and whatever we do, there's always two people signing material in or out. We keep a logbook for each biological, and then we actually do audit checks on the amount of toxins in inventory every quarter. I'll go over everything when we get back to my lab after lunch, but I can't understand how any material went missing."

After lunch the three walked to Waterford's lab to meet his staff and begin the process of identifying how the plasmid had been taken from Plum Island.

24

Darrin Blake sent the e-mail to Dennis Jones early the next morning. The dead drop site chosen by Blake turned out to be a garbage can located in Washington DC, outside the entrance to the DuPont Circle metro station. The replacement document should be folded inside a New York Times and deposited in the trash container at exactly eleven o'clock.

Dennis Jones alerted the surveillance drone group at Andrews Air Force Base, and scheduled the drone's launch for nine o'clock. Alice had been able to arrange for twenty-three FBI agents to follow Blake once he picked up the document.

She positioned several agents on rooftops overlooking the metro station. One agent sat inside an information kiosk at the bottom of the escalator leading to the trains. Another played a violin for tips just outside, and six unmarked cars, two mopeds, and a bicycle were strategically positioned around the metro stop for emergency use. Four additional agents waited on both sides of the metro tracks.

At exactly eleven o'clock, an agent walked out of the DuPont Circle metro stop and placed a folded copy of the *New York Times* into the designated trash container and continued walking west. Everyone waited on heightened alert.

Five minutes later, a homeless man approached the garbage can and removed the paper. He disappeared into the metro station, took the down escalator, and stood waiting on the northbound platform for the next train. Although the rush-hour traffic ended earlier, a large number of people waited for trains.

One of the agents thought he spotted the handoff. It could easily have been missed if you didn't know what to look for, but she did. The bearded homeless man and another man seemed to exchange papers as they boarded the train.

The two then separated and moved to opposite ends of the car. Alice, who had been overhearing the chatter, had her forces split up, with half following the homeless man and the others tracking the man with the document. Unfortunately, neither person looked like Darrin Blake.

Alice's agents were skilled in the art of covert surveillance and kept their distance from both subjects. Alice directed four of the chase cars and two mopeds to advance to the next stops along the metro line, and kept the other agents in reserve. At the Cleveland Park stop, the homeless man left the train, took the escalator to the street level, and immediately turned around and stepped onto the down escalator. The two agents following the homeless man checked in with Alice as they emerged from the station and wisely chose not to follow the man. They did, however, confirm that he stood on the Metro platform waiting for a southbound train.

Alice redirected one of the agents on a moped to enter the DuPont Circle metro stop to reestablish contact with the suspect, but when the train arrived, the man was no longer on board.

The operator flying the pilotless drone reported in. "I have the homeless suspect under surveillance. He has just left the Woodley Park metro station and is walking toward the Marriott Hotel. He's thrown a wig and his coat into a garbage can, and now he's wearing blue jeans, a blue short-sleeve shirt, and a black baseball cap."

This action convinced Alice the homeless man was really Darrin Blake, and she alerted the other agents. Alice and three others took the two remaining chase cars and headed for the Marriott Hotel just off Connecticut Avenue. The drone operator continued his reporting and confirmed the suspect had entered the Marriott Hotel. Alice looked at her watch. Her agents wouldn't be able to intercept Blake before he disappeared into his room. But at least they had confirmed Blake's temporary residence.

As Alice, Brian, and Benny entered the hotel, they looked around hoping Blake would still be there, but he had already left the lobby. Alice presented her FBI ID to the concierge, and asked to be taken to the Manager's Office. Brian stayed in the lobby in case Blake left the hotel. After Alice and Benny introduced themselves to the manager, Alice showed the woman a picture of Blake and explained they needed to find out his room number.

The manager looked up Blake's name in the computer and came up with a blank. Obviously, Darrin Blake used a different name to register. Benny asked, "Do you have a surveillance camera of the registration desk?"

The manager answered yes. She escorted them into a security room located in the hotel's lower level and introduced them to the head of security. He led them to a grouping of dozens of surveillance monitors, sat down at a computer terminal, and showed them the image of the front desk. "We store the pictures for one week, so as long as the person registered within the last seven days, we should be able to see him standing at the front desk.

Benny sat down at the computer and began reversing time. He and Alice scanned the pictures of people. From time to time they stopped the video to take a closer look at a person. Alice feared Blake might be in disguise, but they eventually located their man.

The picture of Darrin Blake stared them in the face, and he had registered at 3:38 P.M. the day before. The hotel manager then looked in a computer database and said, "Only one person registered then, a Mister Jacob Milner. He's in room 1216."

Alice spoke to the manager, "I want to set up shop in the room next to Mister Blake, and I'm going to need a master pass key so we can enter his room later tonight."

The manager said, "I'm sorry, but I'm going to need a court order to grant your request. We value the privacy of our guests."

Alice called Bruce Jacobson's private number and explained the problem. Alice never understood how Jacobson managed to get the most difficult tasks completed as easily as he did, but in less than half an hour a FAX arrived with the necessary court order. The cover letter addressed to the manager also assured her a hard copy would arrive by messenger within the hour.

Unfortunately, a family of three, who were probably on vacation, occupied the room next to Blake. The Manager called them and explained maintenance needed to repair the water line in their bathroom, and they would be upgraded to a large suite to compensate for any inconvenience. It took the family about two seconds to accept the offer, and the Manager sent a bellman to expedite the transfer.

Benny now began moving equipment from one of the FBI cars into the room adjoining Blake's. It took only a few minutes to assemble the eavesdropping devices and begin listening to everything said in Blake's room. Alice dismissed the majority of agents who had helped in locating Blake, and then joined Benny and Brian. They waited for Blake to leave on his mission, ordered lunch from room service, and settled in for what they knew would be a long wait until Blake left.

25

Dan felt totally out of his element. Sally and Paul were speaking in some foreign language, and the scientific mumbo-jumbo left little room for understanding. Frustrated, he finally interrupted, "You're both going to have to speak in words I can understand."

Sally apologized and said, "We were discussing vaccine synthesis, and we're getting ready to discuss security procedures for working with the plasmid and the anthrax."

Paul explained, "We have a logbook we keep in the biological agent storage locker. Two people have to sign out for anything removed from storage and explain the purpose of the experiment, and when the experiment is over two people have to sign the biological agent back into storage or destroy the samples."

Sally asked, "Could a person sneak a sample of the biological agent out of the building without anyone knowing it?"

"I don't think so. To leave the biological laboratory, you have to change clothes, shower and then change into street clothes. Everything is monitored on cameras by Security, even the shower room."

Dan smiled and said, "I definitely want to see the lady's shower room."

Paul, who didn't catch the joke, said, "Only women are allowed to monitor the lady's shower."

Sally said, "So let's suit up and go through a simulated experiment so we can get a feel for how things really work."

Paul called one of his assistants and led the way to the lab area located in the lower level of the building. They met Doctor Rebecca Bauer, a senior scientist, who entered the women's dressing area with Sally while Dan followed Paul into the men's changing room. Dan followed Paul's lead as they stripped, showered, and then put on a disposable gown followed by what appeared to be a self-contained space suit. Paul helped Dan into the protective suit, and after suiting up himself, Paul led them through a sterilizing mist designed to kill any organisms. Paul explained the importance of ensuring the working laboratory remained free of foreign contaminants.

After entering the laboratory area, they hooked up their air lines to an outside air source and met Sally and Rebecca, who were already standing at a lab bench.

Dan looked around the lab. For some reason he had expected to see a room filled with high-tech equipment, but the laboratory was almost totally void of instrumentation. Instead, the place looked like his college chemistry lab, invoking unpleasant memories of those terrible three hours spent each week trying to follow complex recipes for the synthesis of putrid smelling chemicals.

Storage cabinets filled two walls with a variety of glassware. The only high-tech pieces of equipment were a few electronic weigh scales and some microscopes interfaced with computer screens.

Paul began, "When we want to start an experiment we get the sample from the storage locker."

He and Rebecca led the way to a door at the far end of the room. Both Rebecca and Paul entered access codes, and the four entered the biological storage area.

Paul said, "Each access code is person specific, and our computer system keeps track of who enters. The door will not open unless two different code numbers are entered, and only certain people are allowed access."

The cold room contained a large number of liquid nitrogen freezers. He opened a storage container labeled Plasmid X4335 and removed a small test-tube from a rack containing hundreds of test-tubes. Rebecca walked over to a computer and entered the serial number of the test-tube Paul had removed from the freezer, and then filled in the purpose section of the computer logbook with the words *FBI demonstration*. They then both entered their user names and passwords in the computer and brought the sample back to one of the empty benches.

Sally asked, "When you're doing an experiment, how do you follow the experimental protocol?"

"It's all done on the computer. We don't allow paper in here; it's too easy to contaminate."

Paul sat down at the bench and turned on a computer. He entered his user name and a password and opened an experimental protocol he had just finished working on. He pointed out the experimental protocol form required the serial number of the test-tube, and both he and Rebecca had to authenticate the form by entering their user names and passwords at the bottom of the document.

"You can see this experimental protocol took nine days to complete and all of the biological agents were destroyed after the experiment."

Sally asked, "If we want to look at the logbooks for the plasmid and anthrax for the last couple of years, can we see them?"

"Sure, but you'll need to get permission to access the database from Colonel Clarke."

Sally said, "Brad told us he met you in the electron microscope building. You must have taken the samples from here. What's the security for moving the material?"

"Two people have to sign the material out. The same two people then decontaminate the outside of the packaged sample and carry it to the electron microscopy area, where it's placed inside a Class IV containment area. After the sample is viewed, it's burned."

The two scientists returned the plasmid to the storage locker and the four returned to the changing area where they all showered and dressed back into street clothes. They met back in Paul's office where Paul called Colonel Clarke and handed the phone to Sally.

"Colonel Clarke, this is Sally Lawson. We would like access to the logbooks for Plasmid X4335 and Anthrax A6689. Paul indicated you need to grant us permission to access those databases."

Clarke replied, "No problem, but you'll have to access the information from the computer in my conference room. Paul can bring you to my office."

Paul led them up to the fifth floor where Clarke's office was located in a corner with windows overlooking the ocean. Clarke had apparently recovered from his encounter with Jacobson, and he seemed ready, although not eager, to cooperate. He led them to a small conference room adjacent to his office, turned on the computer, entered his access codes, and explained how to use the logbook databases.

Clarke closed the door to the conference room behind him as he returned to his office, and Dan and Sally were alone. Dan asked, "What do we hope to accomplish?"

"I'm thinking their security system seems pretty tight. I think it would be very difficult for one person to sneak out one of the biological samples. At least two people would have to be involved. I want to start at the very beginning and see who actually worked with this stuff."

Sally entered the plasmid database. There were hundreds of entries over the last six years, mostly by Paul and Rebecca but many of Paul's staff seemed to be working with the plasmid. Two entries were of interest. They were identified as *bioreactor feed*. Sally called Paul and asked for an explanation.

"When the inventory of the biological gets too low, we grow more organisms in a bioreactor."

Dan asked, "What's a bioreactor?"

Paul answered, "It's a closed system with special culture media. We can grow the biological agents in the reactor and generate enough fresh material to keep up with the experimental demands. We never let our stock get too low. We're always replenishing the supply."

Sally looked at her watch and said, "Paul, how do we catch the ferry back to Orient Point?"

"Just let me know when you want to leave, and I'll take you to the dock area. The ferry leaves every hour on the hour."

Dan looked exhausted. It had been a busy day. "We can probably catch the four o'clock boat. I'm for closing up shop for the day and looking at the logbooks tomorrow."

Sally agreed, and after they told Clarke they were leaving, Paul escorted them out of the building and along a pathway leading to the western edge of the island. Paul said, "I'm done for the day, so I'll go with you."

A cool offshore breeze made the summer heat almost bearable. They waited at the dock for the ferryboat. Sally asked Paul the procedure for returning to the island in the morning. Paul explained boats left from Orient Point every hour on the half-hour, and he had already added their names to the approved list.

The boat arrived a few minutes before four o'clock, and the boat, with about fifty people onboard, cast off from the quay and headed for Orient Point. The trip took twenty minutes, and as they were leaving the ferry terminal, Dan asked Paul for a recommendation for dinner. Paul answered, "There's a good place just across the street. I have a little time before I need to be home, so I'll have a beer with you."

The restaurant across from the Ferry Terminal wasn't anything special, but it did offer a nice veranda overlooking the ocean. Over beers the three discussed the case.

Paul said, "You know, when I found out the plasmid I developed had been used in the terrorist plot, I denied it at first, but the evidence became too overwhelming. Now I'm living with a burden of guilt beyond anything I could have imagined. You have to figure out who took the material."

Dan said, "We will Paul. It's only a matter of time."

"So how do you know the President?"

Sally answered, "Dan and I were working on a case together. It's how we met. Eventually, the FBI got involved, and they asked us to help them. We agreed, and I can't tell you anything else, except to say everything worked out in the end, and the President called to thank us for our help.

After finishing his beer, Paul left the restaurant and told them he would be at work by nine o'clock.

Alone at last, Sally said, "Let's check in with Jimmy. I want to see how Alice and Benny are doing."

Dan called Jimmy and they exchanged information. They both agreed tomorrow would be a critical day. With any luck, Dan and Sally would have some indication of how the material had been stolen, and hopefully, acquisition of the data on Blake's cellphone and computer would help provide some clarity regarding the terrorists.

By the time they finished dinner and drove back to the B&B, they were both exhausted. Dan called Director Jacobson, briefed him on their investigation, and once again thanked him for his help in clearing away the roadblocks. They set their alarm for seven o'clock, watched CNN for a few minutes before falling asleep.

26

Darrin Blake had just ordered dinner from Room Service. While Benny listened in on the telephone call, Alice immediately talked to the manager about delivering the meal on wheels. The manager secured the right size uniform for Alice, and by the time the kitchen finished preparing the meal, she appeared nicely decked out in the hotel's upscale attire.

She wheeled the food cart down the hallway and knocked on Blake's door. "Room Service!"

Blake opened the door and asked Alice to place the food on the coffee table in front of the TV. As she arranged the food service, she looked around with a critical eye, trying not to be too obvious. She noted a cellphone and i-pad on the desk. After arranging the food on the table, Alice presented Blake with a bill which he signed and returned to her. Alice said, "Just leave the cart out in the hallway when you're done."

Blake thanked her and locked the door after she left. Alice changed out of her uniform and returned to the room next to Blake. "Hey," she said, "I got a ten dollar tip. That's almost as good as overtime pay."

Benny asked, "What did you see?"

"He has a cellphone and i-pad on the desk, but nothing else visible. He probably hasn't dressed yet for the mission."

"Good, I'll have everything downloaded from his phone and i-pad in less than ten minutes. Let's order our dinner. I'm getting hungry."

Alice said, "That's all you ever think about Benny. If you don't watch yourself, you're going to turn into a fat slob."

Benny looked at his belly somewhat defensively. "Okay, I'll have the grilled salmon for dinner and no dessert."

Alice laughed, "I'm going for the steak and fries."

Alice called Brian, stationed in the lobby, prepared to follow Blake if necessary. "Hey Brian, we're ordering dinner; do you want us to get you something?"

"No thanks, I'll eat at the bar. It has a great view of the elevator, and I can watch the baseball game."

Alice laughed, and after placing their orders, both relaxed waiting for Blake to leave for Jacobson's house.

Alice, for a number of years, had considered herself Benny's surrogate mother and protector, and teasing her best friend at the FBI had become a labor of love. "So Benny, how are things going with your girlfriend over at the CIA?"

Benny, always suspicious of Alice's true motives answered, "Oh, you mean Betty; pretty good. Since I'm in DC, I'm going to try to see her."

"Is she the one?"

"You're getting awfully nosey."

"I'm worried about you. I don't want you to wind up being an old mother hen like me."

"Alice, if I don't get married, I'll be an old father cock; and being an old cock sounds like fun."

"Seriously Benjamin, you need to find someone and settle down."

"You sound just like my mother."

"I am your mother when she's not with you, and don't you ever forget it."

Benny walked behind her and patted her on the ass. "Maybe you're the one for me, babe. I definitely like older women."

Alice smiled, "You couldn't handle me; I'd bust your balls."

The arrival of their dinner saved Benny from further abuse.

¤   ¤   ¤

Blake, dressed in black jeans and a black windbreaker, left his hotel room at 1:00 A.M. He took a taxi and headed for the Jacobson residence in Georgetown. Brian, still sitting at the bar in the lobby, watched him leave. He called Benny and let him know he could begin downloading data. Benny used a pass key to unlock the adjoining door and both he and Alice entered Blake's room. They began a systematic search of the entire room. The i-pad and cellphone were nowhere to be seen. Certainly Blake wouldn't have brought the electronic devices with him, and therefore the room's safe seemed the likely hiding place.

Benny called the security people earlier in the day and received the master code number allowing access to the safe. Benny carefully opened the safe and took out a small penlight flashlight from his bag of supplies. He slowly examined the cellphone for any sign Blake had done something to determine whether his phone was tampered with. Benny easily spotted the single human hairs placed on top of the cellphone and i-pad. He remembered seeing James Bond use the same trick in one of those movies. Benny saved both hairs and then removed both items from the safe. It took only five minutes to upload the cellphone data to his computer and another five minutes for the i-pad.

Benny then opened each device and placed miniature transmitters inside each system. Benny removed Blake's watch from the safe and then found something both strange and perhaps important. Neatly folded in the back of the safe, a Herald Tribune newspaper seemed totally out of place. Benny noted the date and quickly scanned the paper to ensure some message wasn't written down on one of the pages, but the paper held no secrets. "Alice, why would he put the newspaper in the safe?"

"I don't have a clue. Maybe he thought the maid would throw it away, and he wanted to finish reading it."

Benny carefully returned everything, being careful to replace Blake's hair. He then opened the safe's electronic section and downloaded the security code Blake had used to lock the safe, and reentered the same number.

Benny looked at his watch. They had been in Blake's room for only twenty minutes. Meanwhile, Alice carefully inspected all of Blake's luggage and clothing. She looked for any hidden compartments or anything holding some important piece of information, but Blake's suitcase and clothing held nothing of value. Benny found a transmitter disguised as a black button in his bag. Benny couldn't sew so Alice took over. She managed to remove one of the less visible buttons on one of Blake's suits and sewed on the homing device. With their work finished, they returned to the adjoining room and called Brian.

¤   ¤   ¤

Blake had easily entered Director Jacobson's Georgetown three-story house just off O Street NW. He hadn't noticed the two FBI agents parked a block away, providing surveillance. Blake, proficient at lock picking, made ease work of the low-tech lock. After opening the door, the break-in artist disarmed the security system. Blake found the safe in the laundry room, certainly a less than obvious location. Blake thought this would be the easiest $100,000 he ever earned.

The safe was easily opened, and the real document replaced with the fake. What incriminating evidence was inside the real envelope? He thought seriously about looking inside, perhaps an opportunity for some good old fashion blackmail, but the decision could wait until later.

The electronic detection system described to him by Dennis Jones was something to remember for future break-ins in high value targets. Five minutes after arriving, he left the house and casually walked down the street in the direction of the FBI agent's car.

Louise Beacon and Deloris Marks had planned for the eventuality and appeared to be making out as Blake passed their car. Knocking on their window broke up the girl's romantic interlude. The girls responded by giving him the finger. He continued on his way laughing at the completion of a successful mission and some unexpected late-night entertainment.

¤ ¤ ¤

Early the next morning, Blake had breakfast at an internet café near DuPont Circle and e-mailed a new dead drop location for the envelope he had taken from Director Jacobson's house. A garbage can in the alley behind the café created the perfect spot. The envelope would be inside a red colored plastic bag at the bottom of the garbage can. After breakfast, Blake dropped off the envelope and walked to the metro stop less than a block away.

27

Dan and Sally awoke to the clock radio blaring out warnings of an evangelist minister lecturing on the numerous opportunities for sin in the world, and the sermon gave Dan the idea for a combined shower. Sally thought the shower area felt a bit cramped, but the tiny space made for a few laughs. The important thing was to get clean, and a liberal amount of scrubbing of all body parts met this key requirement.

They had breakfast at a coffee shop inside the Orient Point Ferry Terminal, and caught the 8:30 A.M. Government ferry to Plum Island. By nine o'clock they were back inside Colonel Clarke's conference room immersed in the combination anthrax/plasmid logbook. There were hundreds of entries, and everyone in Paul Waterford's group seemed busy doing a variety of experiments. Sally crosschecked each log entry against its corresponding experimental protocol. The majority of experiments seemed to be focused on developing a vaccine against the vector spiked anthrax, and as Sally moved from one protocol to the next, she began to understand the complexity of solving the scientific problem. The most recent work focused on using a novel combination of vaccines, one against the vector along with the standard anthrax vaccine, and the results showed they were close to successfully completing animal studies.

One entry in particular caught Sally's attention. A person not in Waterford's group had signed out a vial of material and Colonel Clarke had cosigned the logbook. An experimental protocol number wasn't referenced and the remarks section of the form stated research. She pointed out the unusual entry to Dan who responded by knocking on Clarke's door and asking for a few minutes of his time.

Sally showed the entry to Clarke and asked him to explain. Dan looked into Clarke's eyes and knew they had discovered the answer to the missing material.

Clarke sat down at the conference table and said, "It's a long story."

Dan answered, "We've got the time."

"You need to understand the problem we face as a country. Suppose we are attacked by a terrorist group with a new biological weapon. It would be devastating. It would be nearly impossible to respond with the development of a new vaccine in a timely fashion. That's what our group is about; we develop agents we think could be developed by foreign governments or terrorists, and then develop vaccines and other methods to combat the threat.

But even after a virus is fully characterized, the typical time required to scale up production of a vaccine is six to eight months."

Dan asked, "Why so long?"

"The normal process starts when scientists have isolated and grown the initial seed virus. The virus is then sent out to manufacturers who grow the virus in hens' eggs. Then the virus is purified, inactivated by a variety of processes, combined with some chemicals to enhance the immune response, and packaged into vials.

"Now consider a highly contagious pandemic as a result of some new virus or in our case a vector using anthrax as a host. How would we produce three-hundred-million doses of the vaccine? We'd need hundreds of millions of eggs; it just couldn't be done quickly. So we need a new method of vaccine production to deal with this surge capacity problem."

Sally said, "But I've looked at the experimental protocols in Paul's group. They're working on traditional methods, and it looks like there almost done."

"You're right Doctor Lawson, but their approach still requires the use of millions of eggs. That's where Genccine Corporation comes into the story. They've developed a different approach, a proprietary recombinant process using cells to grow the virus or in our case a plasmid. They don't need millions of eggs, they use mass cell culture techniques, and the scale-up process takes less than a month.

I sent the missing vial of the vector infected anthrax you're asking about to Genccine for them to develop the process for creating the vaccine for this and other biological agents we have discovered; and most importantly, they've been successful. They now have vaccines staged for immediate mass production."

Sally asked, "Does Paul's group know about this program?"

"No, I believe in containing information on a need to know basis."

Dan fought the urge to be visibly upset and said as calmly as he could, "Colonel Clarke, it sounds like you're telling us this Genccine company may in fact be the ones who lost the material; or they may be the actual terrorists themselves."

"No, I know these people, and I've been in contact with them as soon as your people identified the biological agent. They've assured me they can account for all of the material given to them."

Sally interrupted, "Well Colonel, if the material wasn't stolen from here or from Genccine, then how do you explain its presence on the streets of Chicago?"

"I wish I knew Doctor Lawson."

Dan said, "Colonel Clarke, we're going to need to visit Genccine. Where are they located?"

Clarke pulled out a business card from his desk drawer and handed it to Dan. Genccine Corporation, Rod Demming President and CEO, Trenton, New Jersey. Dan wrote down the information and returned the card to Clarke. "Colonel, we're going to visit them this afternoon. Would you please call Doctor Demming and explain the purpose of our visit, and tell him we are cleared to receive all information, whether or not he feels it's confidential."

"I'll do it Agent Lawson, and I assure you, he'll do everything in his power to help you get to the bottom of this."

After a terse goodbye, Sally and Dan left Clarke's office. They remained silent until they had left the building and were alone at the dock waiting for the next boat.

Dan started, "He's a first class jackass. Why didn't he just tell us about Genccine when we first arrived?"

Sally thought for a moment and answered, "I think Clarke believes he's a true patriot, protecting the country from enemies both real and imagined, and anything done in support of his ideological mantra is appropriate. His type is more than willing to torture someone if necessary and believe they're the sole judge of right and wrong. He failed to appreciate his actions may have unintentionally led to the terrorist attack in Chicago and never weighed the consequences of his actions. Clarke justifies everything by believing in the righteousness of his decisions."

Dan said, "When we get back to the car, I'll call Jimmy. We need to have him brief Jacobson on what we've found here."

The arrival of the ferry put a temporary halt to their discussion. Back in the privacy of their car, Dan called Jimmy and briefed him on their findings.

Jimmy listened with growing frustration at the actions of Colonel Clarke. "The idiot created this problem and doesn't even have any sense of responsibility."

Jimmy explained the status of Blake's activities, and asked them to call in for a four o'clock meeting if possible. Dan looked at his watch and did some calculations. "We'll try Jimmy, but we may be in the middle of discussions at Genccine."

Sally took the phone from Dan. "Jimmy, can you do one more thing for me? Could you have Benny e-mail me all the information he can find on Genccine?"

"Will do Sally."

With their call finished, Sally and Dan headed to New Jersey for answers.

28

Benny sat at a computer terminal in the J. Edgar Hoover FBI Building on Pennsylvania Avenue. He had arrived late in the morning after some late-night entertainment with Betty, and began pulling data off of Blake's i-pad and cellphone. His printer had been busy for the last hour printing page after page of information ranging from e-mails to bank account information.

Benny focused on e-mails, but the BennyMeister was having problems with the Washington office's software for resurrecting deleted messages. One of the other techies in the office tried to sort out the problem while Benny moved onto other files, and although some of the e-mails appeared interesting, he wouldn't waste time reading them, at least not now. At this point he only wanted to get printouts and organize everything into easily analyzed stacks of information. Jimmy had scheduled a four o'clock meeting to begin reviewing the documents, and Benny would be pushing it to have everything ready on time.

He had already extracted all of the telephone calls Blake had made or received on his disposable cellphone, and using a proprietary software program had obtained the names and addresses of each caller. Several agents would be needed to determine the relevance of each of the contacts, and he knew it would take weeks to explore every lead.

¤   ¤   ¤

They located Genccine Corporation's office just outside of Trenton on an isolated rural road. The modern concrete and glass structure could have blended in well with the architectural blandness of most industrial parks, but the grass and trees surrounding the building created a pleasant, almost calming environment.

From the number of cars in the parking lot, Dan guessed the employees probably totaled less than fifty. Clarke's call evidently had an effect because the receptionist at the front door had been alerted to their arrival, and had ID badges waiting. She called Demming to announce the arrival of his guests.

A few moments later a middle-aged physically fit man dressed in extreme business casual, in this case safari shorts and a Hugo Boss shirt, introduced himself as Rod Demming and escorted them through dark walnut lobby doors, down a long hallway, and into his corner office. Both Dan and Sally accepted the ritual offering of coffee, and Demming personally prepared the service at an upscale wet-bar. Sally looked around the spacious office. The understated, but elegant furniture, created a comfortable atmosphere, conducive to a relaxed business discussion. The view from the office was breathtaking. A small tree-lined lake and the backdrop of farmland removed a person from the realities of the business world.

Demming set the coffee down on a small table in a sitting area in the corner. "Colonel Clarke briefed me on what happened, and frankly, I don't understand how the biological material could have been taken from here."

Sally said, "We've conclusively shown the anthrax strain and Plasmid vector were developed at the Plum Island facility. The probability of the agent coming from any other source is infinitesimal."

Dan added, "Doctor Demming, we're not saying you or your company had anything to do with this, but we're obligated to fully investigate this facility. We've got to find out who stole the material."

"Well Agent Lawson, I'll help any way I can. Tell me what you want, and I'll try to make it happen."

Sally said, "Why don't you start by giving us an overview of your company."

"Yes, let's do that. Six years ago I started the company with two other scientists. We discovered some proprietary methods for scaling up vaccine production using genetic engineering methods. We decided the scientific community would move away from using eggs to produce vaccines to new methods allowing for rapid scale up. We knew an opportunity to develop vaccines existed when rapid scale up became essential. We approached NIH, and were able to get proof of principle funding, and published on our results. With those results we attracted significant venture capital funding, and then three years ago Colonel Clarke approached us with an opportunity. The government wanted to be prepared to respond to a bioterrorism threat, and agreed to fund work on preparing vaccines for several known biological agents."

Dan asked, "Were these open bid contracts?"

"No, they weren't. The funds were released from the DOD, under a secret black program to preserve the confidentiality of the work. Anyway, those projects succeeded and Colonel Clarke funded other work in an effort to stage vaccine ready cell cultures for all of their biological agents. "

Sally asked, "Would I be correct in assuming none of these vaccines have been approved by the FDA?"

"Correct. The premise has always been the FDA would never be able to react fast enough to a real terrorist attack or worldwide pandemic. If there is a widespread pandemic, then the President would probably declare martial law, and our vaccine could be manufactured without the FDA's approval."

Dan said, "We're going to need to review all of your security methods and talk to your people."

"No problem, we only have twenty-three technical people on staff, and you're welcome to talk to everyone. In fact I'll schedule a meeting with our staff immediately, and let you explain the problem. That'll be the best way to get started."

Demming called his secretary and asked her to call an emergency meeting for all employees in the cafeteria. As they were getting ready to leave

Demming's office, Sally asked for an organization chart. Demming stopped at his computer, found the right database, printed the chart, and handed it to Sally as they left for the meeting.

¤ ¤ ¤

The employees began trickling into the cafeteria, which also apparently served as the company's meeting area. Demming completed a headcount. Demming introduced Dan and Sally as FBI agents, and explained they were here as part of an ongoing investigation of the Chicago attack, as it was now being referred to by the press.

Given the technical nature of the audience, Sally took the lead. "Thank you Doctor Demming. As many of you know, a recent outbreak of both anthrax and hemorrhagic fever took place in Chicago. Work done by the CDC determined these were not naturally occurring strains of the diseases, but rather a genetically engineered biological agent created using Ebola virus DNA inserted into a plasmid, which was then used as a vector inside a unique anthrax strain.

We confirmed the Plum Island facility developed this biological agent, and samples of the agent were also sent to this facility in an effort to develop a manufacture-ready vaccine. We believe some of the material may have been secretly taken from this company. We're going to talk to each of you in an effort to review your security procedures, and I know we'll be able to obtain your full cooperation."

While Demming reinforced Sally's request for full cooperation, Dan looked at his watch. He wanted to be ready for Jimmy's four o'clock meeting. As the employees filed out of the cafeteria Dan asked Demming for a hotel recommendation in the area. Demming suggested the Holiday Inn only five minutes from the company, and he asked his secretary to make a reservation. They left Genccine after the reservation had been confirmed and told Demming they would return in the morning to begin their investigation.

They found the hotel, checked in, and called into Jimmy's temporary office at FBI Headquarters in Washington. Alice, Benny, and Brian had already joined Jimmy in his office. Benny passed out a packet of information taken from Blake's cellphone and i-pad. He told Sally and Dan the same information, along with a complete dossier on Genccine, had been e-mailed to them.

Benny cautioned against drawing conclusions. They were still experiencing some minor software problems, and a lot of e-mails still needed to be removed from Blake's i-pad. It would take at least another couple of hours to complete the downloading and analysis.

It took an hour for everyone to exchange information. Jimmy then made assignments. He wanted to continue to monitor Blake's activities and also wanted agents to discreetly follow up on all of the telephone numbers in Blake's cellphone. Also, he asked Benny to get the Bureau's code breaking experts to begin an analysis of Blake's i-pad documents. Sally and Dan would continue their investigation of Genccine, and they would all meet again tomorrow at the same time.

The hotel recommended a local restaurant nearby, and Sally brought her computer along to go over the information sent by Benny. Genccine was a privately held company. In addition to Demming, who had invested $500,000, two other scientists had each put in $100,000, and then of course the big-time money; one-hundred-fifty-million dollars by a company by the name of NewTech Capital. The Board of Directors consisted of the three scientists and four people who apparently worked for NewTech Capital. The Chairman of the Board for Genccine, Giorgio Baldinni, also served as the CEO of NewTech. Sally read the news clippings Benny located, and it appeared Genccine was exactly as Denning had explained it, a small successful startup company living off lucrative government contracts until the golden opportunity came along.

Their literature proclaimed their goal of leading the scientific community away from the use of egg produced vaccines, to the modern approach of mass cell culture of genetically engineered vaccines. They had certainly developed a novel approach, but Sally knew the protracted lead time required to convince the FDA and scientific community to abandon the proven use of hens' eggs would take years to accomplish.

Sally looked at the scientific papers being published by the company and was impressed with the quality of their work. Their science couldn't be questioned.

During dinner Dan said, "I'm getting worried about another attack, a big one, and I think it's going to be coming soon. After the next attack the terrorists will identify themselves and begin to make demands. We're running out of time."

Back in their hotel room, Sally and Dan began a more detailed study of the hundreds of documents pulled off Blake's computer. It was

eleven o'clock before they turned off the lights
and went to bed.

29

Over breakfast in the hotel's restaurant, Dan scanned the Times of Trenton, the local newspaper. He started with the sports section. His Chicago White Sox had lost another close game to the Minnesota Twins; nothing new. He then moved to the front page where a local journalist had been writing about the recent fire with a loss of two lives in a local industrial park. The two men had apparently died from smoke inhalation. The city's Fire Chief cast the blame on unsafe use of highly volatile chemicals by the people killed in the blaze.

Dan thought the two men probably caused their own deaths with their irresponsible actions, and he then moved onto the national news. The news media had moved away from the Chicago attack, which had occupied so much of their concerns only a few days earlier, and were now fully engaged in the latest DUI arrest of an infamous Hollywood celebrity.

¤   ¤   ¤

They arrived at Genccine at nine A.M. and once again met with Rod Demming. He had arranged for individual meetings with his technical staff, and had given Dan a list of the scheduled appointments. He led them to another part of the building where the R&D people were doing their thing.

They first interviewed Betty Lowery, Genccine's Senior Scientist. She met them in her office with extended cold clammy hands. Dr. Lowery's lips pursed trying to hold back the fear of the upcoming ordeal. She had nothing to hide, but nonetheless, a meeting with FBI was not an everyday occurrence here or in many other companies, and would understandably cause considerable stress.

Sally tried to ease her fears, "Betty, I know this meeting is difficult, but we need to ask some straightforward questions. Mostly to review the security measures you employ here in the lab. Do you have any idea how biological material may have been taken from the lab?"

"No, I don't know how it could have happened. After yesterday's meeting, I've been discussing security with my senior staff, and none of us can figure out how the material was taken."

Dan asked, "Who set up your security system?"

"I think the same group who developed the Plum Island procedures."

Sally and Dan reviewed the complete security methods with Doctor Lowery, and they did emulate the Plum Island system, but with two noteworthy exceptions. First, although removal of biological agents from storage did require two signatures, a second person did not monitor all experiments. Secondly, there appeared to be several blind spots in the surveillance camera coverage inside the men's changing room.

Someone could have removed a sample from the lab, claiming it had been destroyed, and then hidden the material from the cameras in the changing room. At that point the material could have been easily removed from the building. Of course this was not a conclusive explanation of what had happened, only a possible scenario.

Dan and Sally had written down the names of each of the persons who had worked with the vector spiked anthrax. Sally handed the list of people to Betty, and explained they would need to talk to each of the people. Betty scanned the list and said, "No problem, except you won't be able to talk to Ralph Crawford."

Sally asked, "Why not?"

"He died a couple of days ago in a robbery at his home."

Dan's eyes flashed brightly at the new piece of information. "Tell me more."

"There's not really more to tell. The police are still investigating."

Dan asked, "Do you have the name of the investigating officer?"

"No, but Human Resources might. Check with them."

Sally and Dan sat down with the head of Human Resources who confirmed Doctor Lowery's story and gave them Ralph Crawford's home address.

Dan contacted the Trenton Police Department and after being connected to the Homicide Department, talked to the investigating officer,

Detective Brice Collier. They set up a meeting at the police station, and after getting directions from Detective Collier, Sally and Dan left Genccine.

Showing their FBI IDs at the police station's reception desk resulted in an immediate call to Detective Collier. He escorted them back to his desk. The entire office area looked like a clone of Dan's own office, and he wondered whether a single architect designed all of the world's police stations.

After exchanging business cards, Dan started the conversation. "Brice, we're in the area investigating the source of the biological agent used in the Chicago terrorist attack. We believe Ralph Crawford may have stolen the biological material from Genccine. We understand he died in an apparent robbery a few days ago, and my suspicion is this may have been a murder to cover up the trail, and not a simple burglary."

Brice opened the investigation folder and read from some notes. "We were called to the scene by the cleaning lady. She found the body when she came to his apartment. She's there once a week. The coroner set the time of death at twelve hours earlier, give or take a couple of hours. It looked like the back door had been crowbarred open, and the perpetrator ransacked the place. There weren't any witnesses to the crime. We checked with all of the neighbors and nobody heard anything. We looked at the surveillance cameras and again nothing. Our forensic lab is still working the place, but so far we haven't had any luck lifting any prints other than the victim's."

Dan asked, "Do you have a picture of the body."

Brice thumbed through his folder and tossed a few pictures of the crime scene in Dan's direction. Dan looked at a full frontal picture of Ralph Crawford's body. He had been shot in the forehead, another professional shot. Dan showed the picture to Sally and said, "Brice the Chicago terrorist shot two people in Chicago in the head, just like this picture. I'll have our ballistics people send you their workup on those bullets. I'm betting there'll be a match. Can we look at the crime scene?"

"Sure Dan, I'll drive you over myself. I'm not too proud to ask for help from the FBI."

Thirty minutes later they walked through Crawford's apartment searching for evidence; not the kind consistent with a botched burglary, but the type associated with the theft of the plasmid spiked anthrax. Sally said, "If Crawford stole the material, then he's either a terrorist or he did it for the money. I'm betting on the money angle. Let's check on his bank accounts and any unusual activity."

Dan called Benny to have him begin the search. While Dan and Brice looked for evidence, Sally turned on Crawford's computer and began looking at his files. His e-mail file appeared fairly clean; just the usual circulation of sexist jokes to his inner circle of male friends, notification of online bills, the usual spam from an assortment of companies offering amazing opportunities, and messages between friends. Of course Benny's people would have to examine everything in detail, but there didn't appear to be anything incriminating.

Sally opened a desktop Excel file labeled *investments*. It listed all of Crawford's investments going back fifteen years. Sally noticed a marked change in net worth beginning one year ago. An entry labeled as *inheritance* showed eight-hundred-thousand dollars had been received by Crawford and most of it had been invested in a variety of financial instruments, everything from gold to bonds. There were many entries, each for less than ten-thousand dollars.

Sally called Dan, and he studied the data. "It looks like Crawford had received a large sum of money and tried to launder it, but hiding almost a million dollars without raising suspicions isn't easy. We'll have to check to see if he really did inherit the money, but I'm betting he received this money as payment for stealing the material."

Dan got Crawford's social security number from Officer Collier, and a minute later, Benny began digging into the alleged inheritance. Dan turned to Brice, "We're going to have our forensic people come in here. If our people confirm Crawford never received an inheritance, then the money is probably a payment for the biological material."

Detective Collier looked dejected. He had failed to consider this as anything other than a botched robbery, and now the FBI was involved in his case. His boss wouldn't be happy.

Dan knew the problem and said, "Look Brice, you had no way of knowing this could be anything other than what it appeared to be, a robbery gone bad. I would have come to the same conclusion myself. Come on, let's get some lunch. I'm buying. Benny should have the information by the time we finish eating."

Brice took them to a nearby café frequented by the local police force. The cops knew the best places for a meal, and the restaurant managers liked the police presence. Robbers always avoided these places.

After ordering lunch Sally said, "You know, what we're still missing is the place where they manufactured the biological agent in large enough quantities to make the weapon.

Brice asked, "What kind of place are you looking for?"

Sally answered, "Well, it would basically look like an upscale chemistry lab. There wouldn't be a need for very sophisticated equipment. The bioreactors would look like ordinary chemical vessels."

As Sally talked, Brice thought about the recent fire in the local industrial park. He excused himself for a minute and returned with a copy of the local newspaper. The front-page headlines and lead story talked about the fire and two deaths. He tossed the paper in Sally's direction and said, "You mean a place like this?"

Sally scanned the article, focusing on the lab equipment and noted the fire department still had not confirmed the cause. She slapped the paper and said, "Yes, Brice exactly like this. We need to go there and check out the scene."

Brice smiled, knowing he had just come up with an important lead. Dan said. "I read the article this morning, but didn't think much about it, but you're absolutely right; this could be the place where they manufactured the material."

Benny called Dan during their meal. He had some preliminary information on Ralph Crawford. He had never received an inheritance, and Benny couldn't find any other apparent source of the sudden increase in net worth. Benny would continue to gather evidence and get back to them with a complete report by the end of the day.

¤   ¤   ¤

The scene of the fire looked surreal. Pockets of smoldering material still simmered slowly under rubble throughout the remains of the steel structure; the smell overpowered the senses. The entire site had been cordoned off, and a single fire truck stood guard over the area, ensuring the fire wouldn't reignite.

Dan approached the firemen standing by their truck and produced his FBI ID. One of them pulled out a cellphone and made a call. Dan walked back to Sally and Brice. "The Fire Marshall's driving over now.

While they waited for his arrival, Sally looked over the building's remains. Anything combustible had been consumed by the fire, but a number of large metal vessels still stood, blackened but intact. They needed an expert on genetic engineering to be sure, but it certainly looked like the laboratory could have been a cell culture production site. Doctor Lowery could probably render an expert opinion on the activity here.

"Doctor Lowery, this is Sally Lawson. I'm at the site of a fire at an industrial park in Trenton. I'm going to send you some pictures of the equipment still standing. I'd like you to let me know if these large metal vessels could be used to grow the anthrax."

Doctor Lowery answered, "Sure, I'll look at the pictures as soon as I receive them and call you back."

Sally sent a variety of pictures with her cellphone's camera. The quality wasn't great because they were still waiting for the Fire

Marshall before they crossed the yellow tape. Hopefully, they would be good enough to get a preliminary opinion.

The Fire Marshall finally arrived and they gathered near his car to talk about the FBI's interest. Dan explained the circumstances surrounding their search for the manufacturing site. The head firefighter gave them approval to examine the building as long as they were accompanied by one of the firefighters. Dan explained he would have a FBI forensic team examine the site for possible evidence.

Sally's cellphone rang, and Doctor Lowery confirmed the equipment could be used to grow the plasmid spiked anthrax.

Meanwhile, Brice contacted his office and learned the owners of the building confirmed the facility was rented and the names and addresses shown on the rental contract had been obtained. Brice wrote down the information and walked over to Dan and Sally. "We thing we've identified the two victims in the building. Their names are Samari Moudi and Mohammed El Barassa. Let's drive over and see if anybody knows them."

Both scientists lived in the same apartment complex. On the drive over, Dan called Jimmy and requested a full forensic team to examine the destroyed building for any evidence, and Search Warrants for both men's homes. Jimmy assured him the team would arrive in a few hours, and he would get the Search Warrants immediately.

Knocks on the doors of both Moudi's and Barassa's apartments remained unanswered. The three walked over to the manager's office and displayed their badges. Dan explained the situation and asked for information on the two victims.

The manager looked up the two men's application forms. Both listed names of people in Dearborn, Michigan as references. Dan asked the manager to make copies for follow-up. As they talked, Jimmy called Dan and asked him where he wanted the Search Warrants sent. Dan asked the manager for his fax number, and a few minutes later, the manager used his passkey to enter Samari Moudi's unit.

The one bedroom apartment appeared rather Spartan. Although the man had been living there for almost two years, few creature comforts had accumulated. The only indulgence seemed to be a small TV positioned on an inexpensive bookcase facing the bed. The living room apparently served as the man's office with one wall occupied by a large desk holding a state of the art desktop computer.

Sally sifted through a stack of papers sitting on the desk, hoping to find something of value; several unpaid bills, coupons for discounts at a local food store, a copy of the Koran, and what looked like an experimental protocol titled *Production Run 6.*

She thumbed through the five page document and focused on the last page. The table summarized production runs to date and one column indicated five previous production runs had produced a total of twelve kilograms of weapons grade anthrax. "We're in deep shit," she said. "According to this report over twenty-six pounds of weapons grade anthrax has been produced."

Dan looked at the report and asked, "How many weapons will twenty-six pounds yield?"

Sally answered, "I have no idea, but Brian should know the answer. One thing for sure, there's enough material for several more attacks of the type in Chicago. We can't assume the material burned up in the fire either. I'm guessing their deaths and the fire are the work of Blake, and that means he's now in control of the material"

Dan called Jimmy and confirmed they had found the manufacturing lab for the biological agent. Jimmy thought for a moment and said, "I want you both to come back to Washington as soon as possible. I'm going to send some more agents to Trenton and Dearborn to follow up on your leads. Maybe they can find out who really ran the lab. We've been going over the documents we found in Blake's i-pad, and I want your thoughts on where we go from here. Let's start the meeting at eight o'clock tomorrow morning."

"Okay, Jimmy, have your people work with Detective Brice Collier."

"Will do! See you tomorrow."

Dan talked to Brice, and he agreed to cordon off the apartments and place police officers at the scene of the fire. Brice called for some assistance, and after some local beat cops arrived, he drove Dan and Sally back to the police station.

Sally booked a flight out of Newark, and after thanking Brice for his help, they left for the airport and a short flight to the nation's capital.

30

The meeting started promptly at eight o'clock. Director Jacobson congratulated the team on their exceptional work. He planned to meet later in the day with the President and update him on the progress.

Jimmy summarized what had been learned. Director Jacobson interrupted. "What does twenty-six kilograms of weapons grade material yield in the way of potential devastation?"

Brian Sawkowski answered, "The Chicago attack probably used less than a kilo of the biological agent. They now probably have the capability to launch ten to twenty of the same size or a single attack with a huge impact."

The team looked in shock as Brian spoke.

"Okay, with this good news let me continue."

It took almost an hour to summarize the remaining key facts. Jimmy then asked, "What have I missed?"

Benny said, "I have evidence showing conclusively Blake was involved in the plot."

Jimmy said, "Okay dude, you've got everybody's attention."

Benny smiled as he distributed large folders to everyone. "I've been going over everything on Blake's i-pad and cellphone, and I've organized the information by category. Please look at the second tab in the folder. This section pulls together a series of e-mails between Blake's and another computer.

The e-mails clearly show Blake personally oversaw all of this activity. In every case, authentication codes were used by the person sending and receiving each message. The messages describe Blake's role. He was told to choose a location for the attack which could be monitored, and to place the cameras where the license plate of Ali's car would be recorded, and where the police would easily find the camera as part of their investigation.

They ordered him to kill Ali, Ali's girlfriend, Crawford, and the two scientists, and to destroy the laboratory where the biological agents were being manufactured after the weapons grade material had been given to him. So Blake now has possession of the remaining material."

Benny looked around the room to observe reactions. He loved being the person who held all the information cards. He continued, "The final e-mail directs Blake to prepare to activate operation Big Thunder, but I can't figure out what Big Thunder is all about. One more thing, I've looked at all of the e-mail messages and traced the internet routing to the IP address of the originating computer. In every case one computer sent the messages, and always from one of four internet café locations in Italy."

Jimmy asked, "What are the locations?"

"Salerno, Sorrento, Positano, and Amalfi."

After Benny's information had a chance to sink in, Jimmy said, "We have to decide when to pick up Blake, and we need to find out who's been directing all of this. Any suggestions?"

Alice said, "We could get Blake right now, but then we might not be able to find the rest of the anthrax unless Blake talks, and he doesn't seem the type to cop a plea. Picking him up now is just too risky. I think we need to beef up the surveillance of Blake, and arrest him once we're sure he has the material. Then we may also be able to arrest any others involved in the plot."

Jacobson said, "I agree, even though there's risk in not getting Blake now, but the danger of not being able to get the material is greater. And one more thing, I'm going to ask NSA to monitor overseas calls using the words *Big Thunder*. We may get lucky."

Sally asked, "Benny, is there a pattern to which internet café the person chooses?"

"Nope, no pattern I can see."

Sally said, "Then why not station people at each café until the guy shows up. Benny, I'm assuming you can tell us whenever the computer of interest is e-mailing Blake."

Benny answered, "Sure, no problem."

Sally continued, "If we get lucky, we can follow the person, and find out who he is and who he's working for."

Jacobson said, "We'll need to work with the CIA on this and get special approval for the FBI to be involved in another country, but I'm sure the President will give his approval. I like the idea."

Jimmy said, "Okay, then I'll manage the covert surveillance of Blake, and Alice, Benny, Brian, Sally, and Dan can work with the CIA operatives to locate the leader of this operation."

After the meeting, Benny left for the Special Ops lab to pull together any equipment needed to run the Italian operation. While Jimmy arranged for a Government plane to transport the team into Italy, the others decided to pay a visit to the shopping mall near their hotel. They were running out of clothes and covert surveillance in a resort area required casual tourist attire.

Benny on the other hand, needed no special clothing. His basic grunge look would blend in perfectly with the locals.

Meanwhile, Director Jacobson met with the President, the heads of the CIA, and Homeland Security. Following the meeting, the Director of the CIA directed four of his best agents to join the FBI team. Other CIA operatives in Italy would arrange for their smooth unimpeded entry into the country with a variety of weapons and equipment destined for immediate confiscation under normal circumstances.

31

The unmarked Gulfstream G550 jet sat on the tarmac ready to leave Andrews Air Force Base at six o'clock. Benny arrived early with twelve large suitcases filled with enough equipment to monitor the world, and he carefully supervised the loading of his special tools into the plane's cargo bay.

The rest of the FBI team pulled up to the plane a half hour before the scheduled departure, followed closely by a black SUV with darkened windows. It slowed to a stop behind the FBI van. Sally had seen too many movies. She expected to see four macho men with dark sunglasses emerge from the car.

The reality was far different. The two men and two women looked like regular people; all casually dressed, two slightly overweight, one guy with coke bottle eyeglasses, and one clearly muscular woman. The two groups met by the stairs, and after brief introductions and the loading of luggage, they entered the spacious plane's cabin and stowed their carryon baggage.

The copilot greeted them in the cabin and asked everyone to buckle-up. They were cleared for immediate takeoff, and he wanted to make sure they stayed on time. The cabin's configuration easily accommodated nine and not unexpectedly the FBI people sat on one side of the plane and the CIA group on the other. Sally knew they would have to assimilate into one cohesive team if they were going to be successful.

The seatbelt sign came on and the jet engines began to whine. The plane taxied onto the main runway, and after a momentary pause, rushed forward and leaped into the air. Within a few minutes they had leveled off at 40,000 feet and were headed toward Europe.

Director Jacobson had agreed the CIA would run the operation. After all, the team would technically be operating outside of the FBI's jurisdiction. As soon as the pilot turned off the seatbelt sign, the team gathered around a small conference table. Sally offered to get drinks for everyone, and after taking orders, Dan helped her play cabin attendant. Sarah Barker, the slightly overweight woman, explained she had been designated as the team leader, and thought it would be beneficial if everybody explained their backgrounds, and why they were selected to be on the team.

Sarah began, "We're all operating under cover so we'll not be disclosing our real names. My specialty is logistical support for covert operations. I've already made contact with our Italian operatives and they are arranging accommodations as close to the identified internet cafés as possible. We haven't had the time for a full briefing; we were all pulled from other assignments, but the Director assured us you would provide all of the necessary details."

Bob Clemens, the man with the thick eyeglasses, said, "My expertise is covert surveillance and close quarters combat, and I'm also pretty good with a rifle."

Benny said, "Excuse my bluntness, but you don't look the type."

Bob laughed, "Benny, none of us look the type. You've seen too many spy movies. Look at us; none of us look like we could be anything other than ordinary people not capable of exercising lethal force, but I can say with some confidence each of us has demonstrated an ability to act with deadly force when necessary."

Beth Allen was skilled in communications, information technology and hand to hand combat. She certainly looked like she could handle herself in any fight.

Rich Gibbons explained he was an expert in surveillance and the team's designated sniper.

The FBI team then introduced themselves. As Sally explained her background, Sarah turned on her computer and began typing something. A minute later Sarah interrupted Sally and asked, "You're Sally Graff, right?"

Sally, surprised by the question, answered, "Yes, my maiden name is Graff, but how did you know that?"

Sarah looked up from her computer and said, "The name of Lawson struck a chord. A few minutes ago I took your picture and sent it to a friend of mine; he's in the Rockville, Maryland police force. He recognized your picture. You're the lady who disarmed the nuclear weapon, right?"

Sally, with a smile on her face said, "I'm not allowed to talk about that."

Sarah said, "Well let me summarize for my team. You remember the terrorists who wanted to set off a nuclear weapon in Washington. It seems the Lawsons over here were the ones who almost singlehandedly figured out what was going on, killed and captured the terrorists, and disarmed the booby-trapped weapon. Therefore Sally, I assume your real expertise is information analysis."

Sally answered, "I guess my medical profession makes me pretty adept at pattern recognition."

Sarah's revelation of Dan's and Sally's real skill seemed to break the ice between the two groups, and the CIA team members showed renewed respect for the FBI team.

After the introductions, the FBI team presented the details of the case, focusing on the facts and concluding with their suspicions. Over a dinner prepared by the flight crew, Benny reviewed all of the information gleaned from Blake's computer and cellphone.

They spent a great deal of time talking about the exchange of e-mails on Blake's computer. Benny said, "Here's the way they communicate. A person sends Blake a message using a code word to authenticate the sender. Blake then responds with a different code word to verify his presence. The actual message is then transmitted to Blake, and he then confirms he received the message with another code word. Every message uses different code words."

Beth asked, "How much time from the first e-mail to the last e-mail, and do the messages always occur at the same time each day?"

Benny looked at his data. "Usually the message exchange lasts about ten minutes, and messages always begin at 11:00 A.M. or 4:00 P.M., Italy time."

Beth concluded, "That's good news. It means whoever is sending the messages stays at the internet café for at least ten minutes and always at the same time every day. We'll definitely be able to intercept the message and figure out who's sending it. We can follow the suspect without attracting attention."

Benny added, "When I got information off Blake's computer, I also inserted a virus allowing me to see whatever is on his computer screen. We'll be able to have instant real-time access to his computer."

Sarah split up the teams between the four internet café sites. They wouldn't apprehend initially, but only monitor movements. Bob Clemens would join Dan and Sally in Positano, Alice would team up with Rich Gibbons in Amalfi, Beth and Brian would monitor the Sorrento café, and Sarah and Benny would operate out of Salerno.

Sarah explained her operatives in Naples had paid off some customs officials to ensure their luggage remained uninspected, but the plane needed to arrive at the Naples International Airport between eight and nine o'clock in the morning for the plan to work.

Benny had prepared four duplicate boxes of equipment, each one containing everything each group would need to communicate with the others and monitor the suspect's activities. He reviewed the nuances of each device.

After dinner the team tried to get some sleep before their mission really began. Sally thought about her staff back in Chicago and how she missed working with them. She was particularly proud of her team, who had overcome fear and extreme fatigue. They were a great group of professionals. Even Larry Becker had stepped up to the plate. Having had little rest in the last week, Sally fell asleep, and her last thoughts were of Larry Becker trying his best to find thousands of facemasks.

The pilot woke them an hour before the scheduled landing, just enough time to eat a quick breakfast and freshen up in the upscale lavatory in the rear of the cabin.

The plane touched down at 8:26 A.M., and taxied to the private aviation terminal at the north end of the Naples airport. They were directed into an empty hanger, and as the plane came to a stop, the large doors closed behind the plane. Sarah left the airplane and conferred with a uniformed man standing near the aircraft.

She returned and said, "Here's the deal. The customs official will check our passports and ask whether we wish to declare anything. We will each answer no, and he will then clear all of us. Don't talk at all until we leave the airport. We have arranged for four cars to transport each team to their designated hotel. An operative will drive each car and be your local contact. They have been briefed on the mission and are knowledgeable about the area, so listen to them.

They unloaded the luggage, and Benny distributed each group's equipment. They entered the customs area where each person's passport went through a cursory examination and was officially stamped. Ten minutes later the teams left for their designated locations.

Nina Bendinni, the driver for Sally's team, introduced herself and explained she had booked two rooms in a hotel across the street from the internet café. Given it was the height of the summer tourist season; she had been forced to pay off the hotel's manager. Unfortunately, their rooms were the most expensive in the hotel.

Sally had always wanted to visit the Amalfi Coast, and she knew Positano had the reputation as the most beautiful city in the region. She hoped they could mix in a little sightseeing while working on the case.

After leaving the Naples airport, they proceeded in a southerly direction, driving along the A3 autostrada toward Salerno. Mount Vesuvius dominated the view to their left. Sally couldn't imagine intelligent people building homes so close to an active volcano, but many circled the edge of the volcanic mountain. The next eruption would surely destroy most of these upscale houses.

As they passed the outskirts of Naples, the three-lane road seemed to be built alongside mile after mile of mid-rise apartment buildings. Pastel colored concrete buildings pressed up against the edge of the road, creating a narrow canyon-like effect. The national pastime of the residents seemed to be the hanging of wet laundry on wrought-iron balconies. Every imaginable color of clothing in a vast array of sizes danced in the breeze coming off Naples Bay. Large colored sheets waved precariously alongside the autostrata like warning flags at a motor speedway.

They soon passed the city of Naples, and near the excavation site of Pompeii, Nina left the autostrada and began following the signs to

Sorrento. Their car passed through one small town after another. Flowers of every imaginable color decorated the landscape. Almost every home, regardless of size, devoted a large portion of their land to olive trees and grapevines.

Sally asked Nina about the grapes. "You have to understand," she said, "it's something deeply embedded in the culture of these small towns. It's the responsibility of the eldest male in the family to make wine each year, and there are countless arguments between families over who produces the finest wine. It's a matter of honor and pride to claim the best wine in each town. It's said that the person with the shortest life expectancy is a judge at the annual wine tasting festival, especially if they vote for an unpopular family."

The narrow two-lane road gradually wound back and forth as they drove higher into the mountains, always hugging the coast and constantly moving upward. Finally as she navigated past a hairpin turn, Nina pointed out the city of Sorrento far below on the southern tip of Naples Bay.

Large tour buses dominated the road, sounding their horns prior to entering a tight turn, forcing oncoming cars to slam on their brakes to avoid being pushed off the road and over the cliff. The Darwinian laws of survival were at work. Small crosses placed near the edge of the cliff served as monuments to those drivers who were not lucky enough to avoid the buses.

The road now cut into the cliffs overlooking the sea; creating both a picturesque and terrifying view. Sally, looking out of her window, could see waves breaking on the rocks below.

Suddenly, Nina turned off the main road and headed further up into the mountains. After passing through several tunnels, their car finally emerged onto the Amalfi Coast. The view looked absolutely breathtaking as the road wound northeast toward the city of Positano. A turquoise sea pressed against cream colored cliffs, and the water was filled with a variety of boats ranging in size from massive cruise ships to small fishing skiffs.

Finally, they merged onto a narrow two-lane road hugging the coast. Shear mountain cliffs on the left and the Mediterranean Sea on the right created a beautiful contrast in views. Nina said proudly, "It's the most beautiful area in all of Europe."

Sally asked, "Where did you learn to speak such perfect English?"

"I went to Boston College, and worked in Washington DC for a few years in the Italian Embassy. The CIA recruited me as one of their Italian operatives. I'm a double dipper. I have a full time job in Positano, and from time to time the CIA asks me to make arrangements for their agents. I basically get a lot of money for doing very little."

Dan asked, "Are you going to be staying with us?"

"No, I have an apartment just outside of Positano, but I'm available if needed again. I'll leave after I make sure you're in the rooms we've paid for. I reserved them for one week. If you need to stay longer, we'll have to change hotels."

Nina handed out business cards with her cellphone number and issued instructions to call anytime day or night.

After passing a sharp bend in the narrow road, Positano came into view. It was an amazing view. Nina explained the town no longer permitted parking in the center of town, and a porter from the hotel would bring their luggage from the remote parking area down to the hotel. The road wound back and forth as they lost elevation and soon they pulled into a private parking area above the center of town.

Nina walked into a small office in the front of the parking lot and returned with a porter who began loading their luggage into a three-wheeled modified golf cart. Nina paid the parking attendant, and the group followed Nina as the porter sped off with their luggage along a back road. The narrow cobblestone street changed into a series of steps leading ever downward toward the sea.

They passed through a narrow walkway covered with an expansive arbor inundated with what looked like an old vine that Sally couldn't identify. It was like walking in a long dark colorful tunnel. Artists selling a vast array of paintings along with other merchants and musicians had chosen to set up shop in this area protected from the heat of the sun.

As they approached the water, the street opened up into a small relatively flat area. Nina pointed to a small internet café, indicating it was the origin of some of the e-mails. After passing the small restaurant, she turned right and entered the front entrance of the Covo Dei Sarabaldi Hotel. Sally couldn't discern where the hotel ended and the other buildings began. Everything was a collage of mortar, pastel colored stucco and terracotta roof tiles, and the age of each structure was impossible to determine.

The hotel's reception area, although small, had been magnificently appointed with an abundance of antiques and local pottery. Nina began talking rapidly in Italian to the young man on duty behind the front desk. After a brief discussion the man spoke in English, "Welcome to the Hotel Covo Dei Sarabaldi. My name is Giuseppe. Please feel free to ask me for any assistance during your stay in Positano."

He passed out some registration forms as he continued, "After you fill out the registration forms, I will need your passports. The porter will arrive shortly and bring your luggage up to your rooms. Doctor and Mister Lawson, I have given you the larger room, and I am sure you will be pleased with your accommodations."

Nina said her goodbyes as the porter arrived with the luggage. She reminded them to call her if they needed any help during their stay. The three rode a miniature elevator up to the third floor. As Bob entered his room across the hallway, the three agreed to meet in Dan and Sally's room, which apparently overlooked the internet café, in one hour.

Dan opened the door to their room, and they were struck by the charm and elegance of the furnishings. The room, actually a suite with a bedroom and bath off to one side, also contained a large sitting area with windows and a balcony overlooking the harbor.

Sally walked over to the French doors leading out onto the tiled balcony, and swung open the large wooden shutters shielding the room from the glare of the summer sun. The view exceeded spectacular, and was actually the most beautiful hotel room view Sally had ever seen. She grabbed Dan's arm and pulled him onto the large balcony covered with flowers. "Wow," he said, "What a view!"

"I know," she said, "The Mediterranean Sea on our right and the town on the left nestled in the cliffs. I think I could stay here for the rest of my life.

The porter arrived with their luggage and Dan slipped a twenty dollar bill into the porter's hand as he left. Dan realized they needed to stop by an ATM machine for Euros as soon as possible.

Sally unpacked while Dan shaved and showered. He hadn't slept well on the plane, not anything new; he could never sleep on planes. Sally, on the other hand, could sleep anywhere and anytime, a skill she claimed she learned as a Resident.

Sally decided not to unpack Benny's box of covert supplies. Bob, who seemed to be fully trained in the use of all of Benny's technical gadgets, could unpack the goodies.

Sally followed Dan into the shower. With the outside temperature pushing ninety degrees, Sally decided to wear shorts. Extreme casual seemed to be the typical tourist garb, and after all, she wanted to blend in.

While Sally showered, Dan couldn't resist opening up Benny's equipment. He found a pair of binoculars and stepped out onto the balcony. There was an excellent view of the internet café, at least the small outside seating area. Their first stop would definitely be the café. He looked at his watch. They still had over three hours until the four o'clock scheduled communication, plenty of time to set up the equipment and plan their strategy.

As Sally appeared in her summer outfit, Bob knocked on the door and walked into the room. "Wow," he said, "my room's a piece of crap with a view of the cliff behind the hotel, and you guys hit pay dirt. There's no justice."

He walked onto the balcony and Dan handed him the binoculars. "A perfect view," he said, "we can set up the surveillance camera out here and feed it directly into the TV.

Bob began setting up the communications system. Sally studied her earpiece. It looked like the units she had seen the Secret Service use when guarding the President. They each tried on a headset with its wireless power pack, and began testing the audio reception. The equipment seemed to be working fine, at least from this distance, and Benny claimed the reception worked up to three miles.

Benny had included a variety of homing devices capable of transmitting their location for over one-hundred miles. The homers were constructed using magnetic backs to allow them to be easily attached to the undercarriage of cars or other metal objects. Bob carefully removed: a high-tech lock picking kit, night vision equipment, a complete medical kit, and a variety of special components.

Sally picked up the medical kit and looked inside; not your typical Red Cross version. Whoever put the field kit together assumed the person needing help would not have access to a local hospital. There were a variety of useful components to extract bullets and repair wounds, and a complete assortment of drugs for treating ailments from diarrhea to shock, and even a surgical repair kit. She hoped they wouldn't need the supplies, but at least they were prepared.

Bob, with help from Dan, set up the surveillance camera on the balcony. The video linked wirelessly to a small control unit which

Bob placed behind the TV, and he then attached a cable from the control unit to a USB connection on the back of the TV. He turned the TV on, and using the remote control, switched the input to external. A clear picture appeared on the TV. Dan adjusted the zoom lens on the camera, and with input from Bob centered the internet café on the screen. The control unit had a built in seven day record feature.

Dan hid the small camera inside a flower pot. Unless a person looked right at it, it wouldn't be discovered.

Sally said, "How about some lunch? We can check out the internet café."

Bob placed an expensive Nikon camera around his neck. He looked like a typical tourist. A New York Yankees baseball cap created the perfect final touch. As they arrived in the lobby Dan asked Giuseppe for the nearest ATM machine, and after confirming its location, they left the hotel.

32

Enriched with Euros, they walked across the open area to the internet café. About a dozen small tables were placed outside of the small restaurant. The three sat down inside the café. Bob carefully studied the layout of the room and pointed to a small table off to the right in the corner. "That's definitely the place to sit. From there we'll be able to see all of the inside tables and still keep tabs on what's going on outside."

Dan's cellphone rang. Benny called to let everyone know he was good to go and would call as soon as e-mails were being sent to Blake's computer. Benny then gave them a telephone number to be used for conference calls.

Sally hadn't realized how much her body craved food. The time change had screwed up her biological clock. The café offered a variety of exotic coffee concoctions, and a small assortment of sandwiches displayed on the counter. Sally wrinkled her nose at the meager selection and settled on a ham and cheese Panini with a cappuccino.

While they ate their lunch, Bob asked, "Sally, there must be an interesting story about how you got involved with the FBI. What's the deal?"

"It all started several years ago. While walking to work, I stopped to help a man who had been mugged. I brought him to the ER where he later died. He was a genetic anomaly. He had the most iridescent blue eyes you've ever seen, and his hemoglobin levels were higher than anything I had ever seen; and the more we learned, the stranger it got. That's how I met Dan; he worked on the case. Anyway it looked like he had been exposed to radiation, and I got a degree in Nuclear Engineering before I became a doctor, so I stayed on as the medical expert."

Dan interrupted, "What a crock of shit. She begged me to work on the case. She said it was because of the unusual genetic issues, but I know now, she fell in love with my good looking ass. Am I right?"

Sally laughed, "Well it's true; your good looking ass and your teddy bear eyes made you look desirable, but then the medical mystery seemed more exciting. Anyway, the case morphed into a terrorism plot, and the FBI asked me to assist them because of my special skills."

"Well from what Sarah said, I'm assuming there's a bit more to the story, but as you said before, you've been sworn to secrecy."

Dan asked, "What about you Bob? How did you get started?"

"I studied Political Science at Georgetown University, and also happened to be a black belt on the school's karate team. One day a recruiter for the CIA talked to me about the possibility of signing up. At first, I thought he couldn't really be serious, my glasses after all; but he explained my poor eyesight would actually be a perfect disguise. So, one thing led to another, and when I graduated, I signed up. How did you get involved Dan; what's your story?"

"My story is very simple. I went to college with Jimmy Davis. He's the head of the FBI's Chicago Field Office. After I graduated, I joined the Chicago Police Department and eventually became a Detective. When the case Sally was talking about turned to terrorism, I called Jimmy. Director Jacobson wanted Sally and me to continue working, so he made us Special Agents. I guess once we solved the terrorism case, we were in demand."

During lunch they planned their stakeout. Bob said, "Here's the approach I think we should take. One of us will sit at the table over there, and the other two will wander around outside. As soon as Benny calls to tell us the e-mail has been initiated from this café, we'll identify the person using the computer. When the person leaves, we'll follow him and if he gets in a car, we'll attach one of our homers."

Sally asked, "What if more than one person is using their computer? This is an internet café after all; there must be at least four people using their computers right now."

Bob answered, "Then we'll split up. Hopefully there won't be more than three people using their computers. If we get lucky and there's only one person, then we'll keep on switching the person who's tailing the suspect. We'll stay in contact with each other using the communications gear."

Sally said, "Sounds simple enough."

Dan added, "It always sounds simple until the shit hits the fan, and it almost always does."

After lunch they wandered around the town. Bob stopped at a tourist shop and purchased three Positano street maps. They spent the next hour familiarizing themselves with the town and identifying some key landmarks. They briefly returned to their rooms and collected their communications gear, the homers and pistols.

Sally kept her gun inside her purse. Dan and Bob tried using shoulder holsters under lightweight windbreakers, but in the ninety degree heat the jackets looked absolutely ridiculous; so they bought some large *I love Positano* canvas shopping bags to hide their pistols.

◻   ◻   ◻

Sally sat at the optimally positioned table inside the café nursing a cappuccino and munching on a chocolate covered biscotto. Bob and Dan strolled casually around the beach area, staying in constant communication with their headsets. Dan also stayed tied into the other teams using his cellphone. Sally held a paperback book and kept a watchful eye on the people in the café. A young couple, probably tourists, sat outside using their laptop computer, probably checking e-mails. A middle-aged man dressed in a light tan business suit also sat outside drinking a cappuccino and working on his computer. He was apparently writing some type of report. There were others sitting inside, but nobody else using computers.

Sally looked at her watch. She had been sitting for forty minutes and had already finished several biscotti and a third cappuccino. Benny had explained all e-mails to Blake had been initiated at exactly the same times. At four o'clock, Sally began taking pictures of every customer with her cellphone. Dan and Bob were also taking pictures of the customers sitting outside the café.

Dan answered a call from Benny. "Okay guys, an e-mail has just come into Blake's computer and the IP address is the Amalfi internet café. Alice, do you understand?"

Alice answered, "Roger that Benny, Rich and I are on it now. The problem is there are over a dozen people here on their computers. Let me know as soon as the connection is broken."

Dan relayed Benny's message to Bob and Sally. The three met outside the café and walked back to the hotel. Dan kept in contact with Benny on the conference line. When they arrived in Dan's and Sally's suite, Dan put his cellphone on speaker and the three sat on the balcony and listened to Alice's real-time feedback.

Benny finally broke into Alice's dialog. "Alice, Blake just turned off his computer."

"Benny. Here's what we've got. Rich and I have taken pictures of everyone at the café. Eight people just turned off their computers and paid their bills. Rich and I have agreed on the most likely candidates, and we've decided to follow those two people. We'll let you know what we find out as soon as possible. Got to go!"

Alice followed a middle-aged man dressed in a dark-blue jogging outfit. He had been sitting at the café in Amalfi for over an hour and had constantly looked intently at people passing by the café. He had slipped his laptop computer into a backpack and walked deliberately along the town's main-drag. He kept looking at his watch and waved to a woman walking toward him. The two kissed, and the man pointed to his watch. Alice quickly concluded this man was not their suspect. Alice continued to follow the two, who were now holding hands. They entered a small boutique hotel typical of the area. They stopped by the front desk and asked for the keys to room #214. Alice knew she had reached a dead-end, and these people were ordinary tourists enjoying their vacation.

Rich Gibbons had encountered no better luck. He had followed a man who looked ready to enter a professional wrestling match; over six feet tall and at least two hundred-fifty pounds. The bald ugly brute looked like the ideal muscle a terrorist group might hire to do their dirty work. However, after leaving the café, he joined a large tourist group waiting for a tour bus near the center of town. Rich began talking to one of the tourists. "Are you guys traveling in together?"

The young man answered, "We're with a religious group visiting Italy. We just spent time in Rome, and now we're touring the Amalfi Coast."

"And where do you all come from, the U.S.?"

"No, Canada, we go to McGill University, and belong to the same church."

"Well I hope you have a great time on your tour."

Rich reported to Alice, who relayed the information back to the group on the conference call. Sarah Barker asked Alice and Rich to e-mail pictures of all of the people at the café. The teams could look for one of the people who had been at the Amalfi café. If one of them showed up at another café, it would not be a coincidence.

Dan said, "Unless of course different people use the same computer on different days."

Sarah replied, "You're right Dan, so we need to keep an eye out for anyone, not just the people in the picture. We'll do the same exercise tomorrow at eleven o'clock. Any questions?"

Brian asked, "Hey Benny, what did the message to Blake say?"

"It told Blake the Big Thunder operation would begin shortly and to be ready to act. I'm going to contact Jimmy and see if the tails on Blake have discovered anything."

After the meeting, Bob put away much of their equipment. No need getting the maid suspicious. By the time everything was back in Benny's suitcase, Alice had e-mailed everyone nine pictures of people who had been at the café using their computers while Blake sent his messages.

Sally proclaimed, "This is Italy, meaning pasta and wine, and I'm ready for the best Chianti this country has to offer."

They asked their new friend Giuseppe for a dinner recommendation and he extoled the cuisine of a wonderful restaurant just off the beach, and guaranteed we would not be disappointed. Dressed casually, they began walking along the edge of the harbor. Sally soaked in the beauty of the ancient town. She looked back at the cliff and marveled at the difficulty the builders must have faced in carving the town into the face of the mountain.

The restaurant Giuseppe recommended was small and crowded. The maître' d' put them on a waiting list and explained, with a wave of his hand, it would be about an hour before they were seated. He recommended a beachside bar two doors down, and said he would get them when their table opened up.

Waiting at the bar sounded like a good plan. A number of small tables looked out onto the promenade and the sea. Sally ordered a glass of the house Chianti and Dan and Bob both ordered the local beer. A cool summer breeze floated in off the water, and the sun began to set to the west behind the cliffs along the Amalfi Coast. Dozens of water taxis and fishing boats along with a few mega-yachts were anchored in the harbor, creating a mixture of extreme wealth beside working class people. Dan said, "This has to be one of the most beautiful places on the planet. I can see why this is a favorite tourist destination.

They were relaxing, breathing in the early evening salt air when Sally noticed a man in a T-shirt with *show me the money* emblazoned on his back. It wasn't really funny; rather, the words sounded an alarm in Sally's head. She had been trying to think of the case from a different angle, and the bold statement on the tourists back cleared the cobwebs. She tugged on Dan's arm. "Remember you once told me the most important rule in criminal investigations is to follow the money. What if this isn't really about terrorism, but just a criminal act? Who would stand to profit?"

The two thought about Sally's question, but Sally had an answer ready to her own question. "Genccine would be the big winner. Think of it, if the U.S. Government decided to rush the vaccine into mass production, Genccine would be the only company able to respond. Almost three-hundred-million doses would be ordered. At ten dollars a dose, they'd receive almost three-billion dollars. Genccine would instantly go from a small venture capital private company operating at a loss, to an incredibly profitable entity, and they would bypass the FDA review process because the President would declare a national emergency. They could go public and make a windfall profit for the owners."

Dan asked, "Are you saying Rod Demming did this?"

"No, I don't think so. The people who did this have international connections; they were able to hack into an Iranian website and send messages to Ali; they were able to find some Muslim radicals willing to manufacture the biological agent and build the weapon. I mean we're talking about big bucks here. Benny sent me all the information on Genccine, and one of the documents listed the founders and the investors. The biggest investor in Genccine is NewTech Capital. They've got almost two hundred million dollars invested. I'm thinking they may be the ones who are orchestrating everything with the hope of cashing in big-time."

Dan thought about Sally's proposed explanation. "It's certainly worth pursuing."

Sally took out her cellphone and called Benny. She explained her idea in detail and asked Benny to do some research. "I need all the backup information you can get me on NewTech Capital. E-mail me everything you can find."

"You've got it Sally; I'll have the information for you in a couple of hours."

Sally ended the call and downed the rest of her wine. She had a smile on her face that Dan recognized. He turned to Bob, "See this smile." He held Sally's chin and turned her face so it pointed at Bob. "This smile means I'm smarter than you, and I just figured it out."

Bob laughed, "I see it, and it's a beautiful smile; it really is."

Sally stuck out her tongue, and they all laughed.

Eventually, they were summoned to the restaurant by the maître d' and seated at one of the outside tables. Their waiter welcomed them and recited the evening's specials. Sally asked about the regional specialties. "Ah," he said, "without a doubt it's our calamari appetizer. It's sautéed in a garlic and butter sauce, and ours is the best in the area."

He looked up toward the sky as if explaining this gastronomical delight was a gift from the Gods. With this divine recommendation, how could they say no? The waiter then explained the day's selection of fresh fish and recommended the flounder. To emphasize the point, the server wheeled over a cart with a variety of fresh fish and pointed to the flounder. Sally needed no further encouragement. She ordered the flounder but also insisted on sharing Dan's lasagna.

As they waited for their dinners, Bob said, "I can feel it. Tomorrow's the day. It's all going to be clear by the end of the day tomorrow."

Dan answered, "I hope you're right, because I think we're running out of time."

While they were waiting, Dan called Jimmy to brief him on the day's activities, and to disclose Sally's theory. Sally grabbed Dan's phone and said, "Jimmy, it's Sally. Can you do something for me? Have someone check if there are any contracts or commitments the Government has with Genccine. Have there been talks about starting production of the vaccine?"

"Sally, I'll ask Director Jacobson to get the answers to those questions."

Sally handed the phone back to Dan. She looked around at the multi-million dollar yachts lit up in the harbor, the dark grey sea stretching to the horizon, and hundreds of tourists wandering the streets in one of the most beautiful towns in the world. How could life be any better?

Unfortunately the beauty of this town stood in stark contrast to what her country would look like following another biological weapon attack.

The arrival of their appetizer returned Sally from a world filled with bad guys, who for many different reasons were hell-bent on creating wars, chaos, genocide and a variety of other unthinkable things in order to further their own bizarre agendas.

The sautéed calamari had been prepared to perfection by the chef; very tender, and the aroma of the garlic butter blanketed the table. All three agreed they would definitely be ordering this regional specialty again. The maître d' filleted Sally's fish at the table, and after he performed the delicate surgery flawlessly, he arranged the plate of fish and fresh cooked vegetables in front of her.

33

Sally's had almost adjusted to the time change. She woke up as the early morning sun blasted through the bedroom window. After showering, she stood naked in front of the bathroom mirror drying her hair. Dan entered the bathroom, stood behind her, and slipped his hand down between her legs.

"Yes, may I help you?" she asked.

"Well actually yes. You know I'm a hands on kind of guy, and so naturally I thought I'd give you a hand."

Sally reached behind her. "Ah, I see Mister Woody is begging for attention."

"I think you're right. Perhaps we could reach a mutually acceptable accommodation."

Sally turned around and buried her tongue inside Dan's mouth. "Here or the bed?" he asked.

Sally didn't answer but led him to the bedroom.

¤   ¤   ¤

After a late breakfast at the hotel, she sat at the same table in the internet café sipping her second cappuccino and munching a chocolate biscotto. Sally knew she would pay the price for her addiction to the biscotti. She carefully observed the other patrons, looking for the one person who had been at the Amalfi café the day before.

She glanced at her watch for the hundredth time in the last ten minutes. Fifteen minutes before eleven o'clock and nada. Suddenly, a woman, who looked very familiar, walked into the café and ordered coffee. Sally looked at the pictures on her computer, and there she stood, the same woman who had been in the Amalfi café. The picture wasn't perfect, but it was definitely the same woman. "I've got a definite match with the e-mailed pictures from Amalfi. It's a woman. She's buying coffee now. I'll take some pictures with my cellphone and send them to you.

Sally clicked away as the young woman waited in line for her drink. The lady could best be described as a definite knockout; one beautiful woman with exotic Mediterranean features. She wore a white blouse and navy slacks, and except for her good looks, could have been confused with a hundred other locals taking a coffee break. She carried the coffee and a purchased copy of the Herald Tribune. She looked around for an open table and spotted a small one inside of the café by the front window, where she sat down.

She opened the newspaper, turned a few pages, removed a computer from a large flexible green leather briefcase and turned it on. Sally faced the woman's back, so the lady couldn't see Sally watching her every move.

Meanwhile, Dan called the other teams to let them know they had made contact, and he and Bob moved to cover the two streets leading away from the beach area.

At two minutes after eleven, the message from the woman raced across the ether. Blake received the e-mail, and Benny, monitoring the event, alerted everyone. Blake sent a response with the correct authentication code, and then the woman sent the message, *Activate Big Thunder. Start the clock today. Next scheduled communication will be after the completion of Big Thunder.*

She put the computer back in her briefcase and after finishing her coffee, left the café. As Sally followed her out the door, she carefully placed the spoon the woman had used to stir her cup into her purse. Maybe Benny could lift some fingerprints. The tip Sally left at her table more than compensated for the cost of the spoon.

The woman walked up the street leading to the parking lots above the town. Bob followed her from a fifty foot distance for a block and then Dan picked up the tail. Just before she entered a parking lot nestled in a small alcove cut in the cliff, Dan retreated and Bob again took over and closed the distance to twenty feet.

The woman paid the parking attendant and approached a dark-blue BMW 325 sedan. Bob assessed the situation and said, "Dan, position yourself near the street exit. When she tries to leave, step in front of the car. When she slams on the brakes, I'll attach the homer."

"Okay, I'll try not to get hit."

The timing was perfect; Dan stepped in front of the car, and as the car screeched to a stop,

Bob passed behind the rear bumper and placed the homer underneath the car. Unless people knew what to look for, they would have never noticed the placement of the device.

While, Sally took pictures of the car's license plate, Benny announced he was receiving a clear signal from the homer's transponder. The BMW headed out of town along the coastal highway in the direction of Amalfi.

Sarah set up a conference call for noon, and the Positano team assembled in Dan and Sally's suite. Benny had linked everyone's computer to be able to follow the location of the homer. The woman's car had stopped outside of Positano along the main road leading to Amalfi. A military satellite showed it parked inside the compound of a large villa sitting at the edge of a cliff overlooking the sea.

Sarah pointed out what everyone already surmised; the woman was not the big Kahuna. The person in charge would not spend their days moving between internet cafés to exchange messages.

Sarah wanted the team to relocate to the Positano area, close to where the action would likely take place. She gave out assignments. "Dan, Sally and Bob, I want you to rent a car and get a closer look at the villa. She may not spend the nights there, so we need to follow her car to where she probably lives.

We need to try to gain access to her computer tonight. Bob, I want you to figure out how to do it, and Benny you give him technical assistance. I'll have to get directions from Washington. They may want to involve the Italian Government or Interpol. I'm personally going to recommend we take care of this ourselves. Involving the Italians at this stage is just going to create problems. If they agree, I'll have the embassy in Rome supply us with the necessary equipment."

Benny said, "If you can get me the address of the villa, I can find out who the owner is, and Sally, I sent you all of the info on NewTech Capital."

Sarah continued, "Brian and Beth, I want you to help Bob. I'll have Nina get everyone hotels in Positano. Plan on visiting this woman's house tonight."

After the meeting broke up, Sally, Dan and Bob asked Giuseppe for the location of the nearest car rental agency. Giuseppe handed them a business card, "My brother has a place up near the parking lots. It's the only one in Positano. Tell him I sent you, and he'll give you a good deal."

Dan took the card, and the three followed Giuseppe's directions to the top of the main road above the town. After several wrong turns, they found the car rental place. Ronaldo, Giuseppe's brother, gave them a terrible rate for the only car left on the lot, a white Smart Car. Only one problem, the car only seated two, so Sally and Dan decided to try mopeds. Sally chose a pink scooter, and Dan insisted on fire engine red. Bob happily took the car.

Ronaldo provided them with maps of the area and cautioned them to be careful of the tour buses and the crazy Italian drivers who loved to race their sports cars along the winding coastal road.

Staying in constant communication with their headsets, the three traveled along the highway leading to the villa. At full speed, the mopeds were able to reach about thirty on the flat areas, but no flat areas existed; only winding roads, sharp cut-backs, and steep climbs and drops. A combination of buses, taxis, cars and mopeds filled the narrow two-lane road. Ronaldo was right; Porsches and Ferraris played tag with each other as they fought for lead positions on the crowded highway.

It took them twenty minutes to reach the villa where the woman's car had stopped. The blue BMW sat parked inside the compound, barely visible behind an olive grove near the main house. The satellite image didn't do justice to the expansive estate. Villa was an understatement; the twenty-thousand square foot mansion, situated on almost five acres, exuded wealth.

Two guards stood near the gated entrance, providing protection for the owner. Guns were not visible, but Dan knew there would be ample firepower inside the small guardhouse located behind the main gate. A thick ten foot stone wall topped with razor-sharp concertina wire surrounded the compound on three sides with the fourth side protected by the sea. This wasn't an estate, but rather a fortress designed to keep out unwanted guests.

Bob spotted several partially hidden surveillance cameras covering the gate and front wall. He assumed there would be others. The three continued past the villa, without slowing down. They stopped at a cutback in the road alongside a small outdoor restaurant overlooking the sea. From this vantage point, they also had an unobstructed view of the villa, which they could see below and to the right of their position.

Dan called Benny on his cellphone. "Benny, my main dude, the address of the villa is 463 Via Guglielmo Marconi. I'll take some pictures from here, and forward them to you. I'd be willing to trade our meager house back in Chicago for one of the small cottages alongside the main house. We're going to wait here until the woman leaves and then follow her."

Benny said, "I think I already know where she lives from the license number you gave me. It's an address in Amalfi, and since the address says unit 4C, I'm assuming it's an apartment, and by the way, her name's Gina Mormino"

While waiting for Mormino to leave, they decided to have a late lunch. A waitress handed them menus in English; she didn't even bother to ask if they were Americans; she knew. Sally wondered if it was how they dressed or perhaps their unusual smell. Maybe Americans exuded a characteristic odor. They all ordered sandwiches from the menu and watched the villa as they waited.

Sally had a perfect view of the walled estate below the restaurant's patio. A grove of olive trees inside the front gate hid the main villa from any unwelcomed visitors who happened to be looking at the building through the secure entrance. A long circular drive wound its way past a grouping of out cottages and then expanded into a courtyard lined with fountains at the front of the villa.

A large swimming pool, actually cantilevered out beyond the edge of the cliff, afforded a beautiful view of the water below for anyone daring enough to look over the edge. The house looked indestructible, built to withstand anything nature might choose to throw its way.

The exterior of the two-story structure had been crafted with beautiful rose-colored marble. An incredible entranceway, built within a three-story turret, provided visitors with a magnificent first impression. The entire effect could best be described as breathtaking.

After carefully scanning the estate, Sally opened her i-pad and pulled up the information Benny sent her on NewTech Capital. Between SEC filings and a variety of newspaper and magazine articles, Sally pieced together the workings of the company. Three principle investors ran the organization with Giorgio Paldinni as the Managing Director.

The group had assets worth over two billion dollars, with major investments in the military industrial complex, especially firms manufacturing munitions and smart weapons. Giorgio Paldinni was a name Sally had seen before. He sat on the Board of Directors at Genccine. Sally had no doubt; Giorgio Paldinni was definitely involved and perhaps other principals in NewTech Capital as well.

As the waitress set down their lunches, Sally pointed to the villa and asked her, "Does the large villa belong to Giorgio Paldinni?"

The elderly lady looked at Sally with interest. "Yes, madam, señor Paldinni owns the villa. He's a very famous industrialist."

After the waitress left, Dan asked, "How did you come up with his name?"

Sally produced one of her, I'm smarter than you smiles, and pushed her i-pad across the table for Bob and Dan to see information on NewTech Capital.

Bob said, "Well I'll be a monkey's ass. It all makes sense now. Paldinni wins in two ways. If the U.S. Government buys the vaccine he makes a fortune, and if he provokes a war with Iran, he wins again as the provider of essential munitions."

Dan said, "Just remember Bob, I taught her everything she knows."

Benny called as they were on their third cappuccinos. "Hey, it took some real legwork, but I found out who owns the property."

Sally interrupted, "We're betting it's Giorgio Paldinni."

"What? How did you find that out?"

Sally answered, "We have our ways Benny."

Benny, trying to prove his value, added, "It's really owned by a shell company run by NewTech Capital. But Paldinni signed the papers."

Dan said, "I'll call Jimmy and let him know what we've discovered, and I'm sure when Sarah calls her boss, it will influence their decision on what to do next. We'll call you as soon as Mormino leaves."

Dan and Sally were taking a nap while Bob watched the villa. He interrupted their beauty-rest. "She's on the move. Let's settle up and hit the road."

After paying their bill, including a substantial tip, they called Benny who was tracking the car and began following Mormino's car along the coastal road toward the town of Amalfi.

Benny provided directions as the three approached the town. It looked slightly larger than Positano, with only a moderate drop toward the sea. Much of the town consisted of an assortment of large apartments and small single family homes.

As Benny had predicted, they found Mormino's car parked at a multistory apartment building on the Via delle Cortiere, a road overlooking the picturesque town. The residential area teamed with people returning from work or their latest shopping trip. The three parked in a small shopping area near the building and decided to take a walk past the apartment complex. Upon closer inspection, the structure backed up against a steep hill. Bob called Benny. "Benny, it's Bob. Do you have the blueprints for the apartment yet?"

"Yes, do you want me to e-mail them?"

"Send them to Sally. She's got the i-pad and it'll be easier to see the pictures."

"I'm sending them right now."

Sally asked, "What are you thinking Bob?"

"I'm thinking we need to do this in the middle of the night. I want to take a look at the back of the building and the blueprints before we finalize our plan."

They continued walking along the sidewalk past the building. About half a mile past the apartment, a cross-street moved further up the hill. They walked along this street and it eventually wound back behind and above Mormino's building. Bob took some pictures as they walked. He led them into a large parking lot overlooking Mormino's building, and they walked to the back. A steep incline led downward toward Mormino's apartment, now almost directly below them.

Bob asked, "Sally have the blueprints come in yet?"

Sally looked at her i-pad. "Yep, I've got them."

"See where apartment 4C is located."

Sally searched several pictures and finally said, "If you're looking at the front, it's located on the top floor, in the back corner on the left."

Bob took out his binoculars and carefully examined the apartment of interest. A balcony extended across the entire back of the unit. "Is the bedroom on the corner," he asked?

"No, it may be the living room, and a single bedroom is further in. The end of the balcony extends to her bedroom."

Bob then took more pictures of the drop-off leading down to the building.

"Let's find a place to relax while Sarah gets the equipment we're going to need."

They retraced their steps and found a small park nearby. Bob transferred his pictures to Sally's i-pad, and the three looked at them while Bob talked. "I'm going to repel down the steep hill behind the apartment. You can see a large tree is almost directly across from Mormino's balcony. There's only a twenty foot gap between the tree and her unit. I can easily traverse twenty feet. Once on her balcony, I can open the door in the living room. If it's locked, I'll pick the lock. Inside her apartment, I'll use some gas to put her into a deep sleep. Then I'll let you in the front door."

Sally listened intently and now understood Bob was not some naïve fumbling apprentice operative, but the real thing. This looked a lot more like the James Bond adventure she expected. Sally asked, "What kind of sleeping gas are you going to use?"

"We call it *Hypnotrance*. The CIA developed it as an interrogation drug, but it never worked effectively. Then they found out it worked great for putting people to sleep. It's short acting and lasts about two hours, but it's ideal for what we need to do. If it's used after the person is already asleep, they never know it's been used."

Bob called Sarah on the phone and rattled off a list of equipment for the covert operation. She called Bob back twenty minutes later. "Okay Bob, I've located everything you need. Our CIA contact in Rome is going to charter a helicopter and fly the stuff down to you at ten o'clock tonight. The meeting point is going to be a field just west of Amalfi."

Sarah gave Bob the GPS coordinates and directions to the meeting point and asked him to check in with her when they were ready to enter Mormino's apartment.

Alice and Rich arrived a little before six o'clock, and the expanded group met Brian and Beth in an outdoor restaurant overlooking Amalfi's harbor. At dinner Bob reviewed the plan's operational details. Assignments were passed out, and the team then relaxed over dinner.

At nine o'clock, Bob and Beth left to meet the CIA chopper and pick up the equipment at the landing site, while the rest of the team decided to take a brief walk along the waterfront.

¤   ¤   ¤

It took Bob and Beth almost an hour to find the designated rendezvous point. They took the wrong road west of the mountain range hugging the coast near Amalfi, but they eventually located the proper field. They left their car by the side of the road, hidden in a grove of olive trees near a large vineyard, and walked slowly into the center of the field where they waited for the arrival of the helicopter. Shortly after ten o'clock, they heard the unmistakable thumping of an approaching chopper. Bob pointed a flashlight toward the sound and began sending flashes of light at ten second intervals.

The pilot spotted the signal and made a slight change in course. As the helicopter hovered over the flashing light, the pilot turned on the landing lights and slowly settled to the ground. The side door slid open, and a man shouted the code word Galaxy, and Bob responded with the code word Pulsar. A duffel bag fell at Bob's feet and Beth grabbed a second package. The unknown man in the helicopter wished them good luck and shut the door. The helicopter lifted off the ground and headed back toward Rome. The entire transfer had taken less than one minute.

By previous agreement, the entire team met in Brian's hotel room near the harbor. Bob distributed equipment to the team members based on their assignments, and reviewed the plan in detail. Finally, he left to get into position behind Mormino's apartment. After midnight the rest of the team split up and agreed to meet again at 2:00 A.M.

Shortly after one o'clock, Sally and Dan rode their mopeds up the road leading to the apartment and waited in the park they had visited earlier in the day.

Bob, meanwhile, had parked a few blocks away from Mormino's apartment and headed for the parking lot just behind and overlooking her building. Dressed in black, he walked in the shadows. He carefully avoided walking near streetlights and finally arrived at the hill behind Mormino's building.

He removed a black climbing rope from his duffel bag and after securing one end to the trunk of a large tree at the top of the hill, slowly rappelled down the hill to a flat ledge almost directly across from Mormino's apartment. He looked at his watch, almost midnight, and lights still illuminated Mormino's living room. Dark shadows reflected against the translucent drapes.

At 12:30 A.M., the lights were turned off and the lights inside her bedroom came on. After another ten minutes those lights were turned off, and Bob assumed the woman had retired for the night. He called the other team members and updated them on his progress. After the call, he began assembling his equipment and staging items in the order they would be used. He checked his watch and waited for the arrival of the other team members. Fifteen minutes before two o'clock the team began to check in with Bob.

At exactly two o'clock, Beth rappelled down to the small ledge and landed next to Bob. Bob called Sarah to inform her of the start of the operation.

He opened a long telescoping pole, attached a rope with a sophisticated hook at one end, and began advancing the end of the pole toward Mormino's balcony. He carefully released the hook end of the rope when it just reached over the balcony's wrought iron fence, and tightened the other end of the rope with a turnbuckle around the large tree Bob had identified earlier in the day. He tested the line with his weight to ensure it held tight, and then attached a small trolley designed to travel along the rope. He attached a special harness around his waist and hooked it up to the trolley system.

He slowly began pulling himself along the rope toward the balcony. The traverse took less than one minute. Upon reaching the balcony, Bob released himself from the trolley, slipped over the balcony's railing, and rested for a few minutes.

He moved to the bedroom window and placed a device that looked like a stethoscope against the sliding door. He listened for several minutes to the amplified sound coming from the bedroom and concluded Mormino was asleep.

Bob now moved to the door leading into the living room, and much to his surprise, found it unlocked. Slowly he opened the door. It squeaked as he cracked it open. He stopped and reached into one of his pockets. He removed a small can of lubricant and sprayed a liberal amount along the hinges. He tested the door again, and the hinges no longer squeaked. The door now opened easily, and pushing aside the drapes, Bob quietly entered the living room. He placed a gas mask over his face and slowly advanced into Mormino's bedroom.

Gina Mormino lay spread-eagle on her stomach making full use of her narrow bed. Bob removed a can containing the Hypnotrance from a pocket and began dispersing the aerosol drug into the air above Mormino's head. He continued to direct the spray toward Mormino until the can was empty. He waited ten minutes for the drug to take full effect, confirmed she didn't respond to his touch, and then opened her bedroom sliding door to help dissipate the sleeping gas.

Bob walked back into the living room and talked into his headset. "The baby's asleep. Let's advance to phase two."

Beth remained in her position, but the other team members assembled in the front lobby. Dan pressed the call button for Mormino's apartment, and Bob, waiting by the front door, buzzed them into the building.

The team carried out their assignments. Rich Gibbons found Mormino's laptop computer on the kitchen table and uploaded everything to an external hard drive and downloaded a virus allowing Benny to see her computer screen in real time. He repeated the process for a computer on her desk and once again for her cellphone. He moved onto a FAX machine and pulled everything off its memory. Going back to her laptop computer, he exposed the electronic circuit board and attached a miniature device to continuously transmit a GPS signal and also an extremely sensitive audio eavesdropping device.

Dan looked through Mormino's desk. He realized almost everything he found was written in Italian. "Does anyone understand Italian," he asked?

Bob answered, "yes," and they quickly exchanged assignments. Dan now methodically searched every piece of furniture in the apartment for useful information.

Sally meticulously looked through Mormino's closet, once again trying to find any information of value. After the closets, she moved to Mormino's purse, removed a small caliber pistol, and placed it on the kitchen table.

She took pictures of Mormino's credit cards, removed a prepaid cellphone, and then asked Rich to upload all of the data onto his external hard drive. Meanwhile, Sally took detailed pictures of some keys, thinking duplicates could be made from the pictures. The rest of the contents consisted of a variety of cosmetics.

Sally finished her assignments and began a more leisurely search. Large numbers of books, newspapers, and magazines scattered around the apartment, demonstrated Mormino's love of reading. The overflowing shelves behind her desk contained hundreds of books. A copy of the Herald Tribune, an American newspaper, sat on the kitchen table, the same paper Mormino had been reading at the internet café. Sally held the newspaper in her hand. What was so special about an American paper?

Meanwhile, Bob took picture after picture of receipts and invoices in a variety of folders inside Mormino's desk. While all of this unfolded, Gina Mormino slept peacefully, undisturbed by the activity inside her apartment.

¤　¤　¤

Adrian Florentino made his second trip of the night to his bathroom in apartment 4D. His enlarged prostate, typical of a man in his seventies, meant a minimum of four trips each night to empty his bladder. After relieving himself, he walked out onto his balcony craving a cigarette. At his age, he would never break a bad habit. He sat down on a chair, lit up and inhaled the addictive vapors deeply into his lungs.

Beth saw the man emerge and gave everyone a heads up. She froze, trying to blend into the landscape, but without success. If the man turned in her direction, he would definitely see her.

Señor Florentino flicked an ash over the balcony. His eyes were suddenly diverted to moonlight reflecting off of a grey form on the hill behind the apartment. His eyes focused on the object. He had never seen it before and his mind reacted slowly to the new shape. He walked inside his apartment, returned with a flashlight, and directed its light toward the unknown shape. He saw a woman sitting on a ledge in the hill almost directly opposite his balcony. Knowing this was a matter for the police, he made the phone call.

"I've been spotted," Beth announced. "I think he called the police."

Bob took charge. "Beth, remove the rope from the tree and throw it down the hill; then get the hell out of there quick. We'll be out in two minutes. We'll meet in the park."

Beth threw the rope down the hill and climbed back up the hill using the rappelling rope for assistance. Bob rushed onto the balcony and gathered up the rope discarded by Beth. As he reentered Mormino's apartment, Florentino returned with his flashlight and saw Beth scurry over the top of the hill. Bob closed the balcony door as the team made one final check of the apartment to ensure everything had been put back in place. Within two minutes, the team left the building and met Beth in the nearby park. She carried the duffel bag and a variety of ropes. Bob grabbed the bag, and the group split up walking, but not running, to their various modes of transportation.

¤   ¤   ¤

The local police arrived at the scene almost twenty minutes after Florentino made the call. He buzzed them into his apartment and showed them where he had seen the woman hiding on the hill. The police drove to the top of the hill and looked down at the area described by Florentino. Yes, the ground appeared disturbed, but no more so than any other area near the steep incline.

They returned to the back of the apartment and walked around the bottom of the hill. Nothing unusual. They returned to Señor Florentino and explained their search revealed nothing. "I know what I saw," he said.

"I'm sure you did see somebody, but we couldn't find any evidence of a prowler. It must have just been a voyeur. You should feel honored that somebody wanted to look at you."

"Maybe it wasn't me; maybe the person wanted to see the young woman who lives next door."

"Okay, we'll check to see if she knows anything, but thanks for calling in the complaint."

The two policemen knocked on the door of unit 4C, first softly, then more loudly. With no response coming from Mormino's apartment, they left, convinced the old man had been hallucinating.

34

The full team had now transferred to Positano. Dispersed throughout the town in a number of hotels, they met in Sally's and Dan's suite. Bob and Benny transferred files, pictures, and other information from Mormino's electronic equipment. Meanwhile, Sarah briefed her superiors in Washington. They were still trying to agree on the next steps. The other team members analyzed the information being provided by Bob and Benny.

Sally, however, was on a different hunt. A minor observation bothered her and made no sense. Gina Mormino had been looking at the Herald Tribune in the internet café and left the newspaper on her kitchen table. She hadn't been reading it in the café. Rather, she just opened the paper to a page and never touched the paper again. This fact by itself wasn't bizarre, except most of the books on her bookshelf appeared to be written in Italian. Gina Mormino probably understood English, but with all of the news media publications available in Italian, why would she need to look at a newspaper written in English? Sally asked the team, "Gina Mormino had a Herald Tribune when she e-mailed Blake at the internet café, and she had a copy of the paper in her apartment, yet almost everything else in her apartment was in Italian. It looks like with the exception of the e-mails written in English everything on her desktop computer is written in Italian.

Benny looked up from his computer. "Hey, did you say the Herald Tribune? That's strange; Darrin Blake had a copy of the Herald Tribune in the safe in his hotel room."

Sally shouted, "That's it; they're somehow using words in the Herald Tribune to authenticate who's using each computer."

Sally grabbed the latest copy of the e-mails from Mormino to Blake. "The first message used the code word *the*; the response from Blake used *alignment*; the message from Mormino responded with *of*."

Sally began a new mission. She left the hotel and found a newsstand in the piazza. She found the latest copy of the Herald Tribune and asked the clerk whether she had papers from the previous days. What an opportunity to sell outdated papers with no value other than recycling material. The store's manager left the register and searched the storeroom for back issues. She returned in a minute with four old papers. Sally paid for them and returned to the hotel suite.

She found a pen and pulled out yesterday's paper, the same one Mormino had opened at the café. She began searching for the word *alignment*, the most unusual code word of the three. It took her one hour to scan the entire paper, and she found the word only four times. One article in the sports section discussed *alignment* changes in the British football league. Two others were in an article discussing fundamental *alignment* shifts in the political parties inside Belgium. She found the fourth in the daily crossword puzzle under *2-across*. *1-across* started with the word *the,* and question *3-across* started with the word *of.*

Could this be the key? Sally looked at the e-mails from previous days and compared the code words used in the crossword puzzles on those days. The order of words fit.

Sally pumped her fist into the air and said, "I've got it; I've got it."

Sally then shared her findings with the rest of the team.

Dan said, "Please forgive her for being the way she is. I've tried on many occasions to explain she can't be smarter than everyone else. She needs to lean more toward mediocrity."

Everyone congratulated Sally for figuring out the code recognition system. Sarah said, "This means we can send messages to Blake and he'll do what we tell him to do."

Benny added, "It's really much better, because I can now take over both of their computers, and they'll only see the messages we want them to see."

The team ordered Room Service pizzas and reviewed their collective findings. The information could be consolidated into a few facts.

Gina Mormino was thirty-two years old. She graduated with a degree in Economics at Bocconi University in Milan, and started working for

NewTech Capital as Giorgio Paldinni's Personal Assistant. Interpol had no record of her.

Bob summarized the other facts gleaned from the search of Mormino's apartment. "It appears the small laptop computer is only used to transmit e-mails to Blake, and we already have those messages. She used her desktop computer for everything else, but only her own personal stuff. She probably has a computer at the villa she uses for business. Other than breaking the recognition codes by Sally, we've got nothing new."

Sally said, "That's not true. We found the security guard schedule in her desk."

Brian, who had been quiet for much of the discussion, said, "We need to be able to monitor what's going on inside the villa. Any ideas how?"

Bob replied, "I spotted several surveillance cameras, so a frontal approach isn't wise. The villa sits on a cliff overlooking the sea. We could rent a boat and scale the cliff and plant all of our surveillance equipment at night."

Benny added, "I've got some instruments to pick up voices by monitoring the vibrations from windows."

Rich replied, "Benny, I think we actually need to get inside the villa. If we can get in without being detected, we can place audio and video sensors."

Sally asked, "What about the guards?"

Sarah said, "We've got their schedule, and it looks like there're only two guards after midnight. We can monitor their movements tonight and assume they use the same pattern all the time."

Bob said, "We're going to need more mountain scaling equipment to climb the cliffs."

"And I'm going to need more electronic equipment," Benny said.

Sarah said, "I'll get Nina Bendinni to help us rent the boat. From the number in the harbor, it shouldn't be a problem.

By the way, Washington says they need to get the Italian government involved. They want to bring Giorgio Paldinni back to the U.S. for prosecution, and that means working through the Italian legal system. They'll call us as soon as they figure out the logistics. In the meantime, we should continue doing what we need to do."

¤   ¤   ¤

Nina Bendinni arrived at the hotel within the hour, and Sarah explained their requirements. Alice, who knew about boats volunteered to be captain. The team agreed Sally, Dan, Bob and Alice would take the boat to the villa in the afternoon and determine the best method for scaling the cliff. The four accompanied Nina down to the beach.

Nina located a boat rental agency on the edge of the harbor. The manager showed them pictures of four boats. They settled on a high-speed bright red forty foot Azimut yacht. The manager wanted to know who would be driving the boat. Nina pointed to Alice and the manager looked at her suspiciously. Female boat captains were beyond his vision of a properly functioning society. He insisted on checking out her boating skills. As the two walked to the beach, Alice turned to Sally, stuck out her tongue, and gave the manager the finger. Sally laughed and shouted, "You show him girl!"

The manager and Alice took a small ten foot skiff out into the harbor and tied the small boat up to the moored forty foot yacht. After a quick explanation of the instruments, the manager let Alice pilot the boat on a quick cruise around the harbor.

When they returned, the manager smiled, clearly impressed with Captain Alice's boating skills. He gave her a high-five and went back to his office with Nina to complete the paperwork. Alice said, "What a schmuck; typical macho Italian male."

Nina returned and handed Alice the contract, and as they reached the hotel, Nina left them and continued up the hill to her car.

A day on the water had not been in anyone's plans, and the four boaters bought bathing suits, large beach towels, hats, flip-flops, and the highest rated sunscreen at a small boutique near the hotel. Bob brought his Nikon to take close-up pictures of the cliff behind the villa, and the four walked to the harbor and boarded their boat.

Alice started the twin 355 horsepower diesel engines, and while they warmed up, she checked out the boat's instruments. After casting off, they slowly headed out into the harbor, and after maneuvering past hundreds of moored yachts, they left Positano and headed east toward the villa.

A cloudless deep blue sky shinned brightly, and the summer sun quickly roasted the boaters. They applied liberal amounts of sunscreen, and their hats provided some additional protection. After leaving the crowded harbor, Alice advanced the throttle, and the boat leaped forward at a little over thirty knots. The air rushing past the boat's cockpit provided minor relief.

With Dan using Google Earth to navigate, they spotted the villa in the distance as they hugged the coast. A small private dock holding six boats lay in a protected cove near where the villa overlooked the sea. Alice cut the boat's engines about one-hundred yards from the cliff, and the boat drifted to a stop.

Sally looked up at the cliff with complete fascination. "I wonder how these cliffs formed?" she said.

Alice answered, "I took a geology course in college. I remember the professor talking about these types of rock formations. He said a combination of factors: wave action, constant erosion, earthquakes, uplifting caused by tectonic plate shifting, and periodic floods, created the unique cliffs. And then, of course, you need to wait a couple million years."

As agreed earlier, Bob stayed on the boat taking pictures while the others jumped into the water to swim. To any observer, they appeared to be nothing more than four wealthy tourists out for a day's fun on the open water. For every picture Bob took of the three, he took four of the cliff and the surrounding area. After half an hour of picture taking and frolicking in the water, they were ready to leave. Bob wanted to have Dan stand at the bottom of the cliff. He would move the boat further off shore and use Dan as a reference to estimate the height of the cliff.

Sally had a better idea. She folded a piece of paper into a triangle conforming to the angle between the water and the top of the cliff. She then used her i-pad to obtain the GPS coordinates of their position. Alice then repositioned the boat at the base of the cliff and Sally took another GPS reading. She calculated the distance between the two positions. "As soon as we get back to the hotel, I'll measure the angle of the paper triangle, and then I'll use simple trigonometry to calculate the height of the cliff."

While at the base of the cliff, Dan spotted a surveillance camera mounted to the rocks. Alongside the camera, a cave opening appeared blocked by an iron gate. After spotting the camera and noticing it pivoted to follow their movements, Alice moved the boat slowly along the shore leading back in the direction of Positano.

35

The camera at the entrance to the cave presented a problem. It would be almost impossible to bring a boat close to shore without being spotted. Bob concluded they would need to make the final approach underwater. After getting a list of equipment from Bob, Alice and Brian left to find some scuba gear.

Sally did some quick calculations and estimated the cliff height at one hundred sixteen feet.

In the early afternoon, Sarah received another delivery from her CIA contact in Rome. Benny sorted through the new electronic equipment, while Bob inspected the mountain climbing gear. After Bob confirmed his equipment's condition, he began printing the pictures he had taken of the cliff. He studied them with a magnifying glass, laying out a plan for attacking the cliff.

At four o'clock the team sat at the nearby internet café watching Benny send an e-mail to

Darrin Blake using the proper authentication code. Their e-mail directed Blake to delay operation Big Thunder until further notice. They waited for over an hour hoping for a response, but their e-mail went unanswered. Hopefully, Blake was still using his computer. They would try again tomorrow morning.

They finalized the plan by dinnertime. The plan stressed simplicity. Bob and Rich would scale the cliff, and monitor the movements of the security people at the villa while Alice and Dan would stay in the boat providing support.

They found a seaside restaurant with enough outdoor seating for nine and all except Brian ordered the house special, Bouillabaisse. He said he hated fish and settled on the lasagna. After her third glass of wine Sarah opened up. "This whole thing with bringing in the Italian ROS sucks. We did all the work and now they're going to get to be the heroes."

Sally asked, "What's the ROS?"

"It stands for Raggruppamento Operativo Speciale. They're the Italian equivalent of one of our SEAL teams. Anyway, we're all here to serve our country; right?"

The group lifted their wine glasses to toast the ROS, with the exception of Rich and Bob, who hoisted their Pellegrinos.

◘   ◘   ◘

The sleek forty foot Azimut eased out of the Positano harbor shortly after 1:00 A.M. The night was perfectly clear and a nearly full moon lit the water; definitely not good conditions for a covert operation. As they neared the villa, Alice cut the throttle back to a near crawl. She hugged the shoreline, out of sight of the camera above the cave entrance, and tied up at the private boat dock a half-mile from the villa. Bob and Rich, who were already dressed in black wetsuits and scuba gear, slipped over the side and began swimming toward the villa. Bob had viewed some CIA satellite pictures taken of the villa grounds and had decided to scale the cliff on the northern most edge of the compound, totally out of sight of the camera near the cave.

They both carried waterproof sacks containing equipment necessary for scaling the cliff and surveillance. As they reached the northern corner of the villa, they swam further off shore and removed two pieces of specialized equipment from Bob's sack. The first looked like a high-tech cross bow with an unusual arrow shaped projectile, and the second like a shallow barrel with two-hundred feet of high-strength nylon rope coiled to promote rapid uncoiling.

After attaching the end of the rope to the projectile, Bob took aim and shot the arrow over the top of the cliff. After reaching its maximum height, grappling hooks sprung outward from the arrow's sides and struck the ground. Bob pulled back on the rope, and the hooks dug deeply into the ground and held tight. Bob tested the rope, and then he and Rich moved closer to shore.

Rich removed two special motorized climbing devices and attached them to the rope. Bob wrapped a climbing cradle under his arms and attached the other end to the first motorized system. He turned on the silent high-speed motor and ascended the rope to the top of the cliff. After reaching the top, he signaled Rich, who followed him with a waterproof bag dangling from his leg.

Once on top, Rich removed two high-tech night vision systems from his sack. In addition to operating in the infrared spectrum, they also allowed them to visualize any optical security devices placed around the compound.

They had two goals. First, to record the movements and timing of the security guards as they checked the compound. Second, if the opportunity arose, to place some video surveillance equipment on the grounds to monitor movements throughout the estate.

Both men silently moved in different directions, splitting up to observe opposite sides of the property. Bob, after carefully avoiding several optical security sensors located near the cliff, positioned himself behind a grove of trees on the southeast edge of the compound.

Meanwhile, Rich moved along the edge of the cliff and found a group of rocks affording excellent cover. He used his binoculars to focus on a window near the backdoor of the villa. Two guards sat at a console in a small room looking at a variety of surveillance monitors.

Soon, one of the guards left the room and began a walkthrough of the house. He checked doors on the first floor and then walked through several rooms on the second floor. Rich noted the time and traced the path of the guard by following the lights being turned on and off. Ten minutes later the guard returned to the security room and sat down next to his partner.

Bob and Rich waited for the security people to make their rounds. At two o'clock, both guards left the main house and began walking in opposite directions around the property. They met near the front gate and after a minute continued on their routes. It took them ten minutes to walk the property. After inspecting the immediate area around the house, they walked back inside the villa.

The heat from the surveillance cameras was enough to register on both men's night vision equipment. They each made careful notes of the cameras' locations. The placements favored coverage of the front and sides of the property, where an intruder would most likely enter the grounds, although three cameras faced the rear of the compound.

Communication links had been set up between Bob and Rich as well as Alice and Dan, and Dan stayed in contact with the team in Positano on his cellphone. Benny wanted to know the makes of the security cameras being used so he could devise countermeasures. Dan relayed the request, and Bob said he would handle it.

Bob spotted the closest camera, attached to a tree about fifty feet to his left. From his position in the corner of the compound, he could see the camera sweeping slowly back and forth through a two hundred seventy degree arc. Luckily, he had positioned himself in the camera's blind spot. He cautiously approached the tree from behind the camera.

The camera was too high to reach from the ground, so Bob removed a rope from his sack and threw one end over one of tree's lower limbs. He then climbed the rope and pulled himself up over the large branch. From his position, he crawled along the limb to the location of the camera. He took out a small pen light, illuminated the label on the surveillance device, and took pictures with his camera. Then, he noted the precise angle of traverse of the camera as it panned the compound.

Bob then moved to the two other cameras near the rear of the compound, being careful to use trees to hide his approach. Both were located in trees which he had to climb. He took pictures of each camera and noted the sweep angles. Luckily, none of the cameras seemed to be covering the rear of the compound.

As Bob climbed down from the third tree, Rich let him know the guards had reemerged from the villa and were heading off on their rounds. Bob's watch read exactly three o'clock and after repeating the patterns from the previous tour, they slipped back inside the same door.

After the guards were seated in their room, Rich positioned a small surveillance camera in the rocks where he hid. He set the device on a flat spot and moved some smaller rocks to provide camouflage.

The wireless video system required an electronic transponder within one-hundred feet to uplink the signal to a military satellite positioned in the northern hemisphere. Bob had already identified the perfect spot for the relay station, a small ledge about ten feet from the top of the cliff directly below the position where Rich had placed the camera.

Rich slipped a rope around a tree and carefully lowered himself to the ledge. It took a few minutes to establish the link to the satellite, and a green light began blinking on the relay system when the antenna was properly positioned. Rich asked Dan to contact Benny to confirm the video uplink functioned properly. Two minutes later Benny reported excellent signal reception.

Bob and Rich now decided to wait until four o'clock to confirm the security routes were always the same. Sure enough, at exactly the top of the hour, the guards reemerged from the same door and began the search of the grounds.

After the guards completed their search, Rich and Bob returned to the cliff and used the motorized units to slowly descend along the rope. After reaching the bottom of the cliff, Bob took out an electronic device, pushed a button and the grappling hooks were released. Bob then pulled the rope with its arrow over the cliff. The projectile fell into the water near their feet.

After placing all of the gear back into their waterproof sacks, the two submerged and swam back to the boat. When they arrived, Dan said, "Great job. As a reward we'll let you both rest while Alice gets us back to Positano."

Rich said, "Wow, some reward. What do we get when we catch the bad guys?"

Alice answered, "You get an attaboy and a dog biscuit."

They relaxed as Alice retraced their path back to Positano and the comfort of warm beds.

36

The team sat at a small outdoor restaurant near the waterfront having their lunch and making plans for the night's mission. Benny had completed an internet search on the camera. "So here's the deal. You guys were lucky not to be detected last night. These cameras are all the same. They use infrared at night, and switchover to visible light during the day, and they're capable of rotating 360 degrees.

From what Bob indicated, they're probably all programed to use a sweeping pattern providing multiple camera coverage of the entire compound, but Bob's data on the camera's angles of sweep identified several blind spots. Sarah, can you get us the kind of protective suits firemen use when they're entering a burning building?"

"I'm sure our Rome contact can find them."

"Okay then, if we're going in at night we won't be visible on their cameras if we're wearing those suits. We'll just blend into the infrared background."

Dan said, "We only need one person to wear the suit."

Sarah asked, "What do you mean?"

Dan continued, "We send one person up with the suit, and he hides in the bushes near the backdoor. When the guards leave to make their rounds, they probably mute the system's alarms. We take a canister of the sleeping gas you use and rig a remote timer to activate the aerosol.

When the guards leave the building on their outside tour, the person in the suit places the canister inside their monitoring room. We then trigger it remotely when they return. When they're asleep, we temporarily place the security system on pause; and the rest of us enter the house undetected, place cameras, audio sensors, and check for other evidence."

Rich said, "Are you sure you didn't train in the CIA? I like the idea. We can even gas Paldinni while he's asleep and check his bedroom."

Sally asked, "What about the other guards asleep in the cottage?"

Rich answered, "We can gas them too."

Sarah approved the plan and contacted her source in Rome for the necessary equipment to be sent by chopper. Assignments were made; Alice would pilot the boat, Sally and Sarah would stay with her, and the rest of the team would scale the cliff, place the sensors and look for clues to the location of the weapon and operation Big Thunder.

They spent the rest of the day planning the details. Everyone memorized their assignments and reviewed contingency plans, and one thing was certain, with this type of mission the unexpected must be expected.

¤   ¤   ¤

Rich and Bob took Sarah's car after dinner to meet the helicopter in a prearranged location. The transfer of equipment went flawlessly, and they returned to the boat with all the new gear. The entire team crowded onto the yacht.

They left the dock a little after midnight and proceeded to the same GPS coordinates used the night before. Once again Bob and Rich ascended the rope. Once on top of the cliff, Bob dressed in his firefighter's protective suit. He checked his watch. They had about fifteen minutes before the next scheduled search of the grounds by the guards.

Rich wished him luck as he slowly walked across the lawn. He arrived near the backdoor apparently undetected, and rested against the villa's outside wall behind a grouping of bushes. He wrapped a dark camouflage cloth around his body and sat quietly waiting for Rich to give him the all clear signal.

At exactly one o'clock, the two guards left by the backdoor and began their rounds. They followed the exact route they had used the night before, and as they moved out of sight, Rich said, "You're a go Bob. I'll call you if there's a change in their route."

Bob took off the camouflage cover and walked through the backdoor of the villa. He tried to open the guard's monitoring room and found it locked. He took out a lock picking kit and began working the lock. Unfortunately, Bob lacked Benny's skills as an expert lock picker, and the process took almost five minutes before he entered the monitoring room and looked for the ideal location to place the aerosol canister. He chose to hide the sleeping gas behind a waste basket located under the monitoring station's desk.

As he placed the device, Rich said, "Bob, one of the guards is on his way back to the villa. He'll be there in thirty seconds. He'll see you if you come out now, so hide someplace inside.

Bob turned on the canister's remote trigger device and left the monitoring room. Instead of turning left toward the backdoor, he turned right into the main part of the house. Staying in the shadows, he hid inside a hall closet. He sat on the floor in his bulky firefighter's suit and once again wrapped the camouflage cover around his body.

The returning guard passed by the monitoring room and headed for a nearby bathroom. Rich informed Bob the other guard had finished his inspection and was also headed back to the backdoor.

The two guards met in the monitoring room, and reactivated the alarm system. One of them left to inspect the house. He opened the hall closet but didn't bother to look at anything. After closing the door, he continued down the hall, and after another ten minutes, completed his inspection and returned to the monitoring room. Rich gave Bob a running commentary on both guards. After both men were seated watching their monitors, Rich said, "Do it now!"

Bob pressed a button on his remote trigger and waited. At first there appeared to be no reaction from the guards, but after a few seconds both men's heads began bobbing back and forth until no further movements could be seen. Rich said, "The two babies are asleep."

Hearing the good news, Bob left his hiding place and moved down the hallway to the monitoring room and removed his protective clothing. His second attempt at picking the lock only took a minute. He put a small respirator over his face and entered.

Having been trained by Benny in what the computerized monitoring equipment looked like, he deactivated the alarm system and temporarily put the cameras facing the rear and the cave's entrance on pause. Having completed his assignments, he gave the all clear to the others waiting on the boat.

Alice repositioned the boat as close to the rope as possible, and Sally and Sarah assisted the other team members in attaching their motorized climbing harnesses.

Beth motored up the rope and waited at the top of the cliff. Benny followed. Halfway up the cliff, Benny jerked to a stop. He tried adjusting his device, but it he couldn't fix the jammed mechanism. "I can't get it working. I'm stuck."

Alice said, "You're the technical guy; fix it."

"No way Alice; It's jammed."

Beth braced herself behind a rock and began pulling Benny up the cliff. Sarah asked, "Beth, do you need Bob and Rich to help?"

With a labored voice, Beth answered, "No, I can manage myself."

She lifted Benny slowly upward. Without any gloves, Beth's hands began to burn and blood oozed from many small cuts. At one-hundred ninety pounds, Benny was no lightweight, but Beth still managed to slowly lift him up the cliff.

As Benny staggered over the top, Beth collapsed onto the ground, totally spent. Benny disengaged his faulty motorized device, found the cause of the jammed dydtem and told the others to begin ascending the rope. Benny sat next to Beth, patted her on the back, and said, "I don't know how you did it, but thanks."

Beth looked at her swollen, bloody hands and said, "No problem."

Within five minutes, the entire team and their equipment had been hoisted to the top, where they were met by Rich. Meanwhile, Bob had entered the front door of the cottage. He knew there would be four guards sleeping, and he located the two bedrooms. After putting on his gas mask, he emptied two aerosol cans in each room. He left the cottage and returned to the edge of the cliff.

The group now entered the backdoor of the villa and spread out to execute their assignments. Bob, as the person most skilled in the use of the sleeping gas walked up a spiral staircase to the second floor. He assumed Paldinni would be sleeping in the master bedroom, undoubtedly a room with a view of the Mediterranean Sea.

After a few wrong turns, he found the master suite and opened the door. He crept cautiously into the bedroom. Paldinni lay asleep on the bed, but not alone. He and a woman were both naked. The middle-aged master of the villa appeared totally spent from his earlier sexual escapades. The woman on the other hand slept restlessly. She turned onto her back, and Bob caught a glimpse of her face. Surprise, surprise; Gina Mormino lay with her arm extended over Paldinni.

Bob removed another canister and gassed the pair. He then systematically searched every room on the second floor to confirm the rest of the villa wasn't occupied.

Meanwhile, Brian searched the basement. He opened one door, and it led to an expansive wine cellar. Paldinni had stocked it with well over a thousand bottles of reds, whites and champagnes. He left the wine cellar and opened another door at the opposite end of the lower hallway.

Suddenly, a large German Shepard bolted from behind the door and jumped on Brian. He screamed for help as the fierce dog bit his arm and tore into his flesh. Bob arrived first, followed closely by Dan and Beth. Beth pulled out a commando's knife, ready to kill the dog. "Bob pulled her arm back. "If we kill the dog, they'll know we were here."

He pulled out his last gas canister, and sprayed the dog, and in the process, Brian as well. The others backed away, trying not to inhale the vapors. Although most of the spray hit the dog, enough residual reached Brian to also put him to sleep. Dan pulled the dog's mouth open to free Brian's arm.

The wound looked terrible. A deep cut had penetrated down to his bone, and a number of puncture wounds were deep and bleeding profusely. Dan contacted the boat. "Sarah, we've got a problem. A watchdog attacked Brian. He's bleeding from his left arm. We gassed the dog and in the process Brian as well.

Sarah asked, "Is the villa secure?"

"Yes," Dan answered. "Sally what should we do?"

Sally answered, "Is he bleeding heavily?"

"Yes, he's got a long deep tear down to his bone and about eight deep puncture wounds."

"Put a tourniquet on his arm and lower him to the boat."

"Okay."

Beth found a rag in the laundry room off the basement hallway and tore a narrow piece of the cloth to use as a tourniquet. As she twisted the rag tightly around Brian's arm, the bleeding slowed and eventually stopped. Dan then tried lifting Brian over his shoulder, but he was too heavy. Beth pushed Dan aside. "What a wimp," she said.

After planting her feet on the floor in front of Brian, she bent down, lifted him with only a moderate effort, and balanced the deadweight over her shoulder. "I'll take care of this myself," she said. "You can finish up here."

Beth walked slowly out the backdoor to return Brian to the boat below the cliff. Dan couldn't believe what he had just witnessed, but Bob said matter-of-factly, "She's into weights."

After Beth left, the others began cleaning up the blood on the tile floor with towels they found in the laundry room.

When Beth arrived at the edge of the cliff, she pulled up the loose end of the rope floating in the sea. When the rope finally cleared the top of the cliff, she wrapped its end around the upper part of Brian's body, just under his arms, and lowered him slowly over the cliff. As Brian reached the boat, Sarah and Sally released him from the rope and carried him into the main cabin.

Sally pulled off the bedding from the cabin's large bed and together, they lifted Brian up onto the exposed mattress. Sally found a large towel and placed it under Brian's arm. They turned on the cabin lights and drew the blinds on the windows.

Sally opened the medical kit Benny had packed for them back in the states. Luckily, Brian remained in a drugged sleep and wouldn't feel any pain. Sally created a sterile field using two disposable drapes which she taped to Brian's arm. She cleansed the wound with saline and hydrogen peroxide, and while Sarah held a flashlight, loosened the tourniquet. Blood oozed from the deep laceration. She would have to tie off a few bleeders, but determined the wound wasn't life threatening. This emergency would be no more difficult to treat than a thousand other wounds she had repaired on busy Saturday nights in the ER.

Meanwhile, back in the villa, everyone completed their assigned tasks. Benny uploaded the files and data on a desktop computer in Paldinni's library. Dan and Bob searched through files inside Paldinni's desk while Beth and Rich looked through the rest of the house.

Dan looked at his watch. Caring for Brian's injury had taken almost forty minutes of valuable time. They would need to finish in another twenty minutes. In a desk drawer, Dan found a DHL receipt for a letter recently sent to Iran, dated two days ago. He took a picture of the document.

Benny moved into Paldinni's bedroom looking for any cellphones. He found one on Paldinni's nightstand and transferred the data to his miniature hard drive. He looked at Gina Mormino and thought about jumping her bones. She was one gorgeous babe. Why did this guy get all the action, and he always got stuck with the plain Janes of the world? Of course he knew the answer. It all boiled down to money and clearly Señor Sugar Daddy had enough Euros.

Sally had tied off the bleeding blood vessels and closed Brian's wound with the proper suture. She swabbed the injury with a liberal amount of Betadine antiseptic and wrapped his arm in gauze and an ace bandage. Sarah said, "Nice work. If I ever need a field assistant, I'll ask for you."

Sally smiled, "You should see me in action in the ER. I'd blow your socks off."

Inside the villa the team finished up. Benny found a wall safe in Paldinni's bedroom and tried to open it, but without success. The German Shepard had been dragged to its home behind the door, and the team completed a last walk-through to ensure everything had been returned to its original location, and no hint of their presence remained.

As they walked back to the cliff, Benny, with a disappointed look on his face, said, "We need to get a look inside his safe, but it's one of the newest models with electronic locks, and I'll need special equipment to get inside.

The team began the process of hooking up to the rope and slowly descending to the boat below. Bob stayed behind to reset the security system cameras and alarms and removed the empty sleeping gas canister. He then put his firefighter's protective suit back on and walked out to the cliff. After descending the rope, he released the grappling hook, and the rope with the projectile once again fell into the water.

Alice started the boat's twin engines and slowly hugged the shoreline until the boat had moved well out of sight of the camera by the cave. She headed further off shore and set a course back to Positano. Brian, having received only a partial dose of the gas, regained consciousness.

"What happened," he asked?

Sally said, "You're in the boat. A dog attacked you inside the villa and Bob put you and the dog to sleep. You had a pretty bad laceration on your right arm, and you needed stitches, but you're going to be fine."

"I feel like shit. My mouth's dry and I've got a bad headache."

Bob laughed and said, "Yea, but if I hadn't used the gas when I did the dog would have chewed your arm down to the bone. You should be thanking me, not complaining."

Brian, with a smile, reached up to Bob and executed an unsteady high-five.

Sarah said, "We're going to need help translating all of this computer data. I'm going to ask the Rome office for some assistance."

After an uneventful trip back to the dock in Positano, the team split up and agreed to meet in the usual waterfront restaurant at ten o'clock for breakfast.

37

Sarah was the last to arrive at the restaurant. She looked disturbed as she occupied the last remaining seat. "I just talked to the Director, and they've made the decision to arrest Paldinni, and the ROS will now take the lead. The leader of their team is going to meet us in Dan and Sally's suite at three this afternoon. We need to pull all the information together for the meeting. Our group has been asked to assist, but to let the ROS do the dirty work."

Benny asked, "When will the translators arrive from Rome?"

Sarah answered, "At eleven this morning. Nina will also help, but we have so much information on Paldinni's computer, it will be impossible to have reviewed everything by the time the head of the ROS team arrives."

Nina and two agents from the Rome CIA office arrived a little early, and they immediately joined Bob in reviewing hundreds of computer files for possible leads. Dan and Alice examined the telephone numbers taken off of Paldinni's cellphone, FAX machine, and landline.

Most of the calls originating from Paldinni's phone were to a telephone number in Geneva, Switzerland, the international headquarters of NewTech Capital. Many calls had also been placed to a New York number, the U.S. subsidiary of his company. Benny had compiled a list of the other numbers, and had e-mailed it to Jimmy, asking for a detailed investigation by local agents.

Dan studied the HDL receipt for the letter sent to Iran. "Sarah, I think this could be an important lead. How can we find out more about the person who received the letter?"

Sarah called a stateside contact, and after a minute's discussion, e-mailed a picture of the receipt. She said, "Our operatives in Iran will follow the lead."

Sally said, "With the exception of the HDL receipt we're not going to find anything useful. I think Paldinni is too smart to use his computer and telephones to communicate with everyone. Remember, e-mails to Blake were only found on Mormino's laptop. He's being very careful not to have his name linked directly to any incriminating information."

A loud knock on their door interrupted the group. A tall muscular soldier in fatigues and aviator sunglasses strutted into the room. He smiled and introduced himself as Colonel Andre Capinelli. He looked over the group and concluded he was working with amateurs, operatives who had no clue about covert operations, let alone executing even a simple capture mission. After Sarah explained she led the U.S. team, he knew his men would be needed to save the situation. "I've received limited information from my superiors. The first thing I need is a detailed briefing."

It took more than two hours for Sally and Dan to review the early work. Then Sarah summarized the team's Italian operations. She showed him the surveillance cameras and audio sensors operational inside the villa. He looked at the pictures coming through on Benny's computer and seemed both surprised and impressed. "How were you able to place these sensors inside the villa without being detected?"

Sarah answered, "We scaled the cliff behind the villa last night, and the rest is classified."

Andre smiled, "Yes, yes, I'm sure it is classified. It looks like you have enough information on Señor Paldinni to get him extradited. My mission is to arrest Paldinni and any others. I see this as rather straight forward."

Dan asked, "Will you be going in tonight?"

Andre answered, "No, this will be a daylight operation."

Sally pointed out, "You should also be aware of the existence of an underwater cave entrance with a locked gate at the bottom of the cliff."

"Young lady, we'll be inside the villa before anyone has time to leave. If you think it's important, you can wait outside the cave."

Sally looked deep into the eyes of Colonel Capinelli and said, "Colonel, I for one resent your patronizing attitude. We're not looking for a bloodbath here; we want to capture Paldinni alive. He's already killed over a thousand people in Chicago, and has plans for an even larger operation. He may be our last hope to find out how to stop the next terrorist attack. We've been told your team will be leading the operation, but don't assume this is going to be a cakewalk. If we had our way, you wouldn't even be involved; but we were overruled. Just make sure you and your team don't fuck up."

Red-faced, Colonel Capinelli began to say something in response and then thought better of it. Instead he said, "My team will be going in at dawn tomorrow. We will arrest Señor Paldinni; you can count on it!"

◘   ◘   ◘

A heavy fog had moved into the region overnight, and visibility was limited to less than a half mile at best. Just before dawn, Colonel Capinelli's team of twelve ROS soldiers jumped out of their trucks and assembled a half mile north of the villa along the coastal road. It took another minute to assemble their equipment.

The U.S. team had decided to split up. Alice, Bob, and Dan, after a harrowing ride in the dense fog, had stationed themselves in the boat along the shoreline, out of sight of the security camera near the cave entrance. The others, after meeting Capinelli's team, decided to wait near the restaurant overlooking the villa. As previously agreed with Capinelli, they would advance to the villa after the ROS team secured the area.

Unfortunately for the ROS team, a wireless security camera positioned near the assault team's staging area captured the activity on the road with its infrared optical sensor. An alarm screeched on the security system monitor as the computer software detected the unusual pattern. A security guard focused in on the monitor and pressed the emergency button. An alarm sounded in the cottage, arousing the sleeping guards, and alerting them to the pending threat near the front gate. Paldinni staggered out of bed, quickly dressed, opened his safe, and prepared to leave the villa.

By the time the ROS team advanced to the villa's front gate, the security team was positioned to respond to the frontal assault. They held their fire when the front gate blew open with a controlled charge of explosives, and waited until the ROS team charged through the narrow opening into the compound.

As the well-armed assault team squeezed through the chokepoint, they were caught in a deadly crossfire by the villa's security personnel hidden in the olive grove. Of the twelve member ROS team, three were immediately cut down. The others, with Colonel Capinelli protecting the rear, rushed for cover behind a grouping of trees near the compound's entrance.

The ROS team regrouped and identified the defender's positions. Half the team laid down suppression fire while the other half moved to the right in a flanking maneuver designed to circle the defenders and cut them off from the villa. As they rushed to the right, an additional two members of the assault team fell to the ground, hit by a flurry of fire.

The defenders then unleashed their surprise weapon. The large German Shepard raced toward the men attempting to outflank the defenders, and pounced on one of the ROS soldiers.

Meanwhile, Paldinni gathered his critical documents, a false passport, a large amount of cash, and ran to the villa's basement. He pressed a button hidden behind a bookshelf and a secret door slid open revealing a spiral staircase descending into the cave below the villa.

Colonel Capinelli rallied his remaining troops and hurled several flash grenades into three of the defensive positions. His troops, who had now completed their encircling maneuver, began firing on the remaining defenders, who were caught in a deadly cross-fire.

Sally and the others observed the assault from the road above the villa and couldn't believe the carnage taking place inside the compound. Sally, recognizing a professional obligation she couldn't avoid, shouted at the others, "I've got to get down there to help the wounded."

Brian said, "I'll drive."

The others on the team followed Sally and Brian as their car sped down the road toward the villa below and screeched to a stop by the front gate. Sally grabbed the medical kit from the trunk and raced into the compound. The others drew pistols and stayed close to Sally, providing cover. The first two members of the assault team were dead of massive head wounds; and the third soldier screamed in pain, missing part of his left arm. His armored vest had protected him from further injury. Sally cut away part of the man's uniform and created a makeshift tourniquet. She found morphine in her kit and injected him with a sufficient amount to make him comfortable.

Colonel Capinelli ran to Sally. Anticipating his question, she said, "I'm a doctor. I'm going to treat the wounded. Call for ambulances."

Capinelli listened intently and gave orders in his communication set in Italian. He turned to Sally and said, "Thank you!"

Sally left the wounded soldier and ran to the others closer to the villa. The German Shepard lay dead near one soldier who clutched his right arm. Sally pointed to herself and shouted

"Doctor" to the man and began treating his wound. She determined he would need nothing more than a compression-bandage and morphine until he arrived at the hospital. After injecting the morphine, she handed Brian a stack of gauze pads and an Ace bandage and told him to make a tight bandage. Then she ran off with the medical kit to treat some of the defenders who were behind a grouping of trees.

Colonel Capinelli's remaining force had captured the last few defenders and entered the villa with the goal of capturing Paldinni. They carefully advanced room by room, but it soon became apparent, Paldinni had disappeared.

With the shooting over, the rest of the U.S. team advanced carefully to the villa. Capinelli met them at the front door and explained, "Paldinni's not here."

Benny said, "I saw him asleep in his bed on the monitor back at the hotel just before we left."

Capinelli said again, "Well, he's not here!"

Dan's call interrupted the conversation. "Sarah, the gate is retracting. We're moving into position in front of the cave."

Sarah relayed the message to Capinelli who now knew he had failed in his attempt to capture Paldinni.

As the gate cleared the cave entrance, a sleek black speedboat charged through the opening, swerved to the left, and shot past the U.S. team's boat. Alice slammed the throttle all the way forward. Dan almost fell off the stern as their boat responded with over seven hundred horsepower.

As Alice tried to catch-up to Paldinni's boat, Dan contacted Sarah. "Paldinni has left the cave on a boat and we're following. We'll try and capture him alive but I can't guarantee anything."

Paldinni's boat pulled ahead, almost at the limit of visibility in the dense fog. Alice looked at her compass and said, "He's heading for Positano. I know the boat he's using. It's a forty two foot Buzzi, an Italian speedboat, and its two engines put out over one thousand horsepower. It can reach over sixty knots. We won't be able to catch it."

She maneuvered their boat inside Paldinni's wake. The calmer water allowed her to slightly increase her boat's speed, but Paldinni still pulled further into the lead. As Paldinni approached Positano, he headed for a large number of boats moored at buoys near the beach. The area looked like a parking lot; boats all lined up in even rows paralleling the shore and extending almost a half mile from the beach.

Paldinni bore down on the mixture of multimillion dollar yachts and fishing boats at full speed. Alice screamed above the roar of the engines, "He's an idiot. He's going to get us killed."

Dan yelled back, "He knows if we catch him he's dead anyway. He figures he has nothing to lose."

Paldinni aimed at a narrow gap between two rows. The wake from his boat struck nearby boats, setting up a chain reaction of multidirectional waves, creating an area almost impossible to navigate at even moderate speed. The dangerous conditions forced Alice to slow down and move even closer to shore. This diversion allowed Paldinni to extend his lead. After passing through the row of boats, he headed west out into the open sea.

Alice fell further behind Paldinni. His boat, holding only one person, and with the extra horsepower, crept ahead. The distance separating the two boats now stood at more than one-thousand yards. Bob pulled out his long range sniper rifle. "I'll try to hit the engines."

He took careful aim and fired off three shots, but both boats, moving at over thirty miles per hour, were not stable, and none of his bullets came close.

An early morning ferry arriving from Capri sounded its fog horn. Paldinni changed course and headed immediately behind the ferryboat's props. His boat hit the front edge of the ferry's wake and catapulted into the air. As it rose out of the water, the hull rotated with the bow rising further and further skyward. The boat reached an almost vertical position before it struck the behind the ferry and the displaced water almost capsized the sleek speedboat. It finally righted itself and sped off in the direction of the Isle of Capri.

Alice considered following Paldinni and decided the risk was too great. She changed course, and shot across the ferryboat's bow. The captain of the ferry sounded his fog horn in angry protest over the two boats' dangerous maneuvers.

Alice's decision to avoid catastrophe had cost them precious seconds, and Paldinni's boat, now over a mile ahead, had disappeared into the fog. Alice looked at the boat's gas gage. She completed some calculations in her head, and said, "We've got another thirty minutes of gas. He probably had a full tank of gas before he left. I have no idea what the range of his boat is, but I'm guessing he can go a lot further than our boat. We should follow him for another ten minutes and then head back to Positano."

Dan and Bob agreed as the chase continued.

With Paldinni now out of sight, Alice could only follow his boat's wake. Without radar, Alice drove blind in the dense fog. After a few minutes even Paldinni's boat's wake had disappeared and Alice cut back on the throttle. They could hear Paldinni's boat in the distance but could not be certain about the boat's direction. They had lost him.

At the beginning of the chase, Sarah had called for a helicopter to pursue Paldinni's boat, but her CIA contact told her it would take two hours to have a chopper on the scene, and unless the dense fog lifted, pursuit would be impossible.

Sarah approached Capinelli and pulled him away from the others. "You fucked up Colonel. We're going to lose Paldinni because you refused to take advantage of what we had learned. We told you his compound was monitored, and his security force heavily armed, but you had to play macho man and not take our advice."

Capinelli's face turned red as he tried to respond to Sarah's verbal attack, but she wouldn't let him reply.

"You thought we were amateurs, but you're the one who looks totally incompetent. I'm going to report all of this to my superiors, and I'm sure they'll inform yours. I hope your people were at least able to capture Gina Mormino, because she may be our last hope of finding out about their next attack."

Capinelli said nothing and left to talk to his men. He pulled one of his remaining soldiers aside and the man immediately began talking on a radio.

Two military ambulances arrived in the compound. Sally talked to the paramedics and helped load the wounded. Paldinni's two injured security guards were handcuffed to their restraints.

Capinelli, having regained his composure, walked over to Sarah and told her Mormino had been arrested and brought to the local army base for interrogation.

Sarah said, "We're going to want to talk to her right now, and we're going to want to search the entire compound."

Capinelli replied, "I have no authorization for you to question her or to go inside the villa."

"Let me tell you this. You'd better get authorization in the next few minutes or I'm going to do everything in my power to get you demoted, and don't think for a minute I can't make it happen."

Colonel Capinelli, with a smug grin on his face, said, "You have no evidence about what happened here. It will be my word against yours."

"That's where you're wrong, asshole. I taped our discussion back in the hotel and our surveillance video is sending back live feed to Langley. You're toast!'

Capinelli walked away visibly shaken. How could this stout, almost homely woman, exert such an outward display of authority? He didn't doubt for a minute she could, and more importantly, would do everything in her power to bring him down. More importantly, he knew he had made some huge mistakes by not listening to the U.S. team's advice. Three of his men had died needlessly because of his arrogance. He concluded he would allow the U.S. team to question the Mormino woman and search the villa and would do so without talking to his superiors.

While Sarah and the colonel had their heated discussion, Benny had quietly slipped inside the villa and headed to Paldinni's master suite. He stared at the open safe, turned around, and headed back to the security room. After picking the lock, he entered the guard's room and brought the library camera up onto the computer screen. He found a clear view of the open safe on monitor sixteen. Maybe, just maybe, he could find out more about the safe's contents.

After ensuring none of the ROS people were nearby, he pulled a flash drive from his pocket, something no good geek would be without, and copied the most recent data from the library camera. He would analyze the information back at the hotel.

Capinelli returned and agreed to allow an interview of Mormino and their search of the compound, and he then returned to his men.

Sarah thought about the people who should do the interrogation. She was not the type of leader who needed to be involved in everything. She only wanted results. She thought about which of her team would be best suited for the task at hand and settled on Dan, a skilled police investigator.

She ruled out her people. The FBI team members might be skilled in extracting vital information, probably Alice and Brian, but not Benny. Then she thought of Sally; certainly not experienced in interrogation, but a persuasive person, a person who could provide vivid details of the Chicago attack from a personal perspective, and there was something to be said for a woman to woman conversation.

She made her decision and would let the others know as soon as they all met again back in

Positano. Meanwhile, the rest of the group turned their attention to a more thorough search of the compound, including the villa.

38

Darrin Blake grew concerned. His internet contact had been telling him to prepare to initiate operation Big Thunder, then to execute Big Thunder, and the next contact wouldn't occur until the day of Big Thunder. Then he noticed the unexpected e-mail telling him to delay Big Thunder. The message contained the correct authentication code words, but he was under explicit instructions to disregard any instructions to delay the operation once it started. Should he worry about the e-mail?

Blake, by his nature, exercised extreme caution, and constantly looking over his shoulder had allowed him to stay alive all of these years. He ate lunch at a nice outdoor restaurant near the Marriott hotel. His instincts told him to remain extra vigilant.

He looked casually around the outdoor seating. Nothing unusual, perhaps he was being paranoid, but something didn't feel right. After finishing lunch, he left the restaurant and started walking back to his hotel. He casually looked back and noticed an elderly lady about a half block behind. She looked familiar. He had seen her somewhere before but couldn't remember where. On a hunch, he stopped in a drug store and bought a magazine. When he left the store, he noticed the woman had moved across the street and sat on a bench at a bus stop.

He continued walking back to the hotel. The woman, who mumbled to herself, stayed seated. Could someone be following him? He could easily find out. He turned left at the next corner and quickly entered a men's clothing boutique. He positioned himself near the window behind a rack of shirts. While pretending to be perusing the selections, he kept a close eye on the street. A young man hurried around the corner, suddenly stopped, looked down the street, as if searching for someone, and Blake knew exactly who the someone was.

He bought a shirt, not even bothering to check the size or price, and left the store with the shirt wrapped in a plastic bag. He walked down the street and noticed the same man he saw from inside the boutique walking a block behind. He arrived at his hotel.

Once in his room, he began thinking through the problem. He had CNN on the TV, but paid no attention. He knew for certain; he was being tailed; most likely the FBI but he couldn't be sure. If the FBI was following him, then they probably already had planted eavesdropping equipment in his room.

He thought about his options. One thing for certain; he needed to disappear quickly and completely. He reviewed his possessions, and decided he would have to take very few items with him. He assumed his computer and cellphone were already compromised, and a variety of homers were probably placed in many of his belongings. He needed to leave tonight, slip out of town, and acquire a new identity. None of this would be difficult. He had always planned for this eventuality.

In the late afternoon, he left the hotel and withdrew the maximum amount from a nearby ATM. He found a general department store and bought a complete change of clothes; he couldn't be sure what miniature transponders might have been placed in shoes or clothing.

He ate dinner in a restaurant near the hotel, a place he had frequented in the last few days. He needed to appear like a man waiting for instructions, not like a person getting ready to leave town. After dinner, he returned to his hotel room, shaved, took a shower, and watched TV until eleven o'clock. With the lights out, he lay quietly in his bed fully alert. He assumed his room was under video surveillance.

At 2:00 A.M. he got out of bed to go to the bathroom. He slipped on his newly purchased clothes, and quietly left his room. He took the stairway near the rear of the hotel and quickly exited through a backdoor near the waste collection area. He walked a block from the hotel, hailed a taxi, and asked to be taken to the airport.

After arriving, he immediately took another cab to the Greyhound Bus Terminal and purchased a one-way ticket with cash to Chicago, Illinois. He waited anxiously until the bus left the terminal at five o'clock, heading for the Windy City.

At six o'clock, as the early light filtered through the hotel room's window, the agent watching the surveillance camera knew Darrin Blake had skipped town. The word filtered up the chain of command and over the ocean to the team in Italy.

¤   ¤   ¤

Dan, Sally, and Alice arrived at the ROS military base outside of Naples and were escorted to a building near the center of the complex. After passing through a security checkpoint, they were brought to a small room. They sat around a table and waited for Gina Mormino to appear. Dan noticed the one-way mirror on a wall and assumed their interview would be recorded.

In a few minutes, Gina Mormino was brought limping into the room wearing an orange jumpsuit and a set of handcuffs. Her escort left after her handcuffs had been removed. Mormino's face looked swollen. She had obviously been severely beaten. Large bleeding welts around her wrists indicated she had probably been hung by her handcuffs during the interrogation. Gina Mormino looked terrified.

Dan had planned on leading the interrogation, but as soon as Sally saw Mormino's condition, she took over. She said, "Gina, I'm a doctor. Have you been tortured?"

Mormino began to cry and shook her head yes. Sally asked Dan to step outside. Dan knocked on the door and a military guard allowed him to leave.

Sally asked Mormino if she could examine her. Alice helped Sally unzip and remove Gina's jumpsuit. She had obviously been beaten with a blunt object. Both sides of her body were swollen with bruises directly over each of her kidneys. Sally felt large hematomas around Mormino's ribcage. Two ribs appeared to be broken. Mormino grimaced in pain.

Sally knocked on the door, stepped out of the room, and demanded to speak with Colonel Capinelli. The guard entered the next room and Capinelli appeared with a sardonic grin.

Sally moved right into his face. "She's been tortured. She has several contusions and two broken ribs."

Capinelli grinned as he replied, "I think she struggled while being captured."

Sally pushed her thumb into Capinelli's chest. "Listen you no good piece of shit, she's been tortured, and you and your people have violated the Geneva Convention. I'm going to report this. I want one of your physicians here right now."

Capinelli regained his composure. "There'll be no doctors. Question Señorita Mormino and leave. I'm in charge, not you."

Sally and Dan returned to the interrogation room. Alice whispered to Dan, "I took pictures with my cellphone. I don't think they saw me do it."

Dan led the interrogation and set a tape recorder on the small table in front of Mormino. "Do you understand English Ms. Mormino?"

She nodded, so Dan continued. "As you know Ms. Mormino, we're with the FBI. You have been taken into custody because of your involvement with the recent terrorist attack in Chicago. Our Government will initiate the extradition process in the next few days. "

"I had nothing to do with any attacks."

"Well Ms. Mormino, let me review some of the evidence we have collected. It not only implicates you in the attack, but also indicates you are the primary person involved in initiating the attack."

Dan reviewed a substantial amount of the data collected. When he turned to her activities at the internet café, her face became ashen with a look of desperation. Her eyes looked at Dan with increased attention.

"Where is Señor Paldinni," she asked?

Dan answered, "We're not here to talk about your boss. We're here to talk about you. The way I see it, you have two choices. You can cooperate with us, and your cooperation will be taken into consideration at your trial; or you can choose to say nothing and face the full weight of our judicial system. Since this will be considered an act of terrorism, you will be facing the death penalty."

Mormino said nothing. She digested Dan's comments, weighing her options. Dan waited an appropriate amount of time and then looked at Sally, her signal to play good cop.

"Ms. Mormino, I run the emergency room at Northwestern Hospital in Chicago. Thousands of patients exposed to the genetically engineered anthrax were brought to my facility. I watched over a thousand innocent people die; men, women, children, and babies. These people did not die a quick painless death."

Mormino listened intently to Sally as she continued.

"Let me tell you how this biological agent kills people. The hemorrhagic fever destroys a great deal of tissue while the person is still alive. Dead tissue spreads through all of the person's internal organs. The liver turns yellow in color, bulges outward, becomes a liquid, and finally cracks apart. The person's kidneys become clogged with blood clots and dead cells and stop producing urine. The spleen turns into a huge single blood clot. The lining of the intestines and stomach die and become filled with blood."

Mormino looked down at her feet, a sign of total capitulation.

"In men, their testicles swell and turn black and blue and their nipples bleed. In women, the labia turn blue and there is massive vaginal bleeding. In pregnant women, the child is spontaneously aborted. In the final stages of the disease, the patients go into epileptic convulsions. The whole body shakes, their arms and legs thrash around violently. Almost ninety percent of the people exposed to the biological agent died this horrible death, and I worked there, trying to save their lives."

Gina Mormino sobbed quietly as Sally continued,

"We know another attack is being planned, only this time the stakes will be higher because the amount of agent released will be much greater. Tens of thousands of additional innocent people will die, and all of this because Giorgio Paldinni wants to sell a vaccine at an inflated price to the U.S. Government."

Gina Mormino now cried openly as Sally concluded. "Ms. Mormino, we need your help in stopping operation Big Thunder. Will you help us?"

Nothing other than the sobbing of Mormino followed. They waited, not saying a word, all three just staring at her. A minute passed before she looked at Sally and said, "I didn't know what he was doing until I read about the attack in the paper. Then, I finally knew what this was all about."

Dan asked, "What's operation Big Thunder?"

"I don't know. Giorgio never tells anyone everything. He splits up the key information. He's paranoid. He's always been this way; ever since I began working for him."

Sally asked, "Tell us about the code recognition system you've been using."

Sally knew the answer, but the question acted as a good check to see whether she told the truth. Mormino responded to the question with the correct information.

"Tell us about how you communicated with Blake."

I never talked to him in the beginning. Giorgio arranged the details. He asked me to communicate with him only after he arranged everything. If Giorgio wanted to send him a message, he would hand it to me, and I would send it to Blake after we exchanged the authentication codes. Blake rarely originated any messages. The communications were almost always one-way."

Dan asked, "What's the backup plan for communicating if the method you were using became compromised?"

"Giorgio never told me. He said if the authentication code failed, quickly terminate the connection and tell him immediately."

Dan had been trying to decide whether or not to tell her about Giorgio's escape, and thought she might know where he had gone. "Paldinni left the villa during the attack and escaped by boat. Do you know where he might have gone?"

"No I don't, but I know he has a secret hideout. He talked about it once."

Sally asked, "What specifically did he say."

About a year ago, he said he had just acquired it, and if things fell apart, we would be living together in paradise."

Dan asked, "Tell us about your relationship with Paldinni."

Mormino shrugged her shoulders and refused to make eye contact. She hesitated, struggling to find the right words; she was embarrassed. "I guess you could call me his paid escort. He never loved me, and I never loved him, but he paid well."

Dan said, "We found a DHL receipt for a letter sent to Iran. Do you know anything about the letter?"

"I don't know what the letter said, but Giorgio asked me to mail it. I think it was written in Arabic or some other Mideast language. One of the security guards is an Arab. I think he wrote it for him."

"What's the guard's name," Dan asked?

"Kaleb Mohammed."

The interrogation continued for almost two hours. Finally, the door opened and an ROS soldier took Gina Mormino back to the lockup. As they were gathering their tape recorder, Colonel Capinelli entered the room. Dan said, "We would like to speak to one of Paldinni's security Guards."

Capinelli interrupted, "Yes, we overheard the conversation. Unfortunately, he died in the fight."

Capinelli then turned to Sally. "I would like to apologize for my earlier comments. I had no idea you were one of the physicians treating the people in Chicago."

Sally plunged the dagger, "You don't need to apologize to me Colonel; you need to apologize to the families of your soldiers who needlessly lost their lives."

As the final verbal assault pierced the heart of Colonel Capinelli, Dan, Alice, and Sally left the military compound and drove back to Positano.

39

Benny had analyzed his flash drive with the pictures of Paldinni's safe. He found a portion of data showing Paldinni removing what looked like a passport. One frame in particular showed Paldinni opening the document. Benny could almost make out the name of the person below the photo.

Benny called one of his friends in the Washington FBI Office and forwarded the key digitized pictures to be enhanced. Several hours later, the pictures were returned with significantly improved resolution. Benny looked at one picture on the screen and smiled. Paldinni stared at a picture of himself in a fake Italian passport, and the name, now visible on the passport, was Umberto Falvinni.

◻ ◻ ◻

The bus finally arrived in Chicago. Blake took a taxi to the Ogilvie train station and caught the next Metra train to Highland Park. From there he walked the six blocks to his aunt's house. His parents had died when he was very young, and he had been raised by his single aunt. He hadn't seen or talked to her in over four years, but she had been entrusted with a very important document.

He walked to the front door of the small two-bedroom old Victorian house, and rang the doorbell. A shocked Stella McCourtney stood momentarily as recognition set in, and then she threw her arms around her youngest nephew. "I thought I'd never see you again before I left this earth. Where have you been all these years?"

"I've been floating around the world, but I missed you, and thought I would pay you a long overdue visit."

"How long will you be here?"

"I have to leave tomorrow morning."

"Well, you have to stay for dinner and spend the night."

"I'd love to, but first I'd like to take a shower."

"Of course Darrin, and I'm going to fix your favorite dinner."

Darrin followed Stella up the stairs to his old bedroom, and asked, "Aunt Stella, remember the important envelope I gave you for safekeeping four years ago; do you still have it?"

"Of course, Darrin, I keep it right in your nightstand. You'll find it there. And by the way, one of your old friends, I think he said Bill Tucker, came by yesterday looking for you. He said your class was scheduling a reunion and wondered if you could help organize things."

"Oh really, what did you tell him?"

I said I hadn't seen you in years and didn't know how to get in touch with you."

After Stella left to prepare dinner, Darrin Blake sat down on his bed and opened the plain brown envelope. Inside were: a new passport, birth certificate, driver's license, social security card, all in the name of James Massey. Also, an extra key to the car still stored in Aunt Stella's garage, a key to a safe-deposit box, and a stack of one-hundred dollar bills. It was time to assume his new identity, and retire from his mercenary lifestyle after he collected his last fee for operation Big Thunder.

He removed his old high school yearbook from his bookshelf. As expected, he couldn't find Bill Tucker. He now knew this was a visit from the FBI, looking for a way to trace his whereabouts.

After shaving, showering and dressing in clothes he had left in his room four years ago, he walked downstairs and found his aunt preparing one of his favorite meals, fried chicken. He kissed her on the cheek. "It's great seeing you again; I've missed you. I'm going to make a quick trip to the bank. Is my car still working?"

"I start it once a week, like you asked, and it has a full tank of gas."

Blake left his aunt's house and entered the detached garage. His black Jeep Grand Cherokee still looked the same, a little dusty from lack of use, but still as he remembered it. The car started, and he pulled out of the driveway. He made a left turn at the corner, and headed for the downtown area.

He stopped at his old bank and found his high school buddy still sitting at the same desk, doing the same meaningless work year after year. He confirmed a class reunion had not been planned, and his friend had never heard of Bill Tucker. A quick check of Brian's savings account verified he had over one-hundred-thousand dollars with accumulated interest. Most of his fortune was hidden in offshore, well laundered, accounts.

Then, he walked to the bank's basement and entered the safe-deposit box vault. He presented his key and signed in. In the privacy of a small room, he opened the box and removed a Glock nine-millimeter pistol with silencer, shoulder holster, and another stack of one-hundred dollar bills. After closing out his accounts, he left the bank, and returned to his aunt's home, ready to begin his last job and a new life.

¤   ¤   ¤

Sarah's team met again in the waterfront café. Dan played the tape recording of Mormino. Sarah, after listening to Sally's speech, knew she had made the right decision to have Sally help with the interrogation. Sally's description of the horrific effects of the biological agent in Chicago had clearly persuaded Gina Mormino to cooperate.

Benny distributed pictures of Giorgio Paldinni's new identity. "I checked with Interpol and Umberto Falvinni boarded a plane late last night for the island of Martinique.

Sarah explained a CIA operative in Iran had located the recipient of the DHL letter, and after intensive questioning, he admitted to receiving the letter. The man worked for one of Paldinni's munitions companies as their Iranian sales representative. He explained the letter contained another envelope with instructions to mail the second letter at the local post office. He didn't remember the full address, but did remember it was sent to Orlando, Florida.

Sally could only imagine what the term intensive questioning meant and wondered whether the person still lived.

Dan's cellphone interrupted the meeting. Jimmy wanted an update. Dan summarized the events that occurred over the last few hours. After listening to Jimmy for a few minutes the call ended. Dan smiled at the team and said, "Jimmy wants us back. Jacobson and the Director of the CIA have agreed the CIA will pursue Paldinni, and we're going to focus on stopping operation Big Thunder. A plane will be waiting at the Naples Airport to bring us home."

It was more of an emotional departure than Sally would have predicted. Both groups had gained a great deal of respect for the other. Benny said, "Listen, here's the deal; you get that asshole Paldinni and we'll stop operation Big Thunder."

Sarah asked, "Do you want him dead or alive?"

Benny answered, "Personally, I don't give a shit, but if you kill him, make sure it's painful."

Alice smiled and said, "My, my, my, Benny; I thought you weren't in favor of capital punishment."

Benny grinned, "There're always special circumstances."

Sarah's team walked them to the parking lot high above Positano where Nina Bendinni waited in a mini-van. After hugs and kisses all around, the FBI team pulled out onto the road with Nina at the wheel.

The team remained silent during the drive back to the Naples airport, each person contemplating the case and the approach to be used in stopping the next act of terrorism. When they arrived at the restricted hanger at the civilian end of the airport, they thanked Nina.

Once again Sarah's people had handed out the necessary bribes, and they passed through passport control and customs with barely a question.

After clearance from Naples flight control, the Government Gulfstream taxied onto the tarmac, turned onto the end of an active runway, accelerated and lifted gracefully into the afternoon sky. After reaching cruising altitude, the plane headed on a northwesterly course and chased the sun.

Sally had been mulling the problem over and over in her mind, and what spun out at the end of the process made sense.

"So here's what I think operation Big Thunder is all about. We already know the delivery system the bad guys have developed can be camouflaged as fireworks. I guess they could shoot it off anywhere, but the thing is, if it's not part of a fireworks show, then it attracts all kinds of unwanted attention. But if they launch the weapon as part of a fireworks show, then nobody notices anything."

She had the attention of the others now, and they waited expectantly for her bottom line.

She looked at each of them and continued. "Let's assume for a second the person in Iran told the CIA operative the truth. Let's also assume Paldinni still wants to implicate the Iranians in all of this to stoke the fires for another war. He knew we would figure out the e-mails to Ali came from the Iranian terrorist website, and knew we'd be looking there for a message about the next attack. Therefore, he needs another way of sending a message to another Iranian national to force him to plant the weapon against his will. So he sends the letter postmarked from Iran."

She looked around at the others. Dan finally broke the silence. "Where are you going with all this?"

Sally smiled. "Patience Honey, I'm getting there; bear with me. I think the next attack is going to take place in the Orlando area, at a fireworks show, and they need a place that doesn't have a fireworks show once a month or just on the Fourth of July. Nope, they want a fireworks show taking place every night, and one with a lot of people."

Sally looked again at everyone as she reached the punch line. "And that place my friends is Disney World. What better place? It's an American Icon, with tens of thousands of people there each night. It would make one hell of a statement."

She continued, "And here's how I think we can stop them. We look at Disney's payroll and find the names of any employees with Arab names. After all, the letter was written in Arabic. I'm betting there won't be a lot of people on the list. We'll check them all out, and tell each person we talk to the threat in the letter is a fake."

Dan asked, "Why not check out all of the fireworks launchers before each show, or ask Disney World to cancel the shows?"

Sally answered, "We can have people inspect the fireworks before each show, but if we have them cancel the shows, they'll shoot off the weapons somewhere else."

Alice said, "Sally, how can we ever justify not calling off the fireworks shows? If we can't find the weapon and it goes off, thousands of people will die."

"Think about it Alice. Darrin Blake is missing. The weapon may have already been placed and explode before we can find it. If Blake thinks we know where the weapon will be detonated, then he'll shoot it off someplace else, and we won't have a clue where. Our best chance of stopping him is to find it after it's been placed. As soon as we know the location, we can alert people."

Dan had the pilot connect the plane's communication system to Jimmy's office so the entire team could be part of the conversation. Sally reviewed her thoughts with Jimmy and Director Jacobson, who Jimmy pulled into the meeting. They both grasped the logic of Sally's analysis.

Jacobson said, "Sally, if you're right, I'm going to have the President give you a bright shiny gold medal. I'll get the payroll list in a couple of hours. Have the pilot reroute the plane to Orlando, and by the time you arrive we'll have the list filtered for Arab names. I'll also bring in some extra help from the Tampa Field Office. They can focus on working with Disney World management, and begin searching for the weapon while you investigate the Arab names on the list.

After the call, the pilot contacted Air Traffic Control and rerouted the plane into Orlando.

◘   ◘   ◘

Darrin Blake left his aunt's home after two wonderful meals. He had forgotten how much he loved her fried chicken, and the blueberry pancakes for breakfast brought back wonderful memories. They had talked well into the night about old times. He realized it would probably be the last time he saw her alive, and she too must have recognized the timeliness of his arrival as a last chance to revisit wonderful memories. After breakfast Darrin gave his surrogate mother a long almost pleading hug and kiss, and with tears in his eyes, he left his childhood home for the last time.

As he drove the twenty-one hours to Orlando, he couldn't help but think of this last job, and what his life would be like after he received the final payment.

He remembered the first contact with a man representing the mystery employer. He would be asked to do some bad things, the work lasting about four months; and if successfully completed, he would receive in total almost five million dollars.

At first, he failed to believe the messenger, but after receiving an advanced payment of one million dollars, he knew the job was for real. The overall plan had been spelled out in a letter handed to him after he accepted the offer. He understood the importance of the attacks being blamed on the Iranian Government, and he received the names and addresses of the scapegoats to be used for the two attacks.

After receiving the final biological agents from the two scientists, he had brought them to a storage facility outside Orlando, where he had completed the final assembly of the weapons inside his private storage shed. The purchase of the fireworks launching systems and skyrockets had been completed with relative ease. It had all been spelled out in the instructions he received. The glass spheres containing the biological agents had been specifically designed to attach to the top of each skyrocket.

He decided to drive to Orlando rather than take an airplane. If he was being followed by the FBI, most airports and train stations would surely be monitored for his presence.

He planned to drive straight through. There would be no time for an extra night at an out of the way hotel, not with this tight schedule. Allowing for several rest stops and meals, he figured he would arrive in Orlando early the next day. One more day, one more murder, one more job to complete, and then his life of peace and freedom could begin.

He arrived at the Orlando storage facility a little after ten o'clock. He entered his password into the security system at the front gate, and drove to his storage shed. He entered the three code numbers, and unlocked the door to the locker where the assembled weapons were stored. He lifted the door, turned on the lights, and lowered the door behind him.

He assembled the sixteen cardboard boxes and used a box cutter to remove the top of each box. After attaching a fresh battery to each base and turning on the timer, he set the scheduled launch time and lowered each launch system into an assembled box. He carefully attached wires from the skyrocket to the ignition system at the bottom of the launch tube and slowly slipped each weapon down into its launch tube.

He now needed to exercise extreme caution. Each weapon had been armed and any stray electrical spark or discharge could instantly end his future retirement plans.

Using a roll of Kraft paper, he cut out two foot squares and sealed the paper to the top of each box with duct tape. Then, using a black magic marker, he added the *this side up* text to the top of every box and added directional arrows on the sides.

Blake let out a sigh of relief. He had completed the assembly of the weapons without problems. He opened the shed's door and backed his SUV partway into the storage locker. It took ten minutes to load and secure the sixteen biological weapons in the back of his car. After locking the shed, he carefully drove out of the facility and headed for the drop-off point. He exercised extreme caution. Getting into an accident now would certainly result in an agonizing death, and he had no desire to see a premature end to his bright future.

Unlike the last attack, this plan called for him to deliver the weapons in broad daylight. His employer had carefully chosen the exchange point, an abandoned rundown home located on a deserted road twenty miles from Disney World.

He arrived an hour earlier than scheduled, unloaded the weapons, and placed them outside the house's half-demolished garage. The sixteen weapons, exact clones of the one used in Chicago, waited for their new custodian to take possession.

He left the garage and parked his car one mile away in a deserted area off of an unused side road. He had found this hidden spot when he visited the exchange point several months ago. He knew a wooded area overlooked the garage, and he could hide there and confirm the pickup of the weapons.

After walking back to the shack, he sat down on a dead log in the middle of the woods, and waited for the arrival of the unfortunate person who would be delivering the weapon to its final destination.

Shortly after two o'clock, a dark green SUV appeared on the road leading to the old shack. The car stopped in front of the garage and a middle-aged man exited the car and cautiously approached the building. He looked around the dilapidated old structure checking for witnesses and then looked carefully at the sixteen boxes. He obviously knew nothing about their true contents but correctly assumed the worst. He walked around the cardboard boxes, trying to determine their purpose but without success. Once again he scanned the area, looking at the woods, but not paying particular attention to the heavily wooded area where Blake waited.

He reached down and carefully lifted one box, testing its weight. Seeing the box weighed no more than twenty pounds, he walked back to his car and lifted the rear hatch. He then returned to the weapons and began loading all sixteen into the back of his SUV. Blake had deliberately left the tie down straps he had used to secure the weapons in his own car and the man clearly understood their purpose. He also used them to secure the boxes in his car.

After closing the back hatch, the man started the car and slowly drove away from the shack. Blake felt relief after the man picked up the boxes, because the fallback plan called for Blake himself to deliver the weapons, and he knew the backup plan would have been a dangerous assignment. Blake waited a few minutes and walked back to his own car. His work had almost been completed, and he decided to stop for a late lunch at a nearby restaurant. So far, everything had gone exactly as planned.

¤   ¤   ¤

Ahmed al-Hakim had lived in the United States for almost ten years. Having escaped from Iran after the last uprising, he had been granted political asylum. He had embraced his new country with a fervor typical of many new immigrants, and then the letter had arrived from Iran. He didn't doubt its authenticity for a minute. The names of his immediate family and other relatives along with their addresses and telephone numbers were proof enough.

Clearly, whoever sent the letter meant exactly what they said. They would kill every one of them if he didn't follow their instructions. He considered going to the FBI, but the letter said he would be monitored and observed, and any contact with the authorities would result in his family's immediate death.

He carefully followed the letter's instructions and had no idea what evil might be inside the sixteen boxes, but knew it must be something terrible. Yet if he had to sacrifice his own life in order to save his family, he would. Tears flowed down his cheek as he drove his car toward Disney World.

His job as a mechanic allowed him access to most of the park, where he repaired anything mechanical. He entered the grounds of the theme park through the employee entrance, drove along

Floridian Way, and passed the Grand Floridian Hotel.

He turned onto a narrow access road, almost hidden from view, leading off to the right alongside the Seven Seas Lagoon. The gravel road followed the lagoon as it worked its way northeast.

The previous day, Ahmed had taken a small raft from the dock area claiming it needed maintenance. He had left it at a small wooden boat landing, partially hidden by a grouping of mangrove trees. As his car approached the landing, he thankfully spotted the boat still waiting at the wooden dock.

He stopped the car by the dock and looked around for anyone within sight. In the distance, small racing boats rented by the park's visitors raced across the lagoon, their passengers enjoying the beauty of the summer day, totally oblivious to what was about to happen. He carefully transferred the sixteen cardboard boxes onto the raft and started the boat's engine. He freed the raft from the dock and steered out into the lagoon. He followed the shoreline until it intersected with a narrow canal leading north toward the amusement rides.

This section of the canal was not visible from the park, and Ahmed progressed slowly toward his ultimate objective, a small dock near the Big Thunder Mountain Railroad ride. As instructed in the letter, he left the boat tied to the dock and walked to a seldom used maintenance doorway under the ride. He disappeared inside the mountain into the underground labyrinth used by hundreds of employees as they kept the rides functioning and the visitors happy. Using the underground passageways, he then worked his way back to his car and drove to the employee parking lot. He reported to work a few hours late, using car trouble as the excuse.

40

An hour before their plane landed at Orlando International airport, Jimmy e-mailed them a list of three men and one woman with Arab names. They decided to split the team and divide the list between them, each team taking two employees.

They loaded their belongings into two SUVs reserved by Jimmy and headed for the people, who at this point were their primary and only leads. Sally entered the first person's address into the car's navigation system, and Dan followed it's instructions. They had no idea about these employees' work shifts, and so they could be anywhere.

Sally stared at a large digital clock near the airport's exit. Six o'clock; time was running short. They arrived at an apartment complex in the town of Windsor Hills, a small working class community. Amir Muusa, the first person on their list, lived in Unit # 2310. They rang the doorbell to his second floor apartment, and a young boy appeared. The three year old could barely open the door. As it opened, a young man, in his early thirties, shooed the boy away and asked his unexpected guests to enter.

Sally and Dan stood just inside the door and showed the man their FBI identification. The man's expression instantly became rigid and questioning. Dan took the lead. "We're sorry to bother you with this visit Mr. Muusa, but we have a very urgent situation."

Amir's wife poked her head out of the kitchen and her husband explained the visitors were with the FBI. She sat down next to Amir on the living room couch and gripped his hand tightly.

Dan started, "The recent biological agent attack in Chicago was the work of terrorists. What you probably don't know is the people who did this are trying to make it look like the attacks were executed by the Iranian Government."

Amir and his wife listened to the story. They moved closer together and held each other more tightly.

Dan continued to explain the facts concerning Giorgio Paldinni and operation Big Thunder. "The problem we have now is the remaining amount of biological agent has been assembled into a weapon and we believe the bomb is going to be set off in Disney World in the next few days. We're contacting all of the Disney employees with Arabic names to warn them of what is happening. We believe these terrorists will try to do the same thing, and they may have written a letter saying they will kill the person's family if they don't cooperate."

Amir's wife said, "Are you accusing us?"

Dan answered, "Absolutely not, but we feel obligated to explain the situation to everyone, so if they receive a letter demanding cooperation, the person will know it's not authentic and even if they follow the instructions, they will still be killed."

Amir carefully considered his answer, "We are not the person you are looking for. My wife and I don't have any family still living in Iran or any Arab country for that matter."

Sally asked, "Are any of your Arab friends acting strangely?"

Amir answered, "My wife and I keep to ourselves, and all of our friends are Americans. You have to understand, we don't consider ourselves Arabs living here. We are Americans; we're both citizens."

Sally and Dan were convinced Amir Muusa couldn't be the person they were looking for. Dan handed Amir a business card and asked him to call the cellphone number if he thought of anything important, or if he received a letter from Iran.

Sally and Dan regrouped outside the apartment complex, and Sally entered the address of Ahmed al-Hakim into the navigation system. He lived in an area called Summerport Beach, and it appeared the ride there would take about thirty minutes.

¤   ¤   ¤

Ahmed had spent the rest of the day working in a near comatose state. He wanted to finish his work and leave the park as quickly as possible. He had been thinking about what might be inside the boxes all afternoon. He didn't believe they were bombs. Why put bombs in sixteen different boxes? It made no sense, but he knew the boxes were trouble. Why else would the Iranian Government have gone to all of the trouble of writing the letter and doing all of the preparations? After wrestling with the problem for the remainder of the day, he knew it was beyond his ability to understand, so he gave up trying.

He punched out of work at seven o'clock and began his drive home. He barely heard the radio, and accidently ran three stop signs before he finally reached the highway. He finally arrived at his four-flat on a quiet street overlooking a small lake. He parked his car on the street, and walked to his front door.

Dan and Sally had arrived in the neighborhood about the same time as Ahmed. As they located the correct address, they noticed a man leave his car and walk to the front door. He entered the house, the same house they were looking for. They hoped it was Ahmed. They left their car and approached the small home.

Ahmed had picked up the day's mail from the mailbox outside his apartment and began separating bills from junk mail at the kitchen table. He never noticed the shadow move silently across the room. Finally sensing something, Ahmed looked up as Blake fired two shots. The first hit Ahmed in the side of his face, passing through his mouth and exiting through his other cheek. The second hit him in the forehead and lodged in his brain.

Dan heard the muffled popping sounds and recognized them for what they were, a silenced pistol firing two shots. He pulled Sally away from the sidewalk leading to the front door, and dialed Alice's cellphone number after pulling out his holstered pistol. Alice answered on the second ring. Dan said, "I've got two silenced pistol shots coming from Ahmed al-Hakim's apartment. Call in backup. We're going in now."

Dan turned to Sally and said, "Here's the plan. While I wait here, I want you to see if there's a backdoor. If there is, you wait there, and shoot Blake if he tries to leave. If there isn't, then come back and cover my entrance. If you're not back in two minutes, I'll assume you're staying there. Don't let him get away under any circumstances."

Sally understood Dan's plan, and she moved to the left and around to the back of the property. A swimming pool, centered in the back of the four-flat, could be accessed from sliding doors at the rear of each unit. Sally took note of the correct door and positioned herself behind a gas-fired pool heater. It provided meager protection, but it would have to suffice. She drew her pistol and disengaged the safety. She held the gun with two hands, steadying it on the top of the heater.

After waiting two minutes, Dan walked up cautiously to the front door and rang the doorbell. He waited thirty seconds and rang the bell again. He moved to the side of the door, protected by a thick stucco wall and shouted, "FBI! Open the door now."

Blake heard the doorbell and realized escaping from this murder scene would not be as easy as he originally thought. At first, he figured it might just be a friend of Ahmed, but when he heard the words FBI, he reacted instantly. He ran to the sliding glass door at the back of the apartment, looked outside, and not seeing anyone, decided to chance escaping from the rear of the building.

As he slid the door aside and stepped out onto the lanai, Sally fired two shots in rapid succession. The first struck his left arm and passed cleanly through. The second grazed his left side.

As Sally fired her shots, Dan kicked in the front door, spotted Blake at the rear of the apartment, rolled to his left and came up firing while Blake also fired at Dan's moving body.

Two bullets from Blake's gun whizzed past Dan's head. He could feel the heat as they touched his skin. Dan immediately rolled again to his left and positioned himself behind a living room couch.

Darrin Blake, bleeding from Sally's shots and slightly grazed by one of Dan's bullets, backed into the kitchen and locked the sliding glass door leading out to the pool. He hid behind a large island in the center of the kitchen. Blake stared at the blood flowing from his left arm. He reached under the kitchen sink and found a towel. He made a makeshift tourniquet and the bleeding slowed to a trickle. Luckily, his shooting arm was unaffected. Positioning himself near the oven, he had a perfect view of the agent hiding behind the sofa, as well as the backdoor.

He sat there, trying to collect his thoughts. There were probably only two agents. They had obviously come to talk to al-Hakim, and had arrived at a most inopportune time.

He tried to anticipate the agents next steps. They probably had already called in for reinforcements, so he might have as long as twenty minutes before he was vastly outnumbered. He needed an escape plan, and he needed to act on it in the next few minutes.

He looked out the sliding backdoor and couldn't see the FBI agent guarding his escape route, but knew he'd be out there, hiding behind some cover just waiting for him to try to run out into the backyard. He didn't dare risk moving closer to the backdoor to try to locate the agent; he'd only expose himself to the other agent waiting in the living room.

Dan, knowing Blake was trapped in the kitchen called Sally on his cellphone. He whispered, "He's hiding in the kitchen behind the island. I see blood on the floor, so I know he's wounded."

Sally, kneeling behind the pool heater, said, "Let's wait till the others get here. Then we'll outnumber him five to one."

"We can't; he killed al-Hakim; that means the weapon's already in play. We need to get Blake now, so we can find the weapon. We've got to risk taking him now. On the count of three, you start firing through the backdoor. At the same time, I'll rush him from the living room."

"No, too risky; I have a better idea."

Sally knew as an elite Army Ranger, Blake would be well trained in dealing with diversionary tactics. They needed to use an unexpected approach, something he would never anticipate.

She had studied the pool area and noticed the unusual way the four-flat was designed. The four attached homes shared a common second floor balcony overlooking the pool, and each unit had a sliding glass door leading out to the balcony. Sally assumed these doors would lead to the master bedrooms, and the door to al-Hakim's second floor bedroom looked open with only a sliding screen door protecting the house from unwanted bugs and other animals. Sally explained her plan to Dan.

"I like it;" he said, "let's do it; let me know when you're in position."

Sally crept out from behind the pool heater and ran in a low crouch to al-Hakim's next-door neighbor. She knocked loudly on the backdoor and pressed her FBI credentials against the glass. A middle-aged woman approached the door, looked suspiciously at Sally's badge, and finally opened the door.

"I'm sorry to bother you, but I need your help. A terrorist shot Mr. al-Hakim next-door, and I want to enter his house from the second floor balcony."

"You said what? Ahmed is dead?"

"Yes, the killer is inside his house now, and I need to get onto the second floor balcony."

The woman led the way up the stairs to the second floor and her master bedroom and then to the sliding door leading out onto the balcony.

As Sally opened the glass door, she said, "Please call the police and tell them the FBI needs their help."

The woman left to make the call as Sally stepped outside onto the narrow concrete walkway. A flimsy privacy screen separated the two houses. Sally climbed up onto the railing and carefully slipped past the screen onto al-Hakim's balcony.

Luckily, his screen door was unlocked. She slid the door open and silently advanced through the bedroom and out into the upstairs' hallway. Advancing slowly down the stairs, she spotted Dan behind the couch. He saw her and signaled her with a thumb up.

Sally returned to the top of the stairs and lay down in the upper hallway with her head just visible from the living room. She called Dan on his cellphone.

He answered his phone and with a voice loud enough for Blake to hear, said, "Right; move more agents to the backyard; I'm coming out the front door; don't shoot."

Dan then quickly opened the front door, slamming the door behind him.

Hearing the phone call, Blake repositioned himself so he could see a reflection of the front door in a family room mirror. He saw Dan leave the house and knew both front and rear escape routes were blocked. He crawled out into the living room, wanting to get a look at how many agents were now in the front yard.

Sally gripped her pistol with both hands and aimed it at the front door. She saw Blake crawling to the front of the house. She had never killed anyone in her life. Nevertheless, Sally adjusted her gun so it was pointed to the midsection of Blake's body.

Her finger pulled back on the trigger. She hesitated, weighing the Hippocratic Oath she had taken against the need to save many lives. Then she thought of the Morgan family and made her decision.

The shot rang out, and Darrin Blake's body twisted around as he tried to locate the source of the unexpected shot. Reeling from the effects of Sally's first shot, he tried to respond, but he failed to look up the stairs to where she lay on the floor.

Sally fired a second shot, striking Blake directly over his heart.

Hearing the two shots in quick succession, Dan rushed through the front door with his gun ready, not knowing what to expect. He saw Darrin Blake lying unconscious, mortally wounded and near death. Dan moved to his body and kicked his gun away.

Sally sat at the top of the stairs, tears streaming down her face. Her body shook as Dan lifted her into his arms and held her tightly.

"I couldn't pull the trigger and then I thought of the Morgans. I guess it was revenge and I feel ashamed."

Dan continued to hold her until Sally stopped trembling. He then lifted her face toward his and kissed her gently on the lips.

"I'm okay now;" she said, "call Jimmy; we've got to find the weapon."

Dan made the call. "Jimmy, listen carefully. Blake's dead. He just murdered Ahmed al-Hakim. Sally and I are al Hakim's apartment right now. Call an immediate evacuation of Disney World. I'm certain the weapon is already placed and is going to go off tonight during the fireworks show. I'll call Alice, and we'll help look for the weapon."

Jimmy answered, "Will do Dan. The first fireworks show is scheduled for nine o'clock."

Sally and Dan ran from the house as the residents of the neighborhood gathered outside Ahmed's house. Sally approached the next-door neighbor and asked her to explain what happened to the police when they arrived. She handed the lady a business card and then ran to their car.

They sped off at breakneck speed toward Disney World. As Dan drove, Sally called Alice and explained what had just happened and instructed her to meet them at the theme park.

She then called Jimmy and said, "Jimmy, I want you to connect me to the person in charge at Disney World. We need to have help in entering the park without being caught in a traffic jam."

Jimmy told her to hold on while he conferenced with the park manager. It took only a minute for the manager to get on the line. Sally explained her concern. The manager asked, "Where are you now?"

"Just leaving Summerport Beach."

"Do you have a navigation system?"

Sally answered yes, and the manager gave her the address of an employee entrance at the north end of the park. He told her he would meet them at the entrance. Sally asked him to bring several maps of the park to help them search for the weapon.

Sally asked, "Where are the other FBI agents now?"

"They've stationed themselves near the locations where the fireworks are launched. My senior staff is helping them look for the weapon."

Sally asked, "Can you look up one of your employees, an Ahmed al-Hakim. I want to know what his job is at the park."

Several long minutes of silence followed before the manager came back on the line. "He's a general mechanic. He's responsible for the maintenance and repair of rides and equipment."

"Would the job give him access to the entire park?"

"Yes, he is authorized to go everywhere."

"Thanks we'll see you in a few minutes."

Sally called Alice and explained the new meeting point. Dan, without the use of a police siren, pushed the limits. He moved onto the shoulder of roads when they were in heavy traffic, and shot through intersections with a liberal use of the car's horn. As they neared the park, the road became clogged with cars fleeing from the unknown terror.

Dan looked at the bottleneck ahead and pulled the SUV off the road into an orange grove.

Sally, looking at the navigation screen, told him to cut diagonally across the expansive orchard. Dan guided his car between the fruit trees as he raced down a long line of ripening citrus. At the end of the row, he turned sharply to the right and rushed toward the far corner of the field. The car bounced high into the air as the tires struck obstacles in its path. Without seatbelts Sally would have been catapulted into the roof of the car. As it was, she almost lost a few teeth as the car slammed into the dirt and her lower jaw smacked into her chest. Outbound cars were using both sides of the two-lane road. With his horn blaring loudly, Dan wedged his way through a procession of cars and moved back onto the shoulder of the road.

They were now only a half mile from the meeting point. Dan leaned on his horn as they approached the employee entrance, but cars were lined up blocking the gate. Sally jumped out of the car and ran toward the blockage. She pulled out her FBI badge and ordered cars blocking the gate to move to the side. They were reluctant to obey. Against her better judgment, she pulled out her gun, making sure she engaged the safety, and her reinforced message got the cars to move off the road, giving enough room for Dan to squeeze the SUV through the point of congestion.

Sally got back in the car and Dan headed toward the proposed meeting point. A small group of people waiting at an employee checkpoint had a managerial look about them. Dan braked the car to a sudden stop, and they both ran up to the group. A man stepped to the front and asked, "FBI?"

Dan answered, "Yes!"

The man shook his hand and introduced himself. "I'm Marty Olsen, the Managing Director of the theme park."

He laid out a large map of the park on the SUV's hood. "I've circled all of the fireworks launch sites. We have our managers assisting some FBI agents looking for the weapon. They arrived about two hours ago, but haven't found anything yet."

Sally said, "Marty, tell us about where the people usually congregate to watch the show."

In the Magic Kingdom, they tend to congregate by Cinderella's castle and at Epcot Center, around the lake."

Alice's car screeched to a stop near the group and Benny, Brian, and Alice joined them. Dan said, "We need to split up. Marty, I want you to assign one of your people to work with each of us. Three of us will go to Epcot and two will focus on the Magic Kingdom.

Sally said, "Marty, I want one of your people to go to your infirmary and get as many facemasks as they can find. Pass them out to everyone in the park. I'm assuming if a there's a sky-burst it won't be from the fireworks display but the weapons we're trying to find. If there is a sky-burst everybody needs to get inside as quickly as possible."

Olsen said, "Underground tunnels run everywhere in the park. Is that the best place to take cover?"

Sally asked, "Is the air filtered through HEPA filters?"

The head of maintenance answered, "Yes, we have HEPA filters everywhere."

"Good," Sally said, "the anthrax won't get past the HEPA filters, so the tunnels are absolutely the best place to hide if the bombs go off."

Sally teamed up with Bill Munsen, a balding middle-aged calm looking man. Dan split the Magic Kingdom down the middle. He would cover the east side and Sally the west.

Sally looked at her watch. Forty-seven minutes until the beginning of the just cancelled fireworks show. She examined the map with Bill looking over her shoulder. Forty-seven minutes, dozens of rides, dozens of shops, and seemingly hundreds of small kiosks. You didn't need to be an expert to understand the math didn't work out in their favor. There wasn't enough time to check even a few of the possible hiding places in the span of forty-seven minutes. She needed to consider a different approach.

She turned to Munsen and said, "Bill, I'm assuming the park has surveillance cameras all over the place. Is there a central location for all of the monitors?"

Bill pointed to an area inside the employee entrance. "It's located over there."

"When Hakim came to work, would he have been checked in at the employee entrance?"

"Yes, he would have checked in at the employee gate, and then again at the Maintenance Department where he worked."

"Can you find out the times he checked in today?"

Bill led the way as they ran to the security building. Bill used a pass key to enter the main monitoring room. While he sat at a computer looking up Ahmed al-Hakim's timecard database, Sally looked at the hundreds of surveillance cameras around the park. Cars were still streaming out of the area like a herd of stampeding cattle. The park looked mostly deserted except for the senior staff and a few FBI agents, who were searching for the weapon. Would they find it? They were almost out of time.

Bill interrupted her thoughts, "He checked in at the South Gate at 1:35 P.M., and checked in at the Maintenance Department at 2:56 P.M."

Sally did the math. "So he spent one hour and twenty-one minutes doing something, and we can assume he placed the bomb. Can we look back at the surveillance camera at the South Gate when he checked in and follow him? I saw his car today. He had a dark-green SUV."

Bill moved to a central computer system and looked up a list of cameras on a sheet of paper. He entered a number and hooked into the Camera at the South Gate. He entered some commands and the image on the screen changed. A clock in the lower right-hand corner of the screen read 1:35 P.M. A dark-green SUV checked in with the guard stationed at the gate. "That's the car," Sally said, "Can you follow it with other cameras?"

Bill checked his list, entered a new number and time and an image looking north along Floridian Way appeared on the screen. Hakim's car moved north along the road. Bill fast forwarded the pictures until the car left the screen. He then switched cameras and picked up the SUV with the next camera. Sally said, "You seem to be an expert on the use of the system."

"I should be," he said, "I managed the project to upgrade our surveillance system last year."

Bill kept changing cameras, following the dark-green SUV as it moved north along Floridian

Way. It turned right onto a narrow road. Sally asked, "What's along the road?"

"Nothing," Bill answered, "it follows the north side of the Seven Seas Lagoon."

Bill fast forwarded the camera and returned to normal speed when the SUV stopped alongside a small wooden dock. Although the car had moved almost out of range of the camera, they were still able to see al-Hakim transfer what looked like boxes, sixteen of them, from his car to what looked like a small raft.

"What's that," Sally asked?

"It's one of our Tom Sawyer rafts."

After loading the raft, Hakim steered the small barge-like boat along the lagoons northern shore until it intersected with a small canal leading north. The raft turned into the canal and moved out of sight. Bill tried to change cameras but finally concluded no camera covered the canal.

Sally asked, "Where does the canal lead?"

"It goes around the Big Thunder Mountain Railway ride."

"Oh shit," Sally screamed, "operation Big Thunder. How could I be so stupid?"

She called Dan. "Go to the Big Thunder Mountain Railway ride. I've been looking at a surveillance camera of Hakim on a boat from this afternoon. Sixteen weapons are being moved along a canal leading to the ride."

Dan understood the significance of the name of the ride. He said, "We're on our way. I'll call the others."

Sally turned to Bill. "We need a boat to see what happened to the raft."

Bill changed surveillance cameras and after more scanning said, "The closet place is at the

Grand Floridian Resort and Spa Hotel. There're some small speedboats at the hotel's dock."

Bill drove his car. Twenty-two minutes left. Sally did some quick calculations in her head and concluded they would have no more than five minutes to disarm the weapons, if they were lucky. "Faster Bill," she said, "We're probably going to have only a few minutes to disarm the weapons if they're located along the canal, and I'm going to need your help. Are you up to it?"

"Lady, I served as a marine in Desert Storm. I don't know anything about bombs except they hurt people, but I'll do anything I can to help. Tell me what to do, and I'll do it."

The Grand Floridian Resort and Spa looked strangely empty. Bill drove to the north end of the hotel, crashed his car through two closed gates and screeched to a stop near the boat dock. They both ran from the car and jumped onto a boat at the end of the pier. The key was missing. Bob said, "Wait here."

He raced to a cabana near the boat dock and returned with a handful of keys. The fourth key started the boat's motor. Sally threw the two mooring lines onto the dock and Bill pushed the small speedboat's throttle to the limit. Within thirty feet the boat rode up on its plane and accelerated toward the canal.

As they approached the north end of the lagoon, Bill spotted the narrow canal leading to Big Thunder Mountain and slowed down prior to entering the narrow opening. The speedboat slammed against a steep bank, straightened out and then continued along the canal.

The clock on the boat showed ten minutes before the fireworks show had been scheduled to start. If she were Blake, she would have wanted the weapons to launch during the middle of the fireworks show. She figured they might have an extra fifteen minutes, but she couldn't be sure.

As Bill maneuvered the boat along the winding canal, it lurched from side to side as it periodically struck glancing blows against the raised banks. The canal cut off to the right, and in the distance, Sally could see Big Thunder Mountain. Bill accelerated the boat in the straightaway, and after the canal again broke off to the right, Sally saw Tom Sawyer's raft jutting out from a small wooden dock alongside Big Thunder Mountain.

Bill docked the boat alongside the raft and shut down the motor. Sally jumped onto the raft before the boat stopped. Her mind raced as she inspected the cardboard boxes. The top of the boxes were sealed with lightweight Kraft paper. She stopped to consider the problem. The launch tubes were obviously inside each box, and each must contain its own electronic timing device to ignite the fuses. She asked Bill if he had a pocket knife. Bill produced a small knife saying, "No good Marine would be without one."

Sally stood above the nearest box and carefully cut away the Kraft paper. In the early evening darkness she could see a launching tube and inside the tube a glass spherically shaped ball containing the biological agent. She had never seen fireworks of this type, but could imagine there must be an electronic ignition system, and wires leading to the skyrocket to launch the glass sphere containing the agent, and then another timed charge to disperse the anthrax when the rocket reached the highpoint of its trajectory.

She thought about how the device was assembled and concluded the weapon must have been lowered into the launch tube as the last step in the assembly process. She knew what needed to be done.

"Bill help me turnover the box. The weapon should then slide out of the launch tube, and we can cut the wires leading to the ignition system."

Bill held the opened box and slowly turned it upside-down to let Sally catch the weapon. After completely inverting the box, the skyrocket slowly slipped away from the launch tube. It only weighed about ten pounds, but Sally cradled it as if it weighed four times as much. She carefully set it down on the raft after Bill cut two wires leading to the ignition system with his pocketknife.

They had officially run out of time. It was now a question of how much extra time Blake had allowed. Bill began cutting off the Kraft paper from the other fifteen boxes while Sally turned each box carefully on its side. Then Bill inverted each box while Sally caught every device. They worked as fast as they could, but each device still took thirty seconds to disarm. They needed six more minutes, and the question remained whether Blake had delayed the launches by enough time.

Bill cut the last two wires and laughed. "Holy shit, we did it."

Sally gave him a big hug, arranged the devices on the raft, and sat down next to Bill. She called Dan. "Honey, it's over; we've disarmed the bombs. Bill's going to tell you how to find us. It's all over. I'll tell you all about it when you get here."

She handed the phone to Bill and he spoke to one of the other senior staff members, giving them directions to their location.

Sally stared at the sixteen weapons, each containing enough genetically modified anthrax to kill tens of thousands of people. She thought of Giorgio Paldinni, and hoped the CIA team would be able to track him down.

Bill looked at her with a broad smile. "You're one hell of a lady. If I'm ever in another war, I want you at my side."

"You ain't so bad yourself dude. I don't know if I was more terrified of the anthrax or the way you drove the speedboat."

She gave him a high-five as Dan and the others began arriving at the scene. Dan called Jimmy and updated him, and he promised to get the word to Jacobson and the President as soon as possible.

The biological weapons were moved from the raft to a safe location, where custody would then be transferred to an FBI bomb squad being helicoptered in from Miami.

The Disney World staff looked on with relief and a growing understanding of their ultimate fate had the weapons exploded.

Jimmy wanted the group to return to Washington as soon as possible, and as they said their goodbyes to the Disney people, Sally pulled Bill Munsen aside and asked him for a favor. They exchanged some words and then Bill handed Sally something not visible to Dan.

¤   ¤   ¤

The flight to Washington on the Government jet became a party. The pilots joked it was the first time they had ever run out of champagne. The celebration would continue well into the night.

Dan asked Sally about her talk with Bill Munsen. She reached in her pocket and pulled out a small pocketknife. She showed it to Dan. "This little knife saved our lives. If it hadn't been for this, it would have taken another couple of minutes to open the boxes and cut the wires and we would have lost the race. I'm going to ask Director Jacobson to have it gilded and sent back to Bill on a plaque with a thank you letter from the President."

Dan laughed and kissed her lightly on the cheek. "That's why I love you so much. It's your sense of always doing a little extra."

Sally then turned serious. "You know, I met a lot of heroes on this little adventure, but two stand out above all the others. First is Mayor Dobbins. He made an incredibly courageous decision to be totally honest with the people of Chicago. The people believed him and didn't panic, and that alone saved thousands of lives. And then there was this woman I told you about, Mrs. Morgan. I never knew her first name. Her husband was the first person to be admitted to the hospital.

He died and I thought she would too, but her two children needed her help, and so she fought the disease with an unbelievable determination. Somehow, with maybe help from above, she survived. She inspired me to be the best I could be during those difficult couple of days. Whenever I felt overwhelmed and down in the dumps, I walked by her bed and saw her determination to live, and then I would find the courage to continue. When we get back to Chicago, I'm going to talk to her and personally thank her for what she did."

Epilogue

Giorgio Paldinni had been born into wealth. His grandfather had started a munitions factory prior to World War II, and the war made him a wealthy man. By the time Giorgio's father inherited the business, the Paldinni Empire had grown both in size and power. Giorgio, the eldest of three children, took over the family business and began to diversify into advanced weapons technology.

The Cold War and the formation of NATO allowed his businesses to flourish, and Paldinni, who never married, became one of the wealthiest industrialists in Italy. His reputation for being both cunning and ruthless became well-known.

In the 1990s, Giorgio, and a few of his closest friends, formed NewTech Capital and began investing heavily in advanced military industrial technologies. Recent wars convinced him small nations were not capable of advanced weapon development, and biological weapons would become their future weapon of choice.

Eventually the work of Genccine came to his attention. He correctly understood the potential opportunity in preparing defenses against biological weapons, and saw how Genccine's proprietary technology could be the answer to the problem of rapid scale up of vaccines needed to combat the threat of biological agents. NewTech Capital had consequently invested heavily in Genccine.

Iran renouncing its nuclear weapons program and the financial collapse of North Korea had a significant negative effect on his business activities. World peace would bankrupt his companies, and he would face financial ruin.

One evening after talking to Rod Demming and finding out about the Plum Island business opportunity, he devised a daring plan. As one of the conditions for NewTech providing the additional capital to expand Genccine, Paldinni insisted on taking personal responsibility for the initial interviewing of all scientific hires. This request seemed reasonable to Demming since he would still be making the final hiring decisions. He agreed to the deal and an additional one-hundred million dollars was made available to Genccine.

It took less than six months to find two Muslim scientists who were affiliated with a known radical Islamist Masque. His Muslim security guard convinced them to manufacture the biological agents, believing they would be used against their archenemy Israel.

Finding Crawford had been a stroke of luck. He had a reputation as a good scientist, but a background check revealed he was in debt for over two-hundred-thousand dollars to a Las

Vegas bookie. The offer of one-million dollars became too good for him to pass up.

The easiest part of the plan had been the hiring of Blake. People working within the secret world of the black-market weapons industry knew Blake well; and his reputation as a person who would do anything for the right price, led to a quick agreement.

The first phase of his grand plan had gone exactly as predicted. Demming had already called to inform him of the preliminary discussions with the Pentagon and their desire to purchase two-hundred-million doses at a price of eight dollars per dose. Demming had also told him about the FBI's recent visit, and he knew they would discover the burned factory and determine the Muslims had a connection to Iran.

Their conclusion would be obvious; Iran had organized this act of terror, an act of war. He knew from experience that another global conflict would soon breakout, and all of his companies would once again be profitable.

He still couldn't comprehend what had gone wrong with his plan, and he doubted he would ever be able to solve the mystery. At this point, however, he knew he would now live in comfort for the rest of his life.

Umberto Falvinni, aka Giorgio Paldinni, had planned his escape with consideration of every detail. Laundered money removed over many years from a variety of his shell companies, had been used to buy a beautiful villa high on a hill overlooking the Caribbean Sea. His new identity had been crafted by a variety of skilled experts.

What he had not counted on was a chance picture being taken by his own cameras showing his passport picture with his new name. It took

Sarah Barker's CIA team a week to locate his villa, and the team had drawn straws to determine who would do the honors.

Beth had won the opportunity, and now stood outside the new home of Giorgio Paldinni. With the help of Rich Gibbons, she had been able to circumvent the villa's security system, and now she stood facing Paldinni as he slept peacefully in his bed. She removed a wire garrote from her pocket and carefully slipped it around Paldinni's neck, rousing him from a deep sleep. He awoke to the sudden tightening of the death wire. His eyes bulged as he tried unsuccessfully to gasp for air.

Beth looked into his terrified eyes and said, "This is for the people of Chicago!"

These were the last words Giorgio Paldinni heard.

¤   ¤   ¤

It took over two months for the hospital to return to normal. Sally finally found time to fulfill a promise she made to herself.

She drove into the once quarantined area. The decontamination efforts by the army had been successful, but at a terrible cost. The streets were turned into a lifeless state. Trees were without leaves and dying; grass and plants totally destroyed; the exterior of houses instantly aged from the use of the toxic chemicals.

One block from ground zero, Sally parked her car and looked at the empty street. No children playing; no residents walking their dogs; just a horrific sense of emptiness and despair. Mayor Dobbins, knowing full well that Chicagoans would never be willing to buy a home in this section of the city again, was planning on demolishing the homes and converting the entire area into a memorial park. Sally had to agree, nobody in their right mind would ever want to live here again.

She left her car and walked up to the front door of Ruby Morgan's house. The eldest child answered the door, followed closely by the youngest, who had just learned how to walk. Ruby Morgan was astonished to learn she had been an inspiration for Sally. She, in turn, thanked Sally once again for saving her life.

They spent more than an hour crying together, reliving the horrible moments of that terrible week. When Sally left their house, it was with a fresh new perspective on life and a desire to continue to be the best doctor she could possibly be.

63307070R00190

Made in the USA
Charleston, SC
01 November 2016